Readers love *Acsquidentally In Love* by K.L. HIERS

"Hiers rolls worldbuilding mythology, delicious flirting, erotic scenes, and detective work into a breezy and sensual LGBTQ paranormal romance."

—Library Journal

"This book has a bit of everything I love, a good mystery, magic, romance, humor, and Action. K.L. Hiers has me hooked and I can't wait for more!"

—Bayou Book Junkie

A SUCKER FOR LOVE MYSTERY

ACSQUIDENTALLY IN LOVE

K.L. HIERS

"A breezy and sensual LGBTQ paranormal romance."
—*Library Journal*

"It's a great mystery and such a fun book. You guys will really be missing out if you don't read this story. I can't wait to see what comes next."

—Love Bytes

By K.L. Hiers

SUCKER FOR LOVE MYSTERIES
Acsquidentally In Love
Kraken My Heart

Published by Dreamspinner Press
www.dreamspinnerpress.com

Kraken My Heart

K.L. Hiers

DREAMSPINNER
PRESS

Published by

DREAMSPINNER PRESS

5032 Capital Circle SW, Suite 2, PMB# 279, Tallahassee, FL 32305-7886 USA
www.dreamspinnerpress.com

Kraken My Heart
© 2021 K.L. Hiers

Cover Art
© 2021 Tiferet Design
http://www.tiferetdesign.com
Cover content is for illustrative purposes only and any person depicted on the cover is a model.

Trade Paperback ISBN: 978-1-64405-926-5
Digital ISBN: 978-1-64405-925-8
Trade Paperback published May 2021
v. 1.0

Printed in the United States of America
∞
This paper meets the requirements of
ANSI/NISO Z39.48-1992 (Permanence of Paper).

CHAPTER 1.

TED STURM stared up at the spiral staircase that separated him from the dead body awaiting transport upstairs, and he began to have second thoughts about his career in the funeral business.

He'd been working at Crosby-Ayers for almost ten years now, and he was tired.

He was tired of working all night just to go into work at eight o'clock the next morning with no sleep. He was tired of seeing horrible things, fighting off bouts of depression, and wading through unspeakable fluids.

And most of all, he was so damn tired of stairs.

Not that Ted struggled physically. He was a big guy, built like an oak tree, and he didn't even use any magic to work out. His coworkers called him "Teddy Bear," and he was everyone's favorite to go on call with because they all knew how strong he was.

Even so, stairs were a bitch. Spiral in particular, because there was no way to get the stretcher up them safely. It simply would not be able to make the tight turns. They would have to carry the deceased man down in their arms.

Luckily, the man was quite small, and Ted could have easily carried him down on his own. His partner for the evening, Kitty York, was finishing up speaking to the family while he waited by the front door.

Tugging at his tie, Ted sighed audibly. Removals of this kind were always done in a full suit and tie, never mind the physical obstacles ahead of him. It was tradition to show respect for the families and for the person who had passed.

As his balls started to sweat and itch from the generous heat flowing through the house, Ted decided he was not a fan of traditions.

There wasn't much else he could do until Kitty was done, and it sounded like the family had a lot of questions. If the scent of burning sage wasn't a big enough clue, the giant relief of Salgumel over the couch told him the family were almost definitely Sagittarian.

The vivid image of the leering tentacled god was startling, and he swore it was staring at him.

Ted had been raised Lucian by his parents, but working in the funeral home had given him lots of insight into other religions. He knew that Sages always buried their dead after an intimate washing ceremony performed by the family. They wouldn't ever embalm or cremate, and the services would be relatively brief.

The celebration-of-life feast that followed the burial, however, could last days. He'd heard some families kept the party going in their homes for weeks, or at least until a new moon.

A lot of the ritual varied, depending on which gods the deceased and their family favored. Unlike Lucians, who only worshipped the Lord of Light, Sages had hundreds to choose from. Salgumel, God of Dreams and Sleep, was a pretty popular one. There was something about him being the first to go to sleep and taking the other gods with him. It was why people said the religion had died out, but Ted wasn't sure.

He also saw lots of family photographs with smiling faces and plenty of kids and grandkids. There were vacations and visits to amusement parks, and it seemed like the gentleman who'd died had led a pretty full life.

It made Ted smile but also sad. He wasn't thinking about the family who was mourning, but selfishly for his own life.

If he kicked the bucket right then and there, who would miss him?

Maybe his parents, but he barely spoke to them these days, and he hadn't seen his younger brother in years. His last serious relationship had ended miserably, he hadn't had another steady boyfriend in months because of his crazy schedule, and his only friends were coworkers.

Well, he reconsidered, his roommate might miss him.

He and Jay Tintenfisch had met last year at—where else—a funeral. It was for Jay's great-grandmother, and when Jay mentioned that he needed a new place to stay, Ted was happy to offer his spare bedroom.

They both liked the same movies, had similar taste in music, and Jay was a wonderful roommate. He was clean, always paid his share of the rent on time, and they got along great.

Except for that damn cat.

"Ah, that was the grandkids' first beach trip," an elderly man's voice said, interrupting Ted's lonely thoughts. "The tiny one, Macy, she loved it. She was so brave. Just charged right into that ocean like she'd been doing it all her life."

Ted turned to find the picture he was referring to, seeing a crowd of smiling faces on a sandy beach, except one little boy who was screaming.

"That's Junior. He was not a fan," the man explained with a fond chuckle. "We probably took twenty pictures, and he was hollering like hell in every single one of them."

Ted nodded and smiled warmly. He didn't want to openly comment in case any of the family was close by.

After all, the elderly man who was talking to him was dead upstairs.

"My wife," the elderly man said, reaching out to touch an old portrait. His hand went right through the frame, and he recoiled. "I think... I think I'll miss her the most."

The longing in his voice made Ted's heart ache. He could see the man's lips twisting back, as if he was about to cry. He wanted to say something, perhaps try to comfort him, anything—

"Ready?" Kitty's hushed voice asked as she approached Ted with a few family members following her.

"Yes," he grunted, offering the family a polite smile as he followed Kitty upstairs. Each twist of the staircase made his stomach drop, listening to the elderly man following him.

"We met at a movie theater," he was saying. "It was so crowded, and we ended up sitting next to each other… as soon as I saw her, I knew she was the one. Our anniversary was gonna be next month. It would have been fifty-four years…."

Despite the obvious circumstances, Ted realized he was jealous of the dead man. It wasn't that Ted craved a giant house full of nice stuff or a pack of grandkids. He wanted someone, just one special someone, to share his life with.

Every day was the same. Work all night, work all day, try to catch up on errands and bills on his few days off before it was right back to the grind. It didn't help that his job was particularly depressing and he only met new people on what was almost always the worst day of their lives.

Not exactly a great way to find potential dates.

Even when he did manage to get one, he ran into a new set of obstacles. Trying to make time for a boyfriend was a nightmare, and there were always certain expectations he was tired of fulfilling.

Oh, and constantly hearing and seeing dead people. That didn't help either.

He and Kitty wrapped the gentleman in a sheet and worked together to carefully maneuver him down the stairs. They'd left the stretcher at the bottom of the steps and laid him down gently when they got there, Ted quickly moving to adjust the pillow beneath his head.

They secured the straps, covered him with the cot cover, and then Kitty went over to say goodbye to the family while Ted waited again.

He didn't want to talk to the family. Not that he couldn't, but he was awkward, and he never knew what to say. Kitty was a natural with people, always sweet and empathetic to their pain. Even with the most belligerent relations, she could keep her cool and calm them down.

It also didn't help that Ted usually had to contend with his own unique conversations. Trying to talk to a grieving spouse while their deceased partner screamed at them about picking out the right color socks for the funeral was extremely difficult.

Ted and Kitty rolled the gentleman out to their van, and Ted loaded the stretcher into the back. He wasn't sure if the family was watching them, but he made sure to take his time and be as courteous as possible when he shut the door.

He glanced back up to where the family was hovering on their front porch. The elderly gentleman was standing with them, and he waved.

Ted nodded politely in reply and took his seat behind the wheel, waiting for Kitty to get buckled up before beginning to drive back to the funeral home.

"That went well," Kitty chirped. "Nice family."

"Yeah," Ted said absently, focusing on the road. It was after midnight, and his thoughts were all over the place.

"What's wrong?" Kitty asked. She'd always been good at reading people, and Ted was no exception.

"You sure you're licensed for earth magic and not some kind of divine mind reading?" Ted joked.

Anyone who used magic had to be licensed to practice. Just like driving a car, there were tests and fees. There were severe consequences for being caught practicing without one.

Magic was strictly regulated into five schools based on the elements of fire, water, air, earth, and the divine. Divine was arguably the most powerful, as it combined abilities from all the other schools and offered powers considered most unique.

There were also those who couldn't use any magic, and they had to register as voids. Sages called them Silenced, Ted had heard. He was a borderline void. He'd shown only the bare minimum in the school of air with inclinations toward the divine, but nothing had ever really manifested.

Even with wands or staves, he couldn't cast the simplest spell without it fizzling out. He'd given up on having any magic until he started working for the funeral home.

When he encountered his first dead body, he finally learned what his true gift was.

"Did someone say hello?" Kitty asked politely.

Ted sighed. There was no point in hiding it. He'd worked with Kitty for a few months now, and she knew about his ability. It was hard to hide, considering their line of work.

"Yeah," he said, jerking his head back to indicate the deceased gentleman resting behind them. "Someone did."

"Was he okay?"

"He's fine," Ted replied. "He didn't try to follow me or anything. He stayed there with his family. He seemed good, you know, for a dead guy."

"So, you think he'll move on?"

"Yeah."

"I wish I could hear them," Kitty said wistfully.

"No." Ted shook his head. "No, you really don't."

Sometimes Ted regretted telling her. Like most people, she was envious because such magic was rare. People thought he could reach out to long-lost relatives and deliver messages and seek out the wisdom of the other side.

In reality, it was unpredictable, often terrifying, and Ted had absolutely no control over it. It was seemingly random whether he encountered a spirit or not, much less if they were willing or able to communicate.

Some spirits were friendly like the gentleman he'd met earlier, others didn't even seem to notice Ted at all, and then there were the angry ones. They would scream and curse and try to attack Ted, threatening him with violence and endless torture if he didn't help them. They seemed to be under the impression that they were somehow trapped and didn't realize they were actually dead.

Although they were rare, they were also the only ones who would follow Ted home.

Well, except that one little boy….

"Sorry," Kitty said quickly. "I know it must be awful sometimes. I'm just… I'm just so curious. I wish I could talk to them. Ask them questions."

"Like what? What happens when we die?" Ted scoffed. "They don't know any more than we do. Some of 'em tell me there's a bright light calling them. Some of 'em say they see some kind of bridge."

"Xenon," Kitty said.

"Huh?"

"The bridge," Kitty explained. "Sages believe that all souls cross a bridge in a place called Xenon to reach the home of the gods."

"Right. Off to Zebulon or whatever." He leaned back as they approached a traffic light, sighing to himself. "Look, what I'm trying to say is that talking to them ain't what you think it is. They don't know what's going on, and honestly, I avoid talkin' to them."

"Why?" Kitty asked, a note of hesitation in her voice.

"Because, no offense, they're just as bad as the living," Ted replied. "They just want more and more from you. You try to do one nice thing for them, like tell their wife they still love 'em or make sure they get buried in some special skirt, and it's never enough.

"They keep asking and asking, and it just, fuck, it sucks you dry trying to keep them happy. They will never move on as long as they think they can get you to do shit for them. So fuck it. I just ignore them now."

"I'm sorry. I didn't realize it was that bad."

"It's usually not," Ted said, flipping on his turn signal as he drove them into the parking lot by the funeral home's garage. "There's only been a few that have harassed me like that, and it was my fault for trying to talk to them in the first damn place."

"You ever thought about trying to find a specialist witch?" Kitty offered. "Maybe someone who can help you tune them out?"

"Nope."

"Well, why not?"

"Kitty girl, I don't want nobody knowing I got this," Ted said sternly. "Talking with the dead is one step away from necromancy, and I ain't going to jail because some damn ghosts get bitchy about what stupid shit their families bring to bury them in."

Necromancy was forbidden by law and considered extremely taboo. Any information on such forbidden magic had been destroyed and was thought lost to the passage of time. It only seemed to exist in rumors and whispers, but Ted suspected there were still some practitioners working in secret.

After all, ghouls were still being raised. By attaching a human soul to a physical copy of their body after death, a person's life could be extended until the body gave out and went rotten. It was very illegal and quite uncommon, though he had seen a few over the years.

Communication with the dead like what Ted had was even more rare. It wasn't illegal, but it was highly regulated. It had its own special licensure, and Ted had avoided revealing his unique skill. He didn't want the attention or the potential headache.

"Fair enough," Kitty said, waiting for the van to stop at the garage door of the funeral home before getting out to open it.

Ted backed up so they could unload, grateful that Kitty finally dropped the subject once they were back inside. They placed the gentleman in their walk-in cooler, finished their paperwork, and Ted was ready to go home.

"You off tomorrow?" Kitty asked as they locked up.

"You mean today?" Ted smirked after glancing at his watch. "Yeah, I'm off. And all I'm doing is sleeping."

"Doris is gonna be heartbroken," Kitty teased. "She was planning on bringing in cupcakes, and I know she made some strawberry ones just for you."

"Send Doris my regrets, but I ain't comin' back, even for her baking. Just gotta make it through the next few hours without a damn call and I'm free for two days."

"Well, try to get some good sleep!" Kitty laughed, waving farewell as they parted ways in the parking lot. "Night, Teddy Bear!"

"Good night, Kitty girl!" Ted waved, getting settled in his car and making ready to leave. He didn't even glance up when he heard a soft giggle in the back seat.

"Hey, little buddy."

There was a quiet shuffling and then silence.

Cranking the car up, Ted asked casually, "Wanna go down the crazy road today?"

There was an urgent tap on his shoulder.

That was a yes.

Ted smiled. "Let's go."

There were two ways to get back to the apartment he shared with Jay. One was direct and took him through downtown. The other circled around the city, added about twenty minutes, but it went down a long and curvy stretch of road.

That was the crazy road, and it was the route the little boy liked the most.

Ted made sure to take the turns hard and hit every bump and pothole he could, grinning when he heard lots of delighted laughing behind him. "Hang on, little buddy! Big one coming up!"

The boy had been with him for months, though Ted didn't know where he had come from. While he'd sadly encountered his fair share of deceased children in his line of work, he'd never met this boy through his work at the funeral home.

He had shown up in Ted's bedroom wanting to play one night and had simply never left.

The boy didn't ask for much, and he never let Ted see his face. Ted had only seen glimpses of his small figure, a thick scarf, and he could always hear his voice.

Especially when he was driving home.

Ted was actually quite fond of the little boy. In his loneliest moments, it was nice to have a friend. After long days at work when he wanted to break down and cry, he would feel a small hand on his shoulder or see a red ball rolling across the floor to him.

Sometimes he found colorful drawings or toy cars in his room. Ted figured out what music the little boy liked and played classic rock often just to hear his little foot tapping.

It was nice, although impossible to explain to anyone. Not even Kitty knew about the little boy.

By the time Ted parked in front of his apartment, the little boy was gone. He wasn't sure where he went exactly, but he knew he wouldn't stay away too long.

Ted crept slowly into his apartment, doing his best to be quiet. It was very early in the morning, and he didn't want to wake his roommate up. All of his senses were on high alert, searching for a certain pesky feline.

His life had been difficult enough when he was being tortured by ghosts and struggling with the daily trauma of dealing with death, but he hadn't known true horror until the day Jay brought the cat home.

Mr. Twigs.

Mr. Twigs was a fluffy black cat that Jay had rescued and was absolutely obsessed with. Damn thing had followed him home one night, and Jay couldn't refuse him. The feeling was quite mutual between them. Mr. Twigs pranced and purred and adored Jay entirely.

Ted was not so fortunate.

It wasn't weird enough that the damn feline had shown up with small cat-sized sunglasses that hooked around his little ears and insisted on following Jay everywhere. If Ted so much as tried to give Jay a hug, Mr. Twigs attacked him. When Jay wasn't home, Mr. Twigs was set on making Ted's life a living hell.

He tripped him, puked in his shoes, pissed in his closet, and delivered mutilated animals to his pillow. Jay had tried to explain his awful behavior by citing his obvious abandonment and promised to replace anything he messed up, but the undeniable truth remained:

Mr. Twigs hated Ted.

Ted tiptoed through the apartment with no sign of the fluffy monster. He hoped that the damn thing was in Jay's room asleep, but he saw a shadow dart by his legs and knew he wasn't lucky enough for it to have been a ghost.

He got changed into a pair of sweats and felt brave enough to venture back out of his room. He really wanted something to drink, and he was not going to let some crazy cat stop him. He could totally do this.

Ted got a can of soda from the fridge, using the light to scan the kitchen and the living room for the cat. He didn't see him and hesitantly shut the door, casting the apartment into darkness.

Carefully, like he was navigating through a minefield, he tried to sneak back to his room. Despite his diligent and precise pace, his foot collided with a very large ball of fur just as he walked around the edge of the couch.

Mr. Twigs yowled in protest and promptly bit Ted's ankle.

"You stupid cat!" Ted growled in pain, his leg jerking and sending the cat stumbling into the wall. His heart dropped in instant regret, and he hurried to turn on a lamp. "Shit! I'm so sorry! I didn't mean to, little dude! Are you okay?"

Mr. Twigs was glaring at Ted over his sunglasses and growled loudly. A portal suddenly opened up in the living room floor with flashing bright lights and whipping winds.

Ted froze, staring stupidly at the giant black void in the apartment floor. Being able to create a portal was a very rare skill, and he'd never seen one in person before. "What the…?"

As if the swirling hole wasn't crazy enough, Mr. Twigs transformed into a very tall, very skinny, and very naked young man. He flashed a smile full of pointed teeth, hissing, "Oh, that's the last time you kick me, asshole."

"I didn't kick you!" Ted argued indignantly. "It was a fucking accidennnnnttt!" he screamed as Mr. Twigs pushed him and sent him toppling headfirst into the portal.

It was like… going down a water slide filled with pudding.

Ted didn't feel air around him, not exactly, but it was something thick and suffocating. The light all around him was so bright that he couldn't see, and he thought he had to be dying.

His stomach dropped as if he was falling, but he couldn't see anything to track his descent. He grunted when he smacked into something solid and wet, the wind knocked right out of his lungs. He wheezed, trying to draw in oxygen and staring up at a high vaulted ceiling.

Ted watched the portal close above him, and he weakly lifted his head to see where he was. He was lying in a puddle of something sticky, and the room was reminiscent of an old castle throne room.

Big ceilings, lots of stained glass, fancy throne....

He was also completely surrounded by monsters.

Giant scaled things with tentacles, humanoids with spiraling horns jutting out of their foreheads, twisted feline creatures with sharp teeth, and fishlike worms were all around him.

Ted scrambled to stand up, but he slipped in the sticky mess beneath him. He could feel the goo all over his back and hands, sliding around as he struggled to get out of it. He bumped into something cold and whirled around to find a dead body.

It was one of the feline creatures, its eyes lifeless and milky, soaking in a puddle of....

Oh God.

It was blood.

"Pardon me, coming through!" a deep voice growled, echoing throughout the massive chamber. "Stand aside! This is official royal business, so move your ass!"

Ted was nauseated, staring up at a human figure pushing his way through the crowd of monsters.

He was short but broad, thick in stature, and sporting a nasty smile full of pointed teeth. Otherwise, he looked quite normal. His hair was jet black, cut close to his scalp, with a well-groomed beard streaked with silver, and his eyes were a spectacular shade of gold, looking over Ted like he was a tasty piece of meat.

He wore a three-piece suit, but it was a much flashier ensemble than Ted would have worn for his job at the funeral home. The jacket and pants were black, but the tie was an obnoxiously bright purple, and he could see a glittering watch chain hanging from the man's matching purple brocade vest.

"Well, aren't you just a pretty little thing?" the man greeted. "What's your name, darling?"

"I'm, I'm...," Ted stammered, looking around frantically as the monsters backed away. Whoever this man was, he was definitely in charge. There was something about the way he was looking at Ted that made him blush and his heart beat a little faster.

"I'm Ted.... My name is Ted," he managed to choke out. He wondered if he was dead or if this was some sort of nightmare. His mind was having trouble processing that any of this was real. "Where am I? What is this?"

"Welcome to Xenon, darling," the man replied. "I'm Thiazi Grell. I was voted most likely to get detained for illegal activities by my primary class, very avid Tetris player, and reigning Miss Pretty Petunia Pageant champion for the last two hundred years. Oh, and King of Xenon. Obviously."

"Huh?" Ted squeaked.

"Would you like something to drink?" Grell offered. "Something strong. Help you calm down, put some more hair on that luscious chest, come to terms with the murder charges...."

"With the *what*?"

CHAPTER 2.

"Murder charges," Grell repeated, gesturing to the blood.

"No fuckin' way!" Ted shouted as he finally climbed to his feet. His toes were squishing in the thickening liquid, and he hastily stepped out of the puddle. "I didn't kill anyone!"

"You have his blood on your hands," Grell said. "The laws of the Asra dictate that you must now be charged with murder until you can prove your innocence."

There was a murmur of agreement from the monsters.

"That's the stupidest thing I've ever heard! You're not pinning this shit on me, you son of a bitch! I just fucking got here!" Ted snapped. No one said anything, and several beats of silence ticked by before he demanded helplessly, "And what the fuck is an Asra?"

"He was one," Grell said, pointing at the hideous body next to Ted. "And so am I." He flashed a toothy smile. "I'm wearing my pretty human face just for you."

Ted flushed, stammering, "Look, look, please. Please just tell me what the fuck is going on."

"Are you sure you wouldn't like something to drink?" Grell asked. "You seem a bit upset."

"You're charging me with murder and offering me a fucking drink?" Ted scoffed. "Aren't you gonna try... I don't know, aren't you gonna go and lock me up or something?"

"It's not like you can run away," Grell said with another toothy leer. "You wouldn't get very far."

"Fuck." Ted gulped. That felt like a threat. He threw up his hands. "Fine. A beer. No, fuck that. Something stronger. Way stronger."

"I've just the thing." Grell snapped his fingers, and a glass tumbler full of a dark liquid appeared in Ted's hand.

Without hesitation, Ted chugged it back.

It burned, but it was warm and a bit sweet. It was actually really tasty. He blinked as the glass magically refilled, and only then did it occur to him that maybe he should be more careful when accepting mysterious drinks from strange men.

Especially strange men who could apparently cast spells using only their hands. With very few exceptions, people had to speak the words of a spell to use magic, and Ted immediately knew that Grell had to be quite powerful to summon up a drink with a mere snap of his fingers.

"Thanks. It's, uh… it's good." Ted fidgeted, glancing nervously at the strange creatures still lingering around them. His skin was cold where the blood was drying, and he was numb from terror.

Or maybe the liquor was just that good.

"Court is dismissed," Grell suddenly barked, turning his head and baring his teeth. "We'll start the trial tomorrow."

"Does this mean you'll be representing the criminal, Your Highness?" one of the fish-worms hissed.

"Why not?" Grell shrugged. "Could be fun."

"Very well," the fish-worm replied. "We will see you at the trial, Your Highness."

One by one, the monsters vanished, either through portals or through various physical archways, until no one was left but the two of them.

Well, and the corpse.

"Trial?" Ted echoed. "What kind of trial?"

"Murder trial, obviously."

"Come on, this is bullshit!"

"Tsk-tsk! Now! How did an adorable human like you manage to come dropping into my humble little home?" Grell circled around Ted like a tiger about to pounce. "Read any cursed books lately? Piss off any kitty cats?"

"The cat," Ted recalled out loud. "It was that damn cat! He opened up some kind of fuckin' portal, but then he wasn't a cat! He turned into this skinny dude and pushed me in!"

"I thought so," Grell said with a click of his tongue. "Mm, you don't strike me as much of a reader."

"Hey, I fuckin' read!" Ted glared.

"The contents of a bottle of soap while you're having a squat doesn't count," Grell snorted dryly.

"Hey, fuck you, ass hat!" Ted stood up to his full height and glared down at the short king. "You don't know jack shit about me!"

"Mmm, you've got quite a mouth on you, don't you?" Grell laughed. "It's so refreshing! And I know plenty. Look at you. Your little jersey pants have more holes than a Vulgoran hooker, you reek of too much aftershave and death, and that fear in your eyes…."

Ted tensed, his heart pounding in his ears and making his stomach churn violently.

"You're so afraid and still trying to put on a brave face," Grell observed, tilting his head with a sly grin. "And it's a very good face, very lovely. Ten out of ten, would definitely shag. But you're still terrified."

Ted's mouth opened to bite back, but he couldn't think of anything to say. He clamped his teeth together as heat crawled up his neck.

Was this really happening?

Ted took a swig of his drink, grunting defiantly, "Eat me."

"Please, let me buy you dinner first," Grell quipped.

Ted scoffed, hating how his face continued to flush. He could feel the heat all over, and he demanded, "Are you seriously flirting with me?"

"Ah, so there is a brain rattling around in that gorgeous thick skull of yours," Grell teased.

"You're such an asshole," Ted grumbled, licking his lips anxiously.

"Duh. You don't stay king very long trying to be everyone's best pal and making little friendship bracelets."

Ted gulped, tensing as Grell crept closer. There was something about him that made Ted feel so awkward when he managed to meet those golden eyes. "So, uh, where am I again?"

"Xenon," Grell said, a glass of his own appearing in his hand with another quick snap. "Shall I say it slower?"

"No," Ted grunted. "I heard you. I just don't know what that is. I mean, sort of. It's a bridge, right?"

"Really?" Grell's brows furrowed. "Have humans truly forgotten the old ways so quickly?" He pursed his lips. "I suppose it has been a few hundred years. I forget your kind doesn't live very long."

"Okay, that's cool and all…." Ted slurped at his drink. "But that still doesn't answer my question."

"Xenon is the bridge between Aeon and Zebulon," Grell said with a roll of his eyes. He gestured for Ted to follow him as he strolled out through a small side door.

Ted hesitated, glancing around warily.

Was that door even there a second ago?

He didn't seem to have any other choice except to follow Grell wherever he was leading him. The doorway opened up to a large balcony, and Ted almost choked when he looked outside. "Holy shit."

It was night, and the sky was full of millions of brilliant stars and dazzling swirls of galaxies. Even though it was dark, there was a soft purple glow cast over everything as far as Ted could see. The trees were iridescent, shining white like bolts of lightning growing up from the ground.

They were definitely in a castle, a monstrous compound of lavender masonry that sat high above the glowing forest below.

Flowering tendrils were crawling all over the stonework, scenting the air with a spicy perfume that reminded Ted of cinnamon.

Glancing back to the forest, he jerked when he saw a giant bridge looming over the trees. He didn't know how the hell he had missed it before, because it was even bigger than the castle. As he watched, the bridge grew dark and disappeared.

A few moments later, it lit back up, and Ted could see streams of luminous orbs running across it. The bridge was so massive he couldn't tell where it started or where it ended, but the lights all seemed to be moving in the same direction.

It was like looking at a dream he'd had and then forgotten when he woke up. It was eerily familiar, and as fantastic as it all was, it was beautiful.

"So, Aeon is… Earth?" Ted asked hesitantly.

"Part of it. It's the mortal world. All your planets and stars and such." Grell pointed to the mammoth bridge. "When you die, your soul passes through that bridge to reach Zebulon, the home of the gods."

"The gods?"

"Great Azaethoth, Babbeth, Baub?" Grell studied Ted's hopeless expression and sighed. "You're Lucian, aren't you."

"Yeah, kinda, but I know those are all Sagittarian gods," Ted protested. "You're telling me all that old witch shit is right?"

Grell motioned to the bridge again. "Looks pretty right to me, darling."

"Fuck," Ted whispered. His eyes moved back to the bridge, following little blips of light moving along when he could see them. His head was swimming, and he didn't know what to think.

Maybe he was dreaming.

He had never been the most devout Lucian, but he had considered himself a believer. He had accepted the Litany of Light and been baptized as a child, but none of that seemed to matter now.

"What does this mean?" Ted asked. "There's no Lord of Light?"

"Not that I've ever met," Grell replied with a shrug. "He came, he saw, he preached, and he vanished. Can't tell you much more than that, darling."

"What happens to Lucians when we die?" Ted frowned. "Do we go somewhere else?"

"All souls pass through the bridge," Grell said, sounding almost soothing. "Lucian, Sage, Tauri, and even the gods when they die."

"You've seen a god die?"

"Cheeky little fellow with big eyebrows sent one to us not too long ago." Grell laughed. "Looked like a giant rocket shooting down that damn thing."

Ted set his drink down and gripped the balcony railing. "This is... this is a lot."

"Keep drinking," Grell advised.

Ted looked back at the bridge. "It's really beautiful."

"Yes, it is," Grell said softly, but he was staring at Ted.

"So, you're king of all this?" Ted asked, rubbing behind his ear.

"Yes," Grell replied. "I'm king of Xenon and the Asra." Before Ted could ask, he explained, "We were the first race created by the gods to be their servants. That gig turned out to be a bit more like being their slaves, and we rebelled."

"You guys fought a bunch of gods?"

"And won," Grell said proudly. "To end the war, Great Azaethoth gave us sovereignty over Xenon so our people could be free and promised that no living god would ever trespass here. It's ours, and has been for thousands of years."

"That was pretty cool of him, I guess," Ted said, shifting his feet and grimacing when they stuck to the stone floor. "Okay, uh, small request for the prisoner?"

"Within reason."

"Can you, like, snap your little fingers and clean this shit up?" Ted motioned to the blood all over him.

"Why would I want to do that?" Grell looked mortified. "That's evidence for your trial tomorrow!"

Ted groaned miserably and accepted his sticky fate.

"By the gods, you're so gullible."

"Huh?"

"Let's get you freshened up. I'm not that much of a bastard. Come along."

Ted took a step forward to follow Grell and everything suddenly flickered. It was like watching an old DVD skip scenes. In a second, they were no longer on the balcony and were now standing in front of a steaming hot pool. There were some sort of bioluminescent eels swimming in the water, giving it an eerie glow.

"The fuck was that?" Ted demanded. "How did we...."

"A portal," Grell explained. "Mortals have this magic, yes?"

"Uh, I mean, I've heard of it. But isn't there supposed to be a big swirly hole or something?"

"Mine are a bit more tidy than my son's. So good you've experienced both so you can really compare."

"*Son?*" Ted stared. "The cat, that skinny brat? He's your son?"

"My one and only," Grell said in a mockingly sweet tone. His clothes were slowly disappearing as he headed to the edge of the pool.

Ted was frozen, unsure whether he was supposed to be following. He couldn't take his eyes off the king, gulping as he stared at his broad shoulders and the dark hair dusting his powerful chest, his thick stomach, and—

Oh shit.

Ted jerked his eyes away, and he was certain his face was about to catch on fire.

"See something you like?" Grell teased, slipping down into the water with a smirk.

Ted's face continued to toast, and he refused to acknowledge the question. He eyed the eels. "Those things dangerous?"

"No more than me." Grell winked as he sipped at his drink.

Ted grimaced.

He didn't want to strip in front of a total stranger, opting to keep his sweats on as he timidly stepped into the water. Once the warm water hit his toes, he groaned and plopped right in.

It was fantastic.

Ted found a ledge he could sit on, able to sink down and stay submerged up to his neck. He set his drink on the edge and leaned his head back on the lip of the pool. The eels swimming around paid him no mind, and Ted could feel all the tension easing from his body.

The blood was fading away without any scrubbing, and Ted had never felt so clean or refreshed. There was probably magic in this water, he realized, but it felt really good.

"So," Grell chirped, "Ted of Aeon. How does a mortal come to reek of so much death, hmm? Are you a serial killer? Perhaps a vengeful vigilante? I am so enjoying the vision of you in spandex."

"I work at a funeral home."

"Ah, so you're an embalmer? You prepare the dead as the Eldress do?"

"No, I'm a removal technician." Ted had no idea what the hell an Eldress was. "I pick people up when they die. Hospitals, nursing homes, maybe their house. I help dress 'em and casket 'em if they need it, but that's it."

"Ah... not an embalmer, then."

"No," Ted griped. "Look, I tried going to school for it. I was gonna be a director and all that shit, but I couldn't handle the classes and still fuckin' work full-time. Happy?"

"Excessively so," Grell said smugly.

"Right." Ted scoffed. "Of course you are. You're king of your own little magical world, got a real asshole son who pushes people into fucking portals. Bet your queen is just a fuckin' hoot."

Grell's merry expression vanished.

"What?" Ted had definitely just stepped in something.

"How about we focus on your murder trial, hmm?" Grell refilled his glass, only to empty it in one swift chug. "You're allowed to work on your defense for one full lunar cycle. That's one day here—"

"I have *one* day to prove I'm innocent, even though he was already very obviously dead when I got here?" Ted made a face.

"Rules are rules," Grell said with a shrug. "You'll then present your case to the court, and then they'll decide whether you're innocent or not."

"What the fuck happens if the court finds me guilty?"

"Death."

"What?" Ted suddenly forgot how to breathe, overcome with panic.

Grell started laughing. "Oh, you should see the look on your face! Ha!" He clutched his chest. "You really believed me! Whew! Humans are so barbaric. We wouldn't actually kill you."

"What the fuck is wrong with you?" Ted hissed. He was equally relieved and furious that Grell was screwing with him.

"A lot."

"So what would really happen, huh?"

"Oh, pfft, eternity in the dungeon."

"That's so much better," Ted growled. "For fuck's sake…. Fine. Since I have less than a fuckin' day to figure this out, tell me who that guy was. Like, did he have any beef with anybody? Any enemies who woulda wanted to see him dead?"

"His name was Sergan Mire," Grell replied. "He was my first cousin, and he was a complete twat. You'll find he had many enemies."

"And he's… he was an Asra?"

"Yes."

Ted thought back to the feline monster's corpse, asking carefully, "So, that's what you look like underneath that human suit?"

"Sexy, innit?" Grell chuckled. "We Asra can change our shapes as we please, but creatures that favor our true form are much easier."

"Like cats?"

"Ha! They say the first cats of Aeon were actually Asra who'd gone mad from shrinking themselves and forgot how to change back."

"Maybe that's why they're all such little assholes and see shit that isn't there," Ted mused. "They all used to be portal hopping jerkoffs like you, huh?"

Grell laughed and raised his glass in a salute. "Guilty."

"Hey. Speaking of fuzzy jerks, why is your son hanging out and pretending to be my roommate's cat?" Ted demanded, more than a bit worried about his friend. "Is he gonna try and shove him off here too?"

"No," Grell assured him. "My son is there to protect him."

"Protect him from what?" Ted sat up. "If something is going on with Jay—"

"You are not equipped to deal with it," Grell cut in smoothly. "Trust that my son, despite his obvious personality defects, will do everything in his power to protect your friend."

"That really doesn't make me feel any better."

"You have a trial to worry about," Grell reminded him.

"So that's it, then? I'm trapped here until I can prove I'm not a murderer?"

"Look at that," Grell gasped. "Such quick and sound deduction! You might just get out of this after all!"

"You're a fuckin' dick," Ted growled.

Grell laughed. "Ah, but I'm the fuckin' dick who's going to help you."

"Yeah, you've been real great so far."

"What?" Grell blinked. "I've provided you with sustenance and counsel. What more do you want?"

"Answers!"

"To what?"

"Fuck, you're so annoying." Ted swept his fingers through his hair.

"You always talk like that to kings?"

"You're my first." Ted reached back to retrieve his drink. "Okay, this Mire guy. He's a kitty-cat monster like you, you say he's got a lot of enemies—"

"Are you mated, Ted of Aeon?"

"Huh?" Ted didn't think he'd heard him correctly.

"Do you have a mate? A companion?"

"No, not for a while." Ted cleared his throat. "I'm trying to be serious now. Who found the body?"

"I did," Grell answered. "So, single, eh?"

"Yes, but that's not really any of your damn business. Did you hate Mire like everybody else?"

"Of course I did. He was a righteous little bastard." Grell tilted his head curiously at Ted. "Why do you remain unmated?"

"You're not going to drop this, are you?"

"No."

"You always interrogate the prisoners you're supposed to be helping, huh?"

"Only if they're big, beautiful, bulky hunks of flesh such as yourself," Grell purred.

Ted couldn't help it. He laughed. He wasn't used to anyone flirting with him so aggressively. He usually had to do all the chasing and courting.

He was expected to do everything, as a matter of fact, from making the first move to the heavy lifting in the bedroom. Being a guy of his size set up some pretty unfair assumptions, and Grell's advances were weirdly refreshing.

"You trying to tell me I'm your type?" Ted challenged, deciding to turn the questions back on him. "Let me see. You're a king, right? You must get tired of ruling all the time. I bet you like a big, strong man to take care of you, let you be a lil' pillow princess, and rock your little world?"

Grell cackled, something wicked in his smile now as he crooned, "Oh, you precious little human. I rule in every aspect of my life, and if you were ever lucky enough to end up in my bed? It's your precious world that would be rocked." He winked. "Thoroughly and at least three times."

Ted's cock flexed in his sweats.

"Don't you humans have a cute little saying about assuming?" Grell taunted. "I think you're the one who wants to be a princess. You want someone to take charge and worship you, to chase all those pesky fears away.

"You're absolutely aching to love someone and have them love you just as you are, without compromise. Being alone… mmm, that's your greatest fear, isn't it? Even more terrifying than what might happen to you here, you fear that you'll be alone forever."

"Maybe," Ted grumbled, refusing to acknowledge Grell's pinpoint accuracy.

Grell smirked.

Ted took another swig of his never-ending drink, saying briskly, "Look, it's been a long night. I just got off work, and being accused of murder isn't sittin' real well with me. Can I just go to my cell or whatever?"

"As you wish. Get some rest, and we'll start fresh when you wake up. We'll have some time yet to work on your defense. The trial won't begin until the Faedra are shedding their wings and the moon flowers are blooming."

"Huh?"

"Eh, like ten o'clock."

"Oh, okay."

Grell grinned slyly. "Mm, do you need me to come tuck you in?"

"I'm good," Ted replied, mentally commanding his cock to stand down. This was not the time or the place to catch wood, especially not over some crazy cat king.

"Your loss." Grell pouted and snapped his fingers.

The world moved, and Ted was suddenly sitting on a plush bed. He was completely dry, and his drink was still in his hand with not a drop spilled. He stood up quickly to survey his new surroundings.

It was a simple bedroom with a bed, a nightstand, and one door. Ted opened it to find a small bathroom. He walked all around the glowing walls and realized there was no exit.

Trapped.

"Fucking great," he muttered, leaving his drink on the nightstand and flopping into bed. The light around him dimmed on its own, as if sensing how tired he was. All he wanted to do was go to sleep, wake up, and find that this had all been a crazy dream.

He was worried about Jay, what was going to happen when everyone realized he was missing, and if he would even survive this ridiculous trial....

And maybe he was still thinking of bright golden eyes and a wicked smile that made his heart beat a little faster.

He brought the budding fantasy to an immediate halt, and he scrubbed his face with his hands.

This was definitely not how he'd expected his day off to go.

CHAPTER 3.

WHEN TED woke up, the glowing room remained dim. He was grateful for the darkness, finding that his head was pounding. He hadn't slept well, although that was nothing new. He wasn't wearing his sweats anymore, groggily aware that they'd been replaced by a set of silk pajamas. He tried to roll over and go back to sleep, not particularly thrilled to find himself still stuck here.

So much for it all being a bad dream.

There was a tug on his foot, and he jerked, half expecting to see Grell standing there with a smug grin.

Nothing.

There was no one there.

As he sat up and looked around, the glow brightened, and he could see clearly. His new pajamas were bright pink with little hearts all over them, and he was definitely alone. There wasn't really anywhere in here for someone to hide.

Unless....

Ted wiggled to the edge of the bed, reaching his hand down to feel below. "Little buddy?"

Small fingers wrapped around his and tugged.

"Hey!" Ted couldn't believe it, and he gave the boy's hand a gentle squeeze. "What the heck are you doing here? You follow me here, little dude?"

The boy didn't say anything, but he pulled Ted's hand urgently.

"I'm gonna try to get us both home soon, I promise," Ted assured him. "Kinda got myself into a really weird mess, but I'm gonna get it figured out. We'll be back driving down the crazy road in no time, okay?"

The boy let go of him, and then there was movement by one of the walls. The boy's arm was sticking right out from the stones and beckoning him over.

"What are you doing?" Ted swung his legs over and got out of bed with a yawn. He rubbed the crust from his eyes. "Little buddy, I'm not a ghost. I can't walk through a wall."

The boy poked his head through, just for a moment, insistently pointing at the floor.

"What is it?" Ted frowned as he came closer. "What are you trying to show me?"

The boy reached out and grabbed Ted's hand, pulling him forward.

Ted grunted, expecting to smack into a solid wall, but he was able to step right through and found himself standing in a long hallway.

He turned around and touched the wall he'd just come through, dragging his hand down the shimmering stone. It looked and felt solid until his fingers disappeared. There was an opening, hidden right in plain sight.

"Trippy."

Ted turned his head when he saw the boy running down the hall, hissing frantically, "Hey! Where are you going?"

The boy peered around a corner, waved, and disappeared.

Grumbling to himself, Ted chased after the boy. He had no idea how the boy had followed him here, and he was even more clueless as to what he was trying to do.

As he turned the corner, he found himself in another long hallway. He didn't see any doors, and he suspected that any openings were probably hidden like the one for the room he'd slept in.

He saw a little hand waving at him through a wall a few yards away. When Ted touched the wall there, his fingers went right through as before. He took a deep breath and walked forward.

Ted was now in a library, a vast space crammed with hundreds of tall shelves that were positively overflowing with scrolls and books. Every inch was packed to bursting, and Ted breathed in the soothing scent of old paper.

There were two giant overstuffed chairs positioned in the center of the room. Behind them, there was one bit of wall that wasn't occupied by books, and a portrait hung there instead.

Ted recognized the creature in the painting as an Asra, and it had a large crown on its head. It had long beaded earrings and gold caps on its most prominent canines. The frame looked newer than the worn chairs and old shelves, and Ted could only assume it was a recent addition to the room.

He looked around for the boy, wondering why he'd led him here.

Before he could do any real exploring, he heard Grell's amused voice from behind him, teasing, "My, my, aren't you just full of surprises?"

Ted shuffled around to face him, grinning wide as he said, "You've got no fuckin' idea."

His smile vanished when he realized Grell was naked.

"What the hell?"

"What?"

The king's thick chest and stomach were covered in dark hair, all the way down to his—oh fuck, not again. Ted forced himself to look away, finding the ceiling particularly fascinating as his face heated up. "You're, uh, not wearing anything."

"Oh, right. Silly me." Grell snapped his fingers, dressing himself in another gaudy suit. It was red and black, and he had foregone a traditional jacket in favor of a knee-length crimson fur coat. "There, that's better."

Ted tugged at the silken collar of his festive pajama top. "I'm guessing these are from you?"

"Do you like them?" Grell preened. "The magenta really brings out the green in your eyes."

"What happened to my sweatpants?"

"They've been incinerated."

"Hey!" Ted protested. "What the fuck, man? I liked those pants!"

"It was a mercy killing, really. They were a cotton abomination. Now tell me." Grell's bright golden eyes narrowed as he looked Ted over. "How did you get out of your room?"

"We gonna actually work on my case?" Ted countered, trying not to stare too obviously at Grell's sharp teeth or just how well that red waistcoat fit his broad chest. "Or you just gonna harass me and flirt some more?"

"I don't see why we can't do all three," Grell replied smugly.

"How about I ask a question and you give me a straight answer? And then you can ask me somethin'? One for one," Ted offered. "Starting with, what the hell is for breakfast around here?"

A snap of Grell's fingers created a tray of food floating in the air between them. It was full of fluffy scrambled eggs, colorful sausages, and thick strips of what might have been some kind of bacon.

It smelled delicious.

"Thank you," Ted said, gratefully picking up the fork and digging right into the food as the tray remained magically floating in front of him.

"My turn," Grell declared. "Tell me, how the hell did you get out of your room?"

"Found the hole and walked through."

"And then you just walked in here?"

"Ah-ah!" Ted warned, holding up his finger while he finished chewing. "That's more than one question."

"Consider yourself very fortunate that I think you're cute," Grell complained.

"You said you were the one that found Mire's body," Ted said, ignoring the obvious flirting that made him blush. "Can you tell me what happened?"

"I walked in, found his body, the end. Now tell me, in detail, how you got in here."

"You add details first if you want the same," Ted argued, smugly biting into a thick sausage.

Glaring for a long moment, Grell finally replied, "It was late. I received a message that Mire wanted to meet with me. Said it was important. I arrived at court, alone, and he was already dead on the floor.

"He'd been stabbed repeatedly, but there was no weapon that I could see. I called for the guards, and none of them remembered hearing a damn thing. I summoned the court, and they had just finished telling me how none of them knew anything either, and then you dropped in."

"Huh."

"Now, in detail, tell me how the fuck you're navigating my castle," Grell demanded.

"Ah spirith showed meh," Ted replied through a mouthful of food.

Grell grimaced in disgust.

"Sorry." Ted chewed quickly and swallowed before he elaborated, "I was never any good at magic, okay? Like, practically a dud. But then I started working at the funeral home and I met my first dead guy.

"I could see him, standing by his own body, and after that? I saw 'em all the time. They talk to me, yell at me, whatever. Some of them are friendly, and well, it always sounds crazy when I say it out loud."

"You have starsight." Grell stepped closer, brushing the floating tray of food out of his way.

"Hey, I was eating that!" Ted griped.

"How does a precious little mortal like you end up with a gift from gods you don't even believe in?" Grell mused, right in Ted's space now and peering up at him curiously.

Ted ran his tongue over his teeth, swallowing back his last bite of food. "Uh, just lucky, I guess. What, uh, what's starsight exactly?"

"A blessing from Great Azaethoth himself. It manifests in many different ways. Some can see the future, some can read godstongue, some see the dead, and some see all that's hidden."

"Cool." Ted fidgeted. "Are you just gonna stay all up in my bubble or what? Because you're freaking me out a little bit right now."

"May I touch you, Ted of Aeon?"

"Yes—wait, no! Why?" Ted steeled himself for anything, hating how his pulse fluttered. He couldn't quite decipher the way Grell was looking at him. It was hungry and full of danger, and he could feel himself being completely sucked in.

"I promise I'll be gentle," Grell said, his hand hovering over Ted's chest. He reconsidered, adding, "Ish."

"Uh… sure, I guess?" Ted watched the buttons of his pajama top magically open on their own for Grell.

Grell pressed his hand against Ted's chest, right over his heart. He seemed to be searching for something, but Ted had no idea what.

Ted didn't know what to do. Grell's hand was so warm, and it was really nice to be touched. If Grell was taller, they would have been close enough to kiss. As it was, Ted would need to lean down.

He tried to escape the ridiculous urge, finding that Grell's expression was becoming worried. He laid his hand over Grell's, asking urgently, "What's wrong?"

"What are you, Ted of Aeon?" Grell asked quietly, his long fingers reaching up to cradle his face. "What are you… *really*?"

"I'm just Ted," he whispered back, his eyes closing as he leaned into Grell's soft palm.

"You truly have no idea how amazing you are." Grell tilted his head up as his thumb stroked Ted's cheek. "I've never met anyone like you. No one has the balls to speak to me, *a king*, the way that you do. That filthy mouth of yours, your undeniable passion…."

Ted found himself being pulled right in, unable to resist whatever magical force of attraction was burning between them. All he had to do was lean down a little bit more and they'd kiss.

Gulping, he watched Grell's lips part expectantly. He was about to kiss a king, a king who was really a kitty-cat monster but who made him feel like he was the most beautiful man in the whole world.

He felt small somehow, vulnerable, and the air had become electric. He couldn't explain the strength of the new energy, nor could he look away from Grell's bright eyes.

Grell was very handsome, though he appeared quite a bit older than Ted. Not old enough to have been his father, but maybe a teacher or something. Ted really liked the silver sparkling around his temples and the streaks in his beard. The very shape of Grell's nose was quite attractive, small and round like a cat's, a fitting centerpiece for his pleasantly round face.

Even his sharp teeth were alluring in their own way, and Ted briefly wondered what they'd feel like on his skin.

Oh, but it was those eyes of his that really made Ted shiver. More so than his pointed teeth, Grell's eyes reminded Ted that this creature before him wasn't human. The depth of color was beyond any mortal's genetics, shimmering and metallic, a spectacular golden hue that Ted found absolutely hypnotic.

"Grell," Ted said, his voice thick and tense. "Are you...."

"Yes, Theodore?"

Ted smiled at that and shook his head. "My name isn't Theodore, it's—"

"Your Highness!" A giant Asra appeared from the nearby wall, baring its teeth as it shouted, "Urgent news!"

Ted jerked in surprise, staring up at the enormous cat creature. He had been too overwhelmed before, but now he had a moment to get a better look at this incredible monster.

The Asra were built like panthers, and all the ones he'd seen so far were the size of Clydesdales. Their shoulders and front legs were particularly bulky, their backs were arched at an unnatural angle, and he could now see that their long tails split off into a bundle of thick tentacles.

There were small tentacles mounted behind their huge pointed ears, and this Asra had a large and intricately carved bead clamped around one of them. It was then Ted realized what he had mistaken for earrings in the painting were actually these smaller ear tentacles strung with multiple beads.

Whatever significance they had, Ted didn't know, but it helped distract from the giant mouthful of pointed teeth.

Grell scowled, whirling around to glare at the intruding Asra. "Oh, this had better be good," he snarled. "I was in the middle of something. No, not even the middle. I was trying to *start* something, and you've ruined it!"

Ted flushed, turning his head away.

He knew he should have been relieved that nothing had happened, but he was truthfully just as annoyed as Grell.

"I'm sorry, Your Highness," the Asra said hastily. "The court is eager to begin the trial, and Humble Visseract is already done completing his witness statements. He sent me to summon you and the prisoner to court at once!"

Grell grimaced and scrubbed his hands over his face, as if trying to calm down. His body was suddenly growing, bigger and bigger, his shoulders stretching and threatening to tear the seams of his crimson fur coat. "Thirteen fuckin' hours to go and he dares to send *me* a summons? You tell that fucking tuna-faced cunt that we're starting when I'm good and fucking ready!"

The Asra cowered, tucking its long tail between its legs.

"And just for being such an overreaching little anal canker sore, you can inform him that the trial will not begin until the moon hangs in the sky at her most splendid apex and the Mostaistlis have taken their last drink of ambrosia!"

"So… midnight?" the Asra squeaked.

"Yes, midnight." Grell took a deep breath and roared, "Now go! Before I decide to eat you from the inside out!"

"Yes, Your Highness!" the Asra yelped as it retreated.

Grell's fury didn't fade until the Asra vanished back through the wall. He took another deep breath, his body slowly returning to its former proportions. "Well, shit."

Ted had a vague memory of a fish monster with big black eyes and a long body, asking, "This Visser-whatever guy, was he in court yesterday?"

"Yes," Grell replied, smoothing out his coat. "He's a Vulgoran. I believe there's still a large company of them that live in your Mariana Trench."

"Wait," Ted scoffed, "you're telling me that there's a bunch of fish monsters livin' in the ocean?"

"Think about how stupid your question sounds, wait a moment, and then ask me something else."

"You're a dick," Ted growled, instantly annoyed. "Fuck, I'm so glad you didn't kiss me."

"Pardon?" Grell turned around with a short laugh. "I'm sorry, but it was you who was about to kiss me."

"Bullshit!" Ted snapped. "Ahem, mister gettin' all mad because you were trying to start something. You were feelin' up on me, and you were totally begging for a damn kiss!"

"I did no such thing."

"Are you kidding me, jerkoff?"

"I'm sorry that you misunderstood the situation." Grell batted his eyes. "I'll let you down easy, darling. While I'm sure you'd have a splendid time letting me pound your brains out, I'm simply not ready for a new relationship."

"A new relationship? What about your queen?" Ted demanded, hating how Grell's rejection stung. "Is she gonna come try to whoop my ass over this shit, maybe tack on some more murder charges, or is she hanging out in a trench somewhere too?"

"My queen is dead," Grell replied flatly.

"What?" All of Ted's fight evaporated. "Dead?"

Grell pointed to the portrait on the wall. "He died over three hundred years ago. Asra are everlasting, but not immortal. We can still get sick, become injured...." He trailed off quietly.

"I'm sorry," Ted said, recognizing the pain of mourning he'd seen thousands of times. His apologies felt hollow, probably because he'd said them so often at work. He didn't know what else to say, and he hated how more questions were trying to sneak out of his mouth. "Your queen was... a dude?"

"We are Asra," Grell replied with a tired smile. "Although we mate in pairs, any one of us has the ability to give life or to carry it. Humans have such a limited concept of gender, eh? We are whatever we want to be. Some of us are 'he,' some are 'she,' and some are 'they.'"

"I don't mean to offend." Ted frowned, watching Grell's expression continue to sag. "I'm just trying to understand." He looked at the painting. "So, a queen is really just whoever is married to the king? No matter what they choose their gender to be?"

"Now you're getting it."

"How do you know what people want to be called?" Ted asked worriedly.

"Usually, I find it's easiest to open your mouth and ask if you're unsure," Grell said in a loud whisper.

"What about you? You look like a man, but does that mean you like being referred to as male?"

"I do, but ah, good question. Not many Asra take on human forms, but it is still wise not to assume based on appearances. When we're in our natural state, we wear jewelry that explains who we are."

"That little doodle-bobber-on-the-ear thingie?" Ted asked, recalling the one he'd seen on the Asra earlier and the long strands on the Asra in the painting.

"Yes. The very first bead on the right side tells you all that you need to know."

"That doesn't really help me if I can't fuckin' read it. It just looks like a bunch of swirly lines."

"I can teach you, if you'd like." Grell slowly wandered back into Ted's personal space.

"Uh… yeah. I guess that could be cool." Ted gulped, buttoning his shirt up. "We should probably get back to work."

"Hmm?"

"On the case!" Ted said urgently. "We only have until fuckin' midnight, and Visser-ass sounds pretty serious about convicting me, like, fuckin' yesterday."

"Visseract," Grell corrected. "He's the heir to Vulgoran's largest clan and a righteous dick weasel. Don't worry about him. Only I can call for the trial to begin, kingly perks and all that, and oh! I'm also your defense. Lucky you."

"Why is he so eager to convict me?" Ted pressed. "Kinda suspicious, don't you think?"

"A bit," Grell mused, looking thoughtful for a moment.

"You said you got a message that night telling you to meet Mire. Who delivered the message? Was it him?"

"No, it was Thulogian Silas."

"What the fuck is with your names?" Ted muttered as he reached for the floating tray of food. "Why are they all so weird?"

"You're one to talk," Grell sneered. "Human names make absolutely no sense. How the hell do you get Ted from Theodore? Jim from James? It's madness."

"Dick from Richard?" Ted snorted.

"Oh, that's easy," Grell teased. "You buy Richard dinner, show him a lovely time, and bring flowers."

Ted rolled his eyes as he finished up his breakfast. "So, where is this Silas?"

"She lives off by herself in the forest outside the castle." Grell removed the emptied tray with another snap.

Ted looked down and saw that he was now dressed in a fresh T-shirt and jeans. "Uh, thanks." He ran his hands on the denim, noting they were just a smidge too tight. He glared at Grell expectantly. "Ahem?"

Grell smiled sweetly, shamelessly admiring the fit.

"You gonna fix this?"

"Fix what?"

"My pants!" Ted snapped.

"Is there a problem?" Grell asked with a little bat of his eyes.

"Yes," Ted groaned in frustration.

"With what?"

"My fuckin' pants! They're too damn tight!"

"What's too tight?"

Ted could see this was a losing battle and decided to ignore the snug state of his pants and move on. "So, can we just snap on over there?"

"We'll have to get Vizier Ghulk to take us," Grell said. "Silas doesn't like unexpected guests. She's very likely to eat us on sight if we don't let Ghulk escort us."

"But she's the one who brought you Mire's message?" Ted scratched his head.

"Right? I thought it was strange too. She swore it was important."

"But wouldn't say what it was?"

"No."

The library vanished, and Ted found himself back in the castle court. There were a few Asra, a Vulgoran fish thing, and other monsters Ted still couldn't identify. He stayed close to Grell, trying to use the smaller man as a shield.

Mire's body was still present in its black pool of blood, and it was starting to smell. He noticed then that Mire had a lot of the same beads on his ear tentacles that Ted now recognized as Asran jewelry.

There was a gap in the line on one side, and Ted only noticed it because an oddly bright shimmer of violet caught his eye. He didn't want to get too close because of all the blood, but he could see that it wasn't a full bead, but a shard where one used to be. Perhaps it had been broken during a struggle prior to Mire's death....

"Why is that human not in the dungeon?" a large beast with huge tusks demanded, glaring at Ted hatefully.

"Will there be no justice for our beloved Mire?" the Vulgoran cried as it slithered toward him. "Must we drag him down there ourselves?"

"What is it doing over there now? Gloating over its kill?" the tusked monster shouted. "King Grell, we demand justice!"

Other voices joined the tusked monster and the Vulgoran, and the court was quickly becoming an angry mob. Ted had been in enough emotionally charged situations with upset families to see this had the potential to not end well for him. It was one thing to fend off a drunk uncle or a grief-stricken spouse, but up against a pack of monsters? He didn't like his chances.

Ted quickly grabbed Grell's shoulders and steered him in between himself and the monsters starting to crowd around him. "Hey, hey now!" he protested, hoping he sounded more confident than he felt. "Innocent until proven guilty, right?"

"It's more of a guilty until proven innocent sort of situation," Grell corrected.

"For fuck's sake, whatever!"

"Attention, good citizens of Xenon!" Grell shouted, addressing the court. He waited for the roar of voices to die down before continuing, "If you have any thoughts or concerns about how I am handling the trial for our prisoner, please write them down and drop them off in the royal suggestion box. I will not read them, but you're welcome to do so."

"Why is he not in chains, Your Highness?" the Vulgoran sneered.

"Not quite sure if he's into that, but I'll find out and let you know."

Ted had to fight the urge to kick Grell.

"Now," Grell bellowed, his voice taking on a more serious tone, "we still have fifteen hours to prepare our defense, and I will not tolerate interference of any kind. Everyone has the right to a fair trial in Xenon, and I do mean *everyone*. You want justice? So do I. But we need the proper time to conduct an investigation and prepare for the trial in accordance with our laws. I swear to you that if this mortal is responsible for Sergan Mire's death, I will drag him down to the dungeon myself."

The crowd murmured amongst themselves, assorted tentacles and claws still skittering, but Grell's promise appeared to have appeased them for now. However unusual the king was, his court seemed to respect him. Despite the lingering tension, no one spoke out again. They all began to disperse, though several continued to stare Ted down and bare their awful teeth at him as they did.

Ted felt a little better about his chances of survival. Not by a lot, but it was something.

"All right, then." Grell clapped his hands together. "Now that we have all that settled, let's get back to it, eh?" He looked over the departing court, calling out, "Vizier Ghulk! Where are you?"

"Here, Your Highness," a deep voice rumbled. A large and terrifying equine creature lumbered toward them.

It was slimy and slick, as if all of its skin had fallen off, and its mane was a staggered row of sharp horns. The longest one jutted right out of its forehead, and its twisted jaws were full of teeth like needles.

"What the fuck is that?" Ted hissed disgustedly. "A fuckin' zombie unicorn?"

"It's fine, he's an Eldress," Grell griped, shooing Ted away. "Wait for me downstairs."

"Huh? Wait for you where?"

Ted groaned as the world moved again, now standing at a massive gate. Behind him was the castle, and through the gate he could see the forest made out of lightning trees. He was totally alone.

"Great." Ted crossed his arms. "Well, I guess this is an improvement. Not by much, but I'll fuckin' take it."

"Right, like you have it so bad," an annoyed voice complained.

"Huh?" Ted looked all around, but he didn't see anyone there. That wasn't so unusual. He had encountered ghosts who couldn't take on a physical form before. "Hello?"

"Can you…." The voice grew louder, asking excitedly, "Can you really hear me?"

"Yeah," Ted replied. "Hi, name's Ted. I talk to dead people. I'm a little busy at the moment—"

"You're that mortal who came from Aeon!" the voice exclaimed. "The one they're trying to pin that murder on!"

"How the hell do you know about that?" Ted demanded.

"I escaped from the bridge! I've been wandering around this castle for months, and I listen—"

"Who are you?"

"My name is Professor Emil Kunst," the voice said. "You've got to listen to me. You cannot trust the king."

"And I should trust you?"

"You're caught up in something you can't possibly begin to understand!" Kunst warned. "The Silenced souls! They're all gone! They've all been missing for weeks, and the king sent his son off to find out why!"

"Whoa!" Ted exclaimed. "He said he sent his son to protect my friend! My roommate!"

"Is your roommate Silenced?"

"Well, yeah." Ted hesitated. "What does that—"

"You idiot!" Kunst seethed. "Slaves! They take the Silenced souls as slaves! He's not protecting him! He's probably getting ready to—"

"Wait, wait, can you back up for a fuckin' second?" Ted snapped. "You need to slow down!" He groaned loudly, certain he was about to have a terrible headache. "For fuck's sake. I can't get one damn minute of peace."

"Is there a problem?" Grell's smooth voice purred as he appeared right beside Ted with a sly grin.

"Uh…." Ted gulped.

"Why, my dear Theodore," he purred, "you look like you've seen a ghost."

CHAPTER 4.

"DON'T SAY anything!" Kunst warned. "Not yet!"

"What's the matter?" Grell huffed, oblivious to Kunst's presence. He peered up at Ted, and his piercing eyes were stabbing right through him. "Is there something you need to tell me?"

"There's… there's a lot of ghosts running around this place," Ted replied nervously.

"Don't suppose any of them would happen to be Mire?" Grell said wistfully. "And he can just tell us who murdered him?"

"No." Ted's smile was strained. "Not him."

"I'll come for you later," Kunst hissed, whispering as if he was afraid Grell could hear him. "We'll talk when we're alone. Don't forget! You are not safe with him."

That was reassuring.

Grell watched Ted for a moment, and there was something suspicious in the scrunch of his face. "Are you sure you're all right?"

"Yeah, I'm good. Just a little shook up. You know, buncha angry monsters. Scary stuff."

"Right." Grell didn't look convinced, but he didn't say anything else. He snapped his fingers and summoned the zombie unicorn before them. "Are we ready?"

"Of course, Your Highness," Ghulk said, trotting to the gate and pushing it open with his snout. "We should get going right away. Time is not the friend of justice."

"We have to walk there?" Ted scoffed. "Why can't we just do your magical portal thingie through the forest?"

"Aw, come now, Theodore!" Grell laughed. "Certainly a big, bulging specimen of manhood like you isn't afraid of a little bit of exercise?"

"No, I just don't understand why we can't poof through the damn freaky little woods!"

"Because the freaky little woods disrupt portal energy," Grell replied dryly. "If we try to poof through, as you so eloquently put it, half of you might end up back at the castle, and the other half might land up on the bridge."

"Ow."

"Precisely."

"We should be most cautious," Ghulk cautioned. "Silas doesn't like visitors as it is, but she especially detests those who call on her so early."

Glancing up to the night sky, Ted wondered how they kept time here. It seemed to always be dark, and he hesitantly fell into step beside Grell as they entered the forest.

He didn't hear Kunst again, and he assumed he was still lurking behind him at the castle. He wished he'd paid more attention to Sagittarian lore now. He knew there was something different about how Silenced souls crossed the bridge into that Zebulon place, but he couldn't remember.

As they walked deeper into the forest, Ted was mesmerized by the alien beauty. The trees flickered if they happened to brush by them, and the luminous forest floor darkened wherever their feet landed. It left a trail of black footprints in their wake, but each depression slowly lit back up until it was impossible to tell which way they had come from.

It was easy enough to navigate, though. All Ted had to do was look up and he could see the massive castle towering into the sky behind them.

"Did your new ghost friend say anything interesting?" Grell asked casually, his eyes brighter in the shimmering glow of the trees.

"Just somethin' about getting off the bridge," Ted replied. "It's always weird when I meet ghosts who actually know they're dead."

"Oh?"

"Yeah," Ted said, ducking to avoid a low branch. "There's so many of them that just don't get it. They think it's a joke or some kinda trick. I used to try and help them, but it never ended real well."

"Trust me." Grell smirked. "They all figure it out eventually."

"You some kinda soul expert?"

"Something like that. You see, Xenon calls to them and pulls them all here. A pesky few resist, stick around to haunt the living and what have you, and there are some rare bastards that make it here and then escape the bridge.

"Little pricks run around the damn castle making a stink until they finally get with the program and poof off. Screaming, moaning, knocking things over, rearranging cupboards, the full poltergeist wheelhouse. There was one stubborn ass who wouldn't stop singing this stupid song about some bastard and his wives. We can't have a chat with our little ghostie friends like you can, so we had to exorcise his ass to get him back on course."

"So," Ted began, trying to frame his question carefully, "is it possible for souls to leave Xenon?"

"Oh no. Once they're here, they're stuck here." Grell laughed to himself. "There's no way they can ever leave this plane unless it's on that big ol' bridge taking their merry dead asses off to Zebulon."

"Even if someone took them?"

"What a curious question." Grell paused to eye Ted again with a scowl. "Something specific on your mind, Ted of Aeon?"

"My friend," Ted replied immediately. "There's a ghost, a little boy, who followed me here. I wanna make sure he leaves with me when I go."

"Oh, he'll be fine."

"How can you be so sure?"

"I told you. I know souls. That soul is bound to you."

"Bound to me?" Ted frowned. "What do you mean?"

"The same way that souls can be bound to objects like ghouls, your ghost boy was bound to you," Grell explained. "Usually, a soul can't be attached to a living person. Any traumatic accidents or daring heroics that you can recall partaking in recently?"

"No." Ted didn't understand what Grell was trying to imply. "I have no idea who that kid is. He just showed up one day."

"You really believe that, don't you?" Grell looked intrigued.

"Of course! It's the fuckin' truth!" Ted barked, his temper starting to boil. He was so far out of his element, and he hated feeling this frustrated. "If you know something, Mr. Soul Expert, why don't you tell me?"

"I can't tell you what you don't remember," Grell countered.

"You little fuckin' prick!" Ted growled. "Look, that ghost at the castle? You really wanna know what he said? He told me not to fuckin' trust you!"

"Oh?" Grell's eyes narrowed. "What else did he say, hmm?"

"He also said I should tell you to suck my fuckin' dick, you fuckin' douche!"

"Well, while I highly doubt that, I suppose I could be persuaded—"

"Hey! I want some straight fucking answers." Ted stepped forward and got right in the king's face. "Right now!"

"Mmm," Grell hummed, not budging and smiling coyly up at Ted. "The way you're comin' along doesn't feel like you want anything straight from me."

"Oh, don't you get that shit going again!"

"What shit?" Grell asked innocently.

Ghulk glanced back over his shoulder, sighed deeply as if suffering greatly, and kept walking on without them.

"You know what shit!" Ted towered over Grell. "That flirting bullshit! I'm trying to work on a fuckin' murder case that I'm mixed up in because of your stupid laws, we're running out of fuckin' time, and you're fucking with me!"

"I have no idea what you're talking about."

"For just five fucking seconds," Ted groaned, "can you please just—"

"Here," Ghulk hissed, nodding his great head at a large hole in the forest floor. "Silas's lair is here."

"To be continued," Grell purred, tapping Ted's chin with a wink.

Ted watched Grell strut by him to join Ghulk, and he was so angry he couldn't even speak. He straightened himself out, took a deep breath, and grumbled a long string of curse words.

"Come along, Theodore," Grell called back. "You wanted to work on your case, didn't you?"

"I'm fuckin' coming," Ted grunted, joining them at the edge of the hole.

Looking down, he could see a steep path leading deep beneath the ground and a low light flickering from below. His foot moved a little too close to the edge and knocked some of the glowing soil loose.

It crumbled down into the hole, and an inhuman scream roared up from the tunnel. It shook the ground under their feet, and the glow of the surrounding trees dimmed briefly.

"The fuck is that?" Ted hissed, hating how quickly he jumped back to Grell's side.

Grell reached out to take Ted's arm. "It's all right. You're safe."

Ted wanted to believe him and allowed himself to be pulled in a little closer.

"Hello!" Ghulk called down. "Silas? It's me, Vizier Ghulk!"

The roar that replied made Ted's teeth chatter.

"Silas!" Ghulk implored. "Please! It's Ghulk! I'm your friend! Can we please talk?"

The ground trembled again from another low roar, but a snarling voice then shouted, "Enter!"

"Quickly now," Ghulk said, ducking down into the hole and vanishing out of sight.

"Yup," Ted said with a click of his tongue. "This is my life now. Following a zombie unicorn down a fuckin' scary hole to go talk to some other weird monster. Great. This is just swell."

"At least it's not raining," Grell said cheerfully, giving Ted's arm a friendly squeeze before sliding gracefully down behind Ghulk.

"At least it's not raining," Ted mimicked loudly, gritting his teeth together and trying to lower himself into the hole. It was hard to move with such tight pants on, and he lost his footing. He fell face first, stumbled miserably down to the bottom, and tried to get to his feet.

Grell's strong hands grabbed him and helped him stand. "Are you all right?"

"Fuckin' peachy."

The hole was actually a small tunnel that led into a large cave. The light from the glowing soil above them cast pale shadows all over the walls. There was only a single candle flickering, and Ted had to squint to see anything.

"You brought some foolish human here?" Silas snarled in disgust. "And the king?"

"Silas, please," Ghulk was begging. "They need to speak with you!"

Silas reared back, and Ted recognized her as an Asra. Her fur was streaked with matted gray stripes, and the tentacles hanging around her ears were full of colorful beads.

Even in the low light, Ted could see that the top bead on Silas' left ear was a brilliant and luminous purple. It reminded him of mother of pearl, but it had its own light, shining in the darkness. It was beautiful and familiar, but Ted couldn't immediately place where he had seen it before.

"No!" Silas barked, her twisted spine arching up. "I have nothing to say to them! You tricked me, you—"

"Please," Ted shouted. "I need your help!"

Silas hissed, her long tentacled tail flailing like a whip. The sides of the cave shook violently, sending dust down on their heads.

Ted pushed his way in front of Grell and Ghulk, gritting his teeth as he begged, "Hey! Listen to me, please! Yes, I'm some dumb human, but I'm currently facing fuckin' charges over this Mire guy!"

"You didn't kill Mire," Silas spat. "I would have smelled your wretched filth on him. You're innocent."

"Thanks for that," Ted said with a nervous smile. "I, uh, I'm really desperate for some help, okay? Pretty please?"

Silas sat down on her hind legs, regarding Ted with a toothy scowl. "What do you want, human?"

"Why did Mire want to see the king?"

"A very urgent matter."

"And exactly what would that matter be?"

"An urgent one."

"Okay, not so helpful." Ted rubbed his forehead.

"It's why he sent me to the king. There was no one else Mire could trust."

"So, Mire was killed so he wouldn't tell the king about the very urgent thing?" Ted tried.

"Yes!" Silas looked pleased.

"Why couldn't he just go to the king himself?"

"Too many eyes," Silas said with a snap of her teeth. "Too many watching."

"Do you know who killed Mire?" Ted demanded, hoping a direct question would yield better results.

"I know it wasn't you," Silas replied, "but soon it won't matter."

"Oh?"

"Can't have a murder trial without a corpse," Silas purred mysteriously.

"The hell are you on about?" Grell growled. "Eh? You gonna try to give some necromancy a go?"

"I won't need to," Silas declared. "Someone is going to help me. They're going to get what I need, and then none of this will matter."

"Get what for you?" Ted urged.

"The item I need."

"Oh, for fuck's sake," Ted groaned. He turned to Grell and grumbled sourly, "Look, this is a giant waste of fucking time. We should bounce."

"Maybe you're just really terrible at interrogation," Grell suggested.

"You think you can do better?" Ted waved Grell on. "Be my guest!"

"Silas," Grell said, stepping forward to glare up at the giant beast. "This wouldn't happen to have anything to do with those little rumors about the Kindress, eh?"

Silas bared her teeth and roared, "Get out! I am done talking! It will be mine, all mine, and Mire shall return! They all will!"

Ghulk cowered against the wall of the cave, saying quickly, "Apologies, Silas! Please! We'll take our leave now!"

Grell didn't look impressed by the outburst, but rolled his eyes as he conceded, "Fine. We'll go." He wagged a stern finger at her. "If I find out you've been keeping secrets about the Kindress, I promise that even the greatest magic won't be enough to bring you back from where I send you."

Silas growled low, backing away farther into the cave. "I have nothing else to say to you!"

"Fine." Grell turned on his heel to climb back up the tunnel with Ted scooting right behind him. He offered his hand down to Ted once he'd made it out and effortlessly pulled him up beside him.

There was a lingering moment when their eyes met, and Ted swore that Grell held on to his hand a bit longer than necessary. It was over all too quickly, and Ted bashfully cleared his throat.

Ghulk bounded out from the hole like a startled gazelle, bowing his head low. "I'm sorry she wasn't more cooperative, Your Highness. I suppose it could have gone worse."

"Could have been a hell of a lot better," Ted griped. "I'm even more fucking confused now. Was she serious about messing around with necromancy?"

"The art of true necromancy has been lost for ages." Ghulk began to trot back toward the castle, his milky eyes scanning over Ted with a snort. "Silas has clearly gone mad. There is no way to raise the dead once their soul has passed on."

"Cool, cool, uh, yeah, so…." Ted followed after Ghulk as Grell fell into step beside him. "What the fuck is a Kindress? Mind explaining that bit?"

"The Kindress is the true firstborn of Great Azaethoth."

"And that's, like, the big god in charge?"

"Great Azaethoth has always been, always was, and will always be," Grell recited. "The Kindress was his first child, a being of pure starlight that died in his arms—"

There was a loud crack in the trees a few yards away. The glowing branches grew dark, and a low snarling came from that direction.

All the hairs on the back of Ted's neck stood up. "The fuck?"

"Huh." Grell peered into the forest. "How strange."

The noise stopped.

"Your Highness?" Ghulk sounded tense. "Perhaps you'd be good enough to try portaling us back to the castle? We Eldress are quite resilient. The mortal probably won't survive, but—"

"Just a moment," Grell said, taking a step toward the darkness. He seemed to be waiting for something.

"Look, I'm with zombie-corn," Ted pleaded. "Can we just get out of here?"

A dark shadow came crashing through the trees and tackled Grell.

"The fuck!" Ted shouted, watching in horror as the shadow dragged Grell off and out of sight.

Ghulk neighed hysterically and galloped away.

"Hey, hey!" Ted screamed furiously. "You big fuckin' chicken My Little Pony reject motherfucker! Come back here!"

The snarling got louder, and there were more shadowy figures slithering toward him. He didn't see any sign of Grell, and he reached up to grab a glowing branch. He snapped it off, and the wood grew dark in his hands.

Ted raised it above his head, taking a few practice swings as he barked, "Hey, fuckers!" He stood at the ready, determined not to go down without a fight. "Come get some!"

There was a frantic chittering, and the shadows finally revealed themselves. They were the giant fish-worms Ted had seen before in court, like that Visseract guy.

Their lower bodies were undulating worms, and they had too many arms. Their faces were like some horrible monstrous fish from deep in the sea, with gaping maws lined with giant fangs.

"Why the fuck does everything here have fucked-up teeth?" Ted complained, bracing himself to swing as one of the worms came at him. He nailed it right in the side of the head, cheering as it went down.

His victory was short-lived, however, as the worm quickly recovered. It was back up in seconds and sinking its teeth into Ted's calf.

"Owww, oh, you motherfucker!" Ted roared, blinded by pain as he frantically pounded the branch on the top of the worm's head. "Fuckin' let go, right now!"

Another worm was coming right at him, and Ted knew he would be overwhelmed in seconds. He thought of the little boy, and his heart ached when a small hand tugged at his hip.

A mighty roar suddenly shook the very bedrock and cast the entire forest into darkness as the trees shuddered. The worm that had been chewing on Ted's leg let go and frantically tried to retreat, but it didn't make it very far.

A gigantic Asra, by the far the biggest one Ted had seen yet, was bounding through the trees and snapping them like twigs in its wake. It snatched up the fleeing worm in its jaws and bit it right in half.

Ted staggered and fell, still clutching his branch and trying to staunch his bleeding with his other hand. He couldn't look away, staring at the majestic beast tearing through the worms like they were all made of paper.

Slowly, the trees' glow was returning, and Ted could see that the beast who had come to his rescue had shining golden eyes.

It was King Grell!

His Asra body was sleek and black with faint slivers of gray behind his ears and around his eyes. His tentacles were all gilded and capped in gold, shining with dozens of glimmering beads and baubles.

Even the ones on his tail were decorated, and his giant body was practically glittering as he ripped the worms into pieces.

Ted backed up against a nearby tree, panting hard. He was getting dizzy, cold, and he could see where he'd left a trail of blood behind on the ground. It was getting harder to hold on to his branch, and he could hear a small whisper in his ear.

"*The library….*"

Groaning in pain, Ted dropped the branch and nearly fell over. He tried to clamp his hands over the bleeding wound in his leg, weakly wheezing, "The library? What… what about the library?"

"*It's in the library… go….*"

Ted closed his eyes, and the sound of battle was fading away. He could hear a seagull squealing and the rumbling purr of the ocean.

He knew it couldn't be real, but that didn't stop him from feeling sand beneath him or the warmth of sunlight on his face.

Ted couldn't even remember when he'd last been to the beach. How many years had it been…?

"*The library*," the little voice pleaded again. "*It's there….*"

"What's… what's there?"

"Theodore?" Grell's voice was snarling, terribly worried and urgent. "Oh no. No, no, no! Come on, darling. Wake up. Wakey, wakey, let's go!"

"Mmm...?" A cold and damp nose bumped Ted's cheek. "Wahh...." He turned away from it. "Just... just five more minutes...."

"Wake up! Please! You can't go, darling! Not like this!"

"But I have... I have to go get some sunscreen...." Ted's eyes fluttered, vaguely aware of warm paws picking him up and the new feeling of soft fur all around him. Even though Grell was carrying him, Ted still felt like he was somewhere else.

He was looking around in a bag at the beach, trying to find sunscreen. It was so warm and beautiful, an absolutely perfect day. He thought he saw the little boy running into the waves....

But that couldn't be right.

How weird, he thought, right as he passed out.

CHAPTER 5.

WHEN TED woke up, he was snuggling something warm and soft. He wondered if he was dreaming. It was so cozy and comfortable, and he didn't want to move. He held on to it, his fingers gliding through silky, sleek….

Fur?

"Hello, darling," Grell's voice greeted softly. "Hope you slept well."

Ted tried to jerk away and instantly regretted it, his entire body racked with a wave of pain when he tried to move. "Ohhh, *fuck*!"

"Easy," Grell soothed. "You're safe. It's all right now."

Judging by the familiar purple glow and the lack of doors, they were somewhere back in the castle. They were lying in a massive bed together, and Grell was still in his feline Asra body.

Ted had been curled up in his front paws with his head against his broad chest, and he weakly fell back into that position. He wanted to blame the pain and exhaustion, but it was also so good to be held.

He looked down and saw his leg was bandaged, blushing when he realized he was wearing a long tunic and nothing else. "Uh… thank you. You know, for saving me and all that."

"My pleasure." Grell nudged Ted's shoulder with his nose. "You've been asleep for almost an entire day. I was getting worried."

"Shit!" Ted gasped frantically. "The trial! No, fuck! What time is it? Is it moon whatever o'clock?"

"Calm down," Grell soothed. "The court granted an extension for the trial due to the circumstances. We now have until midnight two days from now." He tilted his head. "Although yesterday is now technically today, I suppose. So, ah yes, midnight tomorrow. Again."

"Okay. That's good. I mean, it's not good that I'm still bein' charged with this bullshit, but okay, awesome."

"Seeing as how it's one o'clock in the morning, that gives you nearly a full forty-eight hours." Grell paused. "Well, forty-*seven*, technically."

"It's seriously that late?" Ted peered up at Grell curiously. "Have you... have you been watching over me? All this time?"

"In a perfectly normal mostly non-creepy way, yes."

"D'awww," Ted cooed, unable to resist teasing and laughing when Grell scrunched up his face. "Big ol' tough kitty is a softie!"

"The Vulgora are quite venomous," Grell said stubbornly, ignoring Ted's taunts. "Your leg should heal in a few hours, but the venom will take more time to work its way out of your system."

"That's what those things were? Vulgora?"

"Yes. Too bad Ghulk didn't stick around to find out, the damn coward." Grell scowled. "Would have loved to see them take a bite out of his ass."

"Why did the Vulgorans attack us?" Ted demanded, a lick of fear making his pulse flutter. "Were they trying to fuckin' kill us?"

"Calm down," Grell said, his long tail curling around Ted. "They were definitely trying to kill us, but I don't know why. This is tied to Mire's death somehow. I'm sure of it."

"Did you, like, eh, leave any of them alive to interrogate them?"

"No, I ate them."

"You *what*?"

"I ate them."

"You ate them."

Grell lifted his big head and looked all around. "Is there an echo in here?"

"You actually ate the worm guys?" Ted scoffed in disgust. "Is that a thing here? Eating people? How the fuck is that a thing?" He narrowed his eyes. "Wait, no! Better question! Why aren't you on fuckin' trial for totally murdering the crap out of those guys?"

"It was obviously self-defense," Grell replied. "They attacked us first."

"Wait a second!" Ted felt a spark of hope. "Couldn't I just say that Mire attacked me and I had to kill him? Could that get me off?"

"That's preposterous," Grell snorted. "He was clearly already dead when you got here, so that won't work."

"That's why I'm innocent," Ted groaned as his hope fizzled and his head throbbed.

"Now, as far as getting you off is concerned...." Grell flashed his teeth in a sly smile.

Ted ignored him. "I can't fuckin' believe you ate all those guys. That's fuckin' gross and weird, and it sure woulda been nice to ask who fuckin' sent 'em!"

"I was a bit distressed when you didn't wake up," Grell grumbled like a scolded child, bowing his head back down. "I wasn't thinking clearly."

"Well, I hope you get fuckin' indigestion!" Ted tried to roll over and winced as another flash of pain shot through his body. "Ah, fuck!"

"Be careful." Grell pressed a giant paw against Ted's chest to keep him from moving. "I told you, it's going to take time. By Great Azaethoth's damn horns, you're going to hurt yourself, you stubborn little ass."

"Aw, didn't know you cared so much, you fuckin' jerk." Ted grinned crookedly up at him. He laid a hand over Grell's paw, and his heart skipped a few beats. He should have been terrified, cuddling with a giant cat monster, but all he could feel was a profound sense of happiness.

He didn't have to worry about his phone ringing at four o'clock in the morning to haul some poor deceased soul out of his bathroom and deal with a raging family who wasn't expecting their loved one to die. There were no ghosts here harassing him for answers he didn't have, and he couldn't honestly remember the last time he'd slept so well.

The depressing grind of his daily life had been replaced with a new sense of adventure and excitement, not to mention the surprisingly welcome advances of a very charming king who was equally alluring whether he was a cat or a man. Ted's current situation was beyond insane, but he couldn't shake the feeling that he was exactly where he was supposed to be.

"I'd be quite bothered if anything was to happen to you," Grell confessed, shuffling a little and looking away with a huff. "It's not every day I have to defend someone in a murder case, you know."

"Right, and you've been doing such a bang-up job," Ted snorted.

"What? We have some exciting new leads!"

Ted's good feeling was quick to turn into annoyance. "Which are what exactly? Silas gave us more bullshit riddles! You ate everyone that attacked us! And I still don't know what the hell a Kindress is!"

"Settle down and I will tell you."

"I'm totally settled," Ted protested. "I'm the very definition of fucking settled."

Grell did not look convinced.

"Look, this is… this is fuckin' scary," Ted said with a long sigh. "One second I'm just hanging out, minding my own business, and now I'm here in fuckin' Xenon. I didn't even know any of this, any of you guys, were real."

"And now you're knee-deep in it, hmm?" Grell tilted his head thoughtfully.

"I'm chilling with a giant cat king, and fish people tried to kill me. Pretty sure my new permanent mental status is very confused and endlessly frustrated." Ted started petting Grell's paw and closed his eyes. "It beats the hell out of being on call and dealing with dead people, but this still kinda sucks."

"Don't worry," Grell said, bowing his head to tap Ted's hair with his nose. "I do intend to see this through to the end and win your freedom."

"You know, you're pretty nice when you wanna be." Ted kept petting Grell's paw, and he smiled when it tightened around him. "Kinda makes up for you eatin' all those fish guys."

"Don't tell anyone," Grell whispered. "I have a reputation to uphold."

"Hmph." Ted leaned his head back. "So, the Kindress? What was Silas talking about?"

"All right, my darling Lucian friend, do you understand who Great Azaethoth is?"

"Big head honcho god?"

"Precisely," Grell replied. "Most of the faithful believe that his first children were Etheril and Xarapharos, twins that propagated the entire pantheon of gods."

"But it was actually this Kindress?" Ted tried his best to follow along.

"Yes. The true firstborn of Great Azaethoth was a child of pure starlight, but it died in his arms before it could take its first breath."

"Well, that blows."

"Azaethoth wasn't too happy about it either. His grief was endless, and his tears threatened to drown the universe. A special fountain was built to contain them, hidden away in a secret place."

"A fountain full of… tears?" Ted made a face. "Sounds kinda salty. And gross."

"But very powerful," Grell pointed out. "These are the tears of Great Azaethoth. Their magical potential is nearly endless, quite dangerous in fact, but they exist for a singular purpose."

"Which is what?"

"To kill the Kindress."

"Wait, the star baby? I thought you said it already died!"

"It did," Grell scolded. "But Great Azaethoth is nothing if not a very persistent deity, and he keeps trying to resurrect his child."

"And then he has to kill it? With his own tears?" Ted was absolutely horrified. "What the fucking fuck?"

"Some things are meant to be left alone," Grell said with a sad smile, "but grief is a terrible disease. Great Azaethoth brings back his child to ease his mourning, but his pain corrupts the starlight inside it. It changes the child into a monster.

"The Kindress becomes unstable, dangerous, and is born again only to die by its father's hand before it can destroy the universe."

"That's the most fucking depressing story I've ever heard," Ted grumbled. "And I work at a funeral home. I know fuckin' depressing shit."

"Yeah, it's a real downer," Grell agreed. "More importantly, it's true. Sages get all bent out of shape when you start talking about the little star child, but it's not a legend. It's not some myth."

"And Silas is after it?"

"Most likely. Amongst the Kindress's many magical powers, it's said that it can return life to the dead. Conversely, it also takes life from what's already alive. Real fun."

"So she thinks she can use it to bring back Mire," Ted mused.

"Mmhmm."

"Where is this damn thing at?"

"Last one should have popped up almost twenty years ago," Grell replied, rolling his broad shoulders in a shrug. "Haven't seen any trace of it. Could be hiding, could already be dead, who knows."

"But you said something about there being rumors?" Ted accused. "What do you know?"

Grell drew his lips back and bared his fangs, chiding, "Clever little imp, aren't you?"

"Not really that clever, since you said it right in front of me." Ted scoffed. "Come on. Give."

"Fine!" Grell's tail whipped in annoyance. "The Kindress is like Great Azaethoth. Always was, always is, and always will be. Its cycle of birth and death is absolutely endless and impossible to predict, but it seems to especially love dying right after a big ol' fancy celestial event. We never know when it's actually alive and bopping about, you see, but we do know when it dies.

"Unlike other gods, the Kindress's soul completely blacks out that bridge when it passes through. Takes months for it to light back up. Now, there was a pretty impressive celestial event nineteen years ago, perfect time for the Kindress to get itself murdered, but nothing happened. Another magnificent celestial event occurred last year with absolute nada.

"And yet there are still some very strange things going down. Things that haven't happened in centuries. Gods are waking up and walking Aeon again. By both of Great Azaethoth's curly horns, gods are even being *killed*. Not to mention all the damn souls missing from the bridge—"

"Souls missing?" Ted frowned, his mind tracking back to what Kunst had told him. It was too easy to get caught up in Grell, especially when he was being so kind, and Ted had nearly forgotten the warning. It made the current snuggling awkward, and he tried to pull away from Grell's hold.

Not that he had any reason to trust Kunst over Grell, but he'd never known a ghost to lie.

His attempt to move sent a fresh wave of agony throughout his body, and he groaned. "Fuckkk, fuckity fuck fuck!"

"What's wrong?" Grell asked, clearly concerned and nosing at Ted's shoulder.

"Nothing! I mean, fuck! Ow, that fuckin' hurts like hell!" Ted fussed, struggling to get comfortable as Grell wrapped him back up between his paws to keep him from moving. "Okay, can we cut back on kitty cuddles?"

"You need to stop moving," Grell scolded.

"I'll quit fuckin' moving if you just, ugh, stop aggressively snuggling me with your big giant paws! Could you, you know, be, like, a dude again maybe?"

"Fine," Grell said, his body shrinking down and his sleek fur melting away until he was back in his human form.

Ted was now perched on Grell's broad chest, and moving was definitely the last thing on his mind. He could feel the heat of Grell's body against his own, and the gentle way Grell's strong hands settled on his back made his face heat up.

"Is this better?" Grell asked, his usual swagger replaced by genuine concern.

"This is... uh... this is good." Ted didn't dare look down, because he already knew Grell was naked, and he couldn't stand to make this situation any more awkward for himself.

Except it really wasn't that strange. He felt safe, and there was something about the way Grell was looking at him that made him want to stay right here forever.

"I thought you wanted to move?" Grell quirked a brow.

"I'm good." Ted cleared his throat. "Uh, so, about these missing souls?"

"What about them?"

"Oh, don't start that stupid crap again." Ted narrowed his eyes. "We were having such a nice fuckin' chat, and there you go, answering questions with questions again."

"Ask the right questions and you shall receive the answers you seek," Grell said smugly.

"Are these souls Silenced?" Ted challenged, pleased when the smug smile dropped right off Grell's face.

"Now how would you know that?" Grell scowled. "Don't suppose it would be your little ghost friend who told me to suck your dick?"

Hearing those words spoken so casually made them even more obscene, and Ted gulped. He licked his lips, countering, "I don't know, maybe. Why? You thinking about it?"

"Thinking about what?"

"You know."

"Sucking your dick?" Grell's smile only grew as Ted blushed, flashing his teeth. "Can't even say it out loud, can you."

"Maybe I just don't want to," Ted argued. "Maybe I would rather talk about those Silenced souls and what your crazy-ass son is really doing with my roommate."

"Ohhh, this was a very chatty little ghost, indeed!" Grell laughed, his fingers dragging up Ted's spine. "Mmm... I suppose if you insist that we discuss it...."

"I do," Ted confirmed.

"Then I must tell you that I'd like to take you to dinner before we explore any carnal pleasures," Grell said seriously.

"Oh, for fuck's sake!" Ted tried to roll away and cried out in pain as his muscles screamed their protests. "Ow, ow, ow, fuck!"

"Aw, my darling Theodore!" Grell cackled and pulled Ted back into his arms. "Easy now! I'm sorry, I couldn't resist!"

"You're such a douche!" Ted found himself even closer to Grell now, practically on top of him.

"Guilty." Grell was beaming, stroking Ted's back warmly.

Ted was exhausted from the simple tussle and had to lay back down. His head found Grell's shoulder, and he flopped in surrender. "Ulgh. I give."

"So, dinner, then?"

"Huh?"

"You'll let me take you to dinner?" Grell asked without missing a beat. "We can continue discussing souls, monsters, gods... mmm, what else?"

"Grell." Ted hesitated. "We don't exactly have a whole lot of time. I don't know...."

"Oh, and the tempting proposition of fellatio, of course."

"Seriously?" Kunst's voice drawled in disgust. "I try to give you some sincere advice and you're in bed with him?"

Ted's face caught on fire, and he wasn't sure how to defend himself to a ghost. He chose to ignore Kunst for now, but got back on track by asking, "Why are Silenced souls so important?"

"Their steps power the bridge," Kunst grumbled impatiently.

"They're the source of power that keep the bridge running," Grell replied at almost precisely the same time. "Now, is that a yes to dinner?"

"Only if you tell me why a bunch of those souls missing would be a big deal."

"I don't know if you've noticed, but it's looking a little dim out there lately. It's not so much that the souls are missing in the sense that they've been taken, but missing in that none of them are coming here. Something is happening in Aeon, and Silenced people have stopped dying. Once the ones here hit their hundred-year mark, there's none to replace them."

"Hundred-year mark?"

"All Silenced souls—" Kunst began.

"All Silenced souls walk the bridge for a hundred years," Grell said, his voice easily overtaking Kunst's.

Kunst grunted in annoyance.

"Because they don't have magic of their own, they have to earn their passage," Grell went on to explain, not hearing Kunst's fussing. "It takes at least a century for them to gain enough of a spark to poof on over to Zebulon. Now, dinner tonight?"

"So they're not slaves?" Ted asked pointedly.

"No, of course not," Grell replied, his expression betraying how hurt that question left him.

"Ah! He's a liar!" Kunst exclaimed. "Ask him what Visseract and Gronoch have been doing! Ask him about the pits!"

"So." Ted touched Grell's chest, "I gotta be honest right now. The ghost I told you about?"

"No, no! Don't you dare tell him!" Kunst hissed. "We have a real chance here to help people—"

"The one who told me not to trust you?" Ted went on, having to raise his voice to hear himself over Kunst. "Well, he's here right now, and he's insisting that you're lying and wants me to ask you about Visseract and Gronoch and some fuckin' pits."

"Gronoch?" Grell's eyes widened in shock and promptly narrowed.

"Who's that?"

"God of healing and attrition, second eldest son of Salgumel and Urilith."

"Oh," Ted said. "Well, that doesn't sound so bad."

"It's bad," both Kunst and Grell said in unison.

"For fuck's sake," Ted griped, pointing in the general direction of Kunst's voice. "You! Stop talking for a damn second!"

"The nerve!" Kunst gasped.

"Okay!" Ted took a deep breath. "Gronoch is a bad god, and Visseract is that fish guy who really wants to convict me, right?"

"Yes," Grell replied with a snarl. "That's the one."

"The pits!" Kunst snapped. "Never mind all that nonsense! I know what I saw! Ask him about the pits!"

"Shut up about the damn pits!" Ted hated how crazy he looked talking to someone Grell couldn't see. "Fuck, this is annoying."

"Hold on a moment." Grell snapped his fingers. A large glass orb appeared in his hand, and he held it up in the air. "Come along, ghostie. Take a little peek inside and we can all have a nice chat."

"That's a trap," Kunst said with a growl.

"He says it's a trap," Ted echoed.

"Of course it's a trap," Grell drawled. "It's a spirit box. It'll bind his ass in here, but he'll be able to talk." He looked around, perhaps trying to detect Kunst's presence. "Would you like that, little ghostie? You have so much to say about me, how about you say it to my face?"

"Oh, I'm going to regret this." Kunst growled in frustration, but the orb suddenly lit up, filled with a milky blue light. "Now, you listen to me, Your Royal Highness! My name is Professor Emil Kunst, and I witnessed the most heinous fiends conspiring down in the pits!"

"Congratulations! I don't know if you've noticed, but 'conspiring' is one of the top ten most popular activities in Xenon. There's even a club. They have T-shirts."

"What the fuck are the pits?" Ted demanded.

"Underground interdimensional channels that run beneath Xenon," Grell replied quickly. "Some of them are in Xenon proper, some of them are far beyond it, and a few are in between."

"Huh?"

"Spaces between worlds, darling." Grell patted Ted's shoulder.

"So, what would a god and fish dude be doing down there?"

"They were making arrangements for Silenced souls," Kunst said, the orb flickering with his fury. "I heard them! Gronoch has found a way to create slaves using people who are Silenced, and he wants Visseract to give him more!"

"Ha!" Grell scoffed. "There's no way to remove souls from Xenon once they've come here. And in case you didn't notice, we're running a bit short. You must have misunderstood them."

"I know what I heard!" Kunst fumed. "And I know those planes are restricted, except to members of the royal family! You must have let them in there! Which also puts you in direct violation of your own treaty that no living god shall set foot in Xenon!"

"Anything else defamatory and exciting you want to share?" Grell asked dryly.

"You must know that whatever Gronoch is planning with those Silenced souls, you can bet that he means to awaken Salgumel and destroy the world. His brother, Tollmathan, already tried once before, and I died stopping him! I will not allow it to happen again, not while I can still fight!"

"Tragic, really. Thanks for that. Very educational. We'll chat more soon. Bye-bye now!" Grell snapped his fingers, and the orb disappeared. "Irritating little thing, wasn't he?"

"Hey!" Ted protested. "Don't you think that might have been important?"

"What?"

"Gods trying to end the world! Doesn't that sound kinda like a big deal to you?"

"Meh," Grell scoffed, waving his hand. "One crisis at a time. We have a new suspect in Mire's murder to focus on."

"We do?"

"Humble Visseract just jumped to the top of the list," Grell replied. "Ghostie was right in that only members of the royal family can enter the pits." He held up a finger. "Except I recently granted Mire a special key so he could investigate some of the ancient crypts there."

"So if you didn't let them in, and I'm assuming your crazy son didn't since he's been busy annoying me as a cat…."

"That only leaves two possibilities." Grell sighed, reaching up to massage his brow as if trying to fend off a headache. "Either Mire was in league with them, or, more likely, he was a victim of their scheming."

"What's the matter?" Ted frowned. "Isn't this good? This means I'm totally freakin' innocent!"

"It also means I have to decide whether or not to declare war on Zebulon."

"War?" Ted's stomach lurched.

"No living god is permitted to set foot in Xenon," Grell said with a wry smile. "It's part of the treaty that Great Azaethoth signed that gave us this world as our own. There's nothing actually stopping the gods from coming here, but to do so is considered an act of war."

"War, as in, fighting a bunch of gods?" Ted tried to sit up and grumbled as his muscles cramped. The pain took his breath away, but he kept struggling. "No, come on! Fuck! You can't be serious!"

"I'm very serious," Grell said, watching with a scowl as Ted squirmed. "Will you stop that? It hurts to look at you when you do that."

"The pits," Ted said urgently, crying out as he managed to pull himself up, only to fall flat on his back. "Ah, shit!"

"I told you to stop!" Grell growled, rolling over to pin Ted against the bed.

"Listen to me!" Ted barked, completely helpless beneath Grell's firm hold. "There has to be another way!"

"That's my problem, not yours," Grell grunted.

"The pits, you said some of them aren't actually in Xenon!" Ted panted. "Right?"

"Yes," Grell replied carefully, as if wary of a trap.

"So technically, you don't know if that Gronoch guy actually came to Xenon!" Ted went on with an earnest smile. "No need to start a war over that, right?"

"Why, Theodore," Grell purred in delight, "you're a lovely little genius. I could kiss you."

"Yeah?" Ted zeroed in on Grell's lips and swallowed thickly. At that moment, he didn't even care that Grell kept screwing up his name. The thought of correcting him was the very last thing on his mind.

There was no way to escape that Grell was very much naked and very much on top of him, and Ted's body was responding accordingly. He felt vulnerable and weak, but Grell also made him feel so safe.

He felt… *wanted.*

Ted hadn't known such desire in so long, and the air between them was instantly electrified. Grell's eyes were moving over his body as if seeing Ted for the first time, and he was leaning in, only stopping when he was a breath away from Ted's lips.

"Yeah," Grell echoed, his nose lightly bumping Ted's. "I could kiss you… if you wanted me to, of course."

"Well, only if you really want me to want you to," Ted replied, inhaling shakily. "I mean, did you brush your teeth after eating all those fish dudes?"

"Flossed too." Grell's mouth hovered over his, neither retreating nor advancing, and the torment made Ted's insides clench.

They had been here before, so close to kissing and yet worlds away, and Ted didn't know if this was a wise decision. Considering he'd almost died and had just talked Grell out of starting a war, perhaps a kiss was another unnecessary risk.

"Hmm," Grell hummed, licking his lips so Ted could feel the briefest swipe of his tongue. "I suppose I only want you to want me to want you to do it if you truly want to—"

Oh, fuck it.

Biting back the brief flash of pain, Ted surged upward to connect their lips in a passionate kiss.

CHAPTER 6.

GRELL'S RESPONDING kiss was fierce. He pushed Ted down into the plush pillows, owning every inch of his mouth with a long swipe of his rough tongue. Grell's tongue was barbed like a cat's, slick and scratchy, and it was hotter than Ted could have ever dreamed of. He would be replaying this moment in his mind for years to come.

A few days ago, he'd been caught in the soul-sucking grind of a depressing job, quite literally haunted by ghosts, and left longing for any lowly scrap of affection. Now he was kissing a handsome king in a glowing castle floating out amongst the stars.

Sure, he was still fighting asinine murder charges and the king could turn into a giant cat monster, but it was still an improvement.

Ted moaned, reaching up to grab Grell's shoulders. He loved the rough texture of Grell's tongue sliding against his own. He couldn't get over the softness of his lips or how strong his hands were as they explored the broad lines of his body.

Ted wanted to wrap himself all around Grell, and ow, ow, ow!

Right.

Still full of nasty fish-people venom.

"Fuck!" Ted growled, his muscles seizing up in pain and forcing him to break the kiss. "Ugh, I'm sorry."

"Don't be," Grell said softly, smiling with such a warmth that he seemed decades younger. He gently nuzzled Ted's cheek, placing a tender kiss there as he said, "Mm, just relax... and try not to move."

"Wh-what are you doing?" Ted asked nervously.

"Taking care of you," Grell replied, his golden eyes shining brightly as he glanced down over Ted's thick chest. His hand slid over the thin fabric of his tunic, finding his nipple and petting it slowly.

Ted groaned, shivering and twitching, his cock growing hard with absolutely nowhere to hide. He couldn't relax, feeling the urge to move and take over, to take control. "Grell, shouldn't I...."

"Theodore," Grell said firmly, tilting his head back down for a sweet kiss. "If you want me to stop, then tell me now. Otherwise, lay back, relax, and let me rock your little mortal world, hmm?"

"O-okay," Ted said, his hands unclenching by his sides. "I can do that. Totally."

"The constant expectation to take control has left you feeling inadequate when you're put in this position, hmm?" Grell gently dragged a single finger down Ted's chest to his hip, the tunic magically fading away. "You want someone else to take over, and yet it's been so long that you don't know how...."

"Fuck," Ted whispered, watching his chest tremble as Grell started to kiss his way down to his stomach. His cock flexed, and he whimpered, secretly thrilled that he couldn't move. It made it easier to give in and let Grell do what he wanted, and Ted whispered, "Yes."

"It's all right," Grell promised, lavishing the crest of Ted's hipbone with wet smooches. "I've got you. I'll take care of everything."

"What, uh, what are you doing?" Ted asked, excited and curious.

"All this talk about sucking dick has given me the most lovely idea," Grell teased slyly. He ran his hands over Ted's muscular thighs, getting settled between them as he licked his lips. "I think I may in fact—" He dropped his voice to a sultry whisper. "—suck your dick."

Ted could not look away from Grell's tongue. Flicking it out like that over his lower lip wasn't so unusual, but Ted had never noticed before just how long it was. It had several inches on a normal human's, and it looked even bigger.

Grell noticed Ted staring and stuck out his tongue with a lecherous wink. Yup. Definitely long, thick, and absolutely made for sinful things.

"Oh fuck," Ted gasped without meaning to.

"Oh yes." Grell eyed Ted's cock and bowed his head. He nuzzled against his hard shaft, breathing him in with a luxurious sigh. "Mm, I just know you're going to taste fantastic."

"Fuck, that's hot," Ted panted. "Just…." He couldn't even finish the thought, faltering for a conclusion that didn't sound lame.

Just what? Be gentle? Be patient? Don't be surprised if it's over in seconds?

"Don't worry, darling. I'll still respect you in the morning," Grell teased, opening his mouth wide and sinking down on Ted's cock with a loud groan.

The sudden wet heat made Ted moan, and he had to remind himself that he couldn't move much without it hurting. He watched in awe as Grell took every inch of him without hesitation, squeaking, "Holy crap! That's, that's so good!"

Grell sucked him slowly, stroking with his tongue from base to tip inside his mouth. The rough texture of the barbs was weird, but not at all uncomfortable. It was an incredible feeling, and Ted feared he wouldn't be able to last very long. He took a few deep breaths, focused on enjoying himself but trying not to bust too fast.

Then Grell did something that Ted couldn't explain: His tongue began to wrap *around* his shaft, spiraling down and squeezing as he sucked.

"F-fuck!" Ted wheezed, his hands fisting into the sheets. Nothing had ever been this intense, and he was lost in the lovely warmth and pulsating pressure of Grell's wicked tongue wrapped so intimately around him.

Grell somehow managed to look smug, glancing up at Ted as if to gauge his pleasure. He kept his tongue going, twisting and untwisting down Ted's cock as he bobbed his head, stuffing his own throat as far as he could go.

Which, apparently, was all the fucking way.

Ted's hips jerked up despite his best efforts, and he moaned in a mixture of pleasure and pain. He gasped when Grell pushed him down to pin his body against the bed, and that made all of this even hotter. His balls were already tightening up, and he was doomed. Oh, he was so freakin' doomed.

Grell never slowed, apparently determined to make Ted absolutely lose his mind. He squeezed Ted's sides, his powerful hands sliding down his hips and thighs as he gave him the best blowjob of his entire life.

"Grell!" Ted cried out in warning, shaking and twitching as the king's hot mouth dragged him over the edge. He couldn't stop, coming hard and groaning as his back arched right off the bed. The bliss blinded the discomfort, and he pulsed repeatedly down Grell's tight throat.

Growling possessively, Grell grabbed Ted's ass and held him suspended off the bed, swallowing back all that he had to offer and sucking more passionately, as if he could milk out more if he just tried hard enough.

"Hunghh… oh… oh God!" Ted sounded hysterical to his own ears, his toes curling up as Grell kept taking and taking. He was waiting for the agony of overstimulation to steal his joy, but it never came. He was totally enslaved by Grell's wicked tongue, and his climax seemed never ending.

He breathed in—still coming.

He breathed out—still coming.

Ted could feel tears in his eyes, and he clawed at the bed, not sure whether to cry or scream or both. He heard Grell growl, and the intense explosion of sensation finally faded. It was a steady drop, like a feather floating down on a light breeze, and left him totally exhausted.

Grell returned his hips to the bed and finally pulled off with one last lick, giving Ted full view of his especially dexterous tongue.

"Holy… fuck…," Ted managed to wheeze, his bones sinking into the mattress as Grell climbed back up to claim a kiss. Ted's lips were tingling as they kissed, and he was buzzing from the fantastic orgasm.

"Consider your world rocked," Grell taunted with a gorgeously smug smile, pecking Ted's nose. "Mmm. You tasted even better than I thought you would, Theodore."

"Awesome," was all Ted could manage.

"Just wait until you have my cocks," Grell purred.

"*Cocks*?" Ted echoed.

Grell had certainly misspoken.

There was no way….

Grell was grinning very proudly.

"Oh fuck."

Ted didn't know if he would survive, but fuck if it wouldn't be fun to try. "Do you wanna…?" He gestured vaguely. "You know? Get yours?"

"Mmm, I don't think you could handle me in your current state." Grell chuckled as he rolled off beside Ted. "I really don't mind, darling. I enjoyed myself thoroughly."

"Yeah?" Ted grinned.

"Absolutely," Grell promised. He looked every bit the cat who had gotten the cream. "Feeling good, love?"

"Uh-huh." Ted carefully shuffled onto his side with minimal discomfort, his face still hot from the thrill of climax. "You were not kidding, huh? Because *damn*, Your Royal Highness."

"Oh, it was nothing," Grell said, clearly very pleased. He snapped his fingers and summoned a glass of liquor to his hand. "Anytime."

"It's been a while for me," Ted confessed. He didn't know if the Asra were big into pillow talk, but he was uncertain as to where this left them.

Maybe it was nothing.

Maybe it was something....

"It's also been a long time for me," Grell said, snapping his fingers to summon a second glass for Ted. "Despite my dashing charisma, it's not often I find myself desired by others... not unless they want something for themselves."

"You mean because you're king," Ted supplied, cringing as he tried to sit up to take a sip.

"Precisely." Grell wiggled his nose and a long, looped straw appeared so Ted could drink without moving.

"Thanks."

"Why has it been so long, hmm?" Grell eyed Ted curiously. "You're a gorgeous specimen. You don't smell particularly bad. You're even tolerable to talk to."

"Mmm, just keep pouring on the compliments."

"I'm serious!" Grell protested.

"Look, I've had some dates, you know!" Ted frowned, slurping at his drink through the swirly straw. "I had a really bad breakup last year, and since then, it's just been hard to get serious with anyone."

"What happened? Did they break your precious heart? Carry on a torrid love affair?"

"No, he proposed." Ted grimaced.

"Wait," Grell scoffed. "Your relationship ended because your partner offered you marriage?"

"I wasn't ready," Ted explained hastily. "We'd only been dating for a year—"

"A year? Isn't that a pretty significant chunk of lifespan for humans? Don't you only live for half a century or so?"

"Hey, we can live for, like, I dunno, eighty years!" Ted was flustered, trying to explain himself. "Look, it was very significant.

I really loved him, but I wasn't ready for all of that. I got scared. And when I told him no, well, he dumped me."

"Ouch."

Ted sucked hard on the straw, gulping back the booze and groaning. "Look, I've had plenty of time to beat myself up over it. Pretty sure that was my one shot at a happily ever after, and I fucked it up."

"What makes you say that?" Grell frowned.

"I can't meet anybody new," Ted replied sadly. "And on the actual freak occasion I do meet someone, trying to make time for a date around my schedule is almost impossible. Guys get tired of waiting around, and they just move on.

"I can't stop thinking, what if I had just said yes? I wouldn't be alone right now. I wouldn't be so fucking miserable, watching everybody else around me hanging out with their happy families and shit. I mean, my job would still suck ass, but at least I'd be going home to someone."

"Well," Grell said thoughtfully, "I'm rather thankful you didn't get married."

"Ugh. Why?"

"If you had accepted the proposal, you wouldn't very likely have the roommate that you do now," Grell replied. "You wouldn't have been around to annoy my son, and he wouldn't have sent you through the portal. In essence, we wouldn't have ever met."

"Shit." A blush crept up Ted's neck. "Yeah, I guess not." He took another sip of his drink. "What about you?"

"What?" Grell blinked.

"I work all the fuckin' time, and the smell of formaldehyde isn't a big turn-on for most people. That's why I'm still single. So what about you?"

"I also work all the time and because no one could ever compare to my mate, I suppose," Grell said with a bittersweet smile. "After he died, I was… angry. For all my power, I couldn't save him."

Even though it hurt, Ted moved his arm to take Grell's hand.

Grell laced their fingers together as he went on, "It was a plague that took him. Hundreds of our people were sick and dying, and his stubborn ass insisted on going to help." He laughed bitterly. "Caught it himself, that dumb bastard."

"I'm sorry," Ted said, wishing the words didn't sound so hollow.

"He was my light." Grell smiled sadly. "The whole kingdom was a little less bright after he died." He drained his glass. "Our son didn't take it particularly well either."

"So," Ted said carefully, "he wasn't always such a brat?"

"Ha!" Grell actually laughed. "No, he definitely was. But it got worse after Vael died."

"That was his name?"

"Mmhmm." Grell's thumb brushed over Ted's knuckles. "Vael Crem. We were together for six hundred and fifty-six years."

"Holy fuck," Ted murmured, eyeing Grell curiously. "Six hundred... how old are you?"

"A lady never discusses her age." Grell batted his eyes.

"You Asra really live for a while, huh?"

"Indeed," Grell said. "And as long as I've lived, I've never met anyone else like Vael...." He smirked. "Well, until I met you, of course."

"Me?" Ted was flattered. "I really remind you of your husband?"

"Yes," Grell said. "You're both hopelessly stubborn bastards."

"Sweet talker."

"And you make me laugh," Grell said more sincerely, leaning in to kiss Ted. "It's been a very long time since I've laughed like this. It's been a long time since I've felt... well, anything like this. Thank you for that."

"Yeah," Ted murmured, his chest flooded with a new warmth as he gazed over at Grell. "No problem."

Grell was smiling at him so sweetly, and Ted melted as he came back in for another kiss. He shifted his body, aching to be closer, and winced when he felt another stab of pain.

"Fuck!"

"Mmm, perhaps we should exercise a bit of patience with regards to more exciting carnal activities." Grell backed off with a departing kiss.

"Yeah, probably," Ted mumbled. There was a tug at his leg, and he glanced up to see the familiar shadow of the little boy out of the corner of his eye. "Mm, hey, little guy."

"Your friend?" Grell asked politely, sitting up and refilling his drink so he could take a healthy gulp.

"Yeah," Ted said, glancing around the room to figure out where the boy had gone. "He's acting like he wants me to follow him." There was another hard tug. "Yeah, definitely."

"To where exactly? Back to the library?"

"Maybe." Ted tried to concentrate. "There's something… fuck, I can't remember. He was trying to tell me something. If he's trying to get me to go again, there's gotta be something there."

"Does he often show you where to find things?"

"No," Ted replied, hissing in pain as he tried to move. "Ow, fuck. No, he doesn't, but it's just this feeling I have. Like it's really important."

"Well," Grell tutted, "whatever it is, it can wait until you're feeling better."

"Oh, come on!"

"Nope." Grell shook his head. "You're staying right here until I deem you well enough to continue investigating."

"I'm fine!" Ted argued.

"Really?" Grell grinned, smacking Ted's shoulder. "Go on, then! Go follow your little ghost friend. Let's see how far you get."

Determined and agitated, Ted summoned all of his strength. He would show that damn king what he was made of. He ignored the aches and the pain in his leg, grunting with massive effort as he forced his body to function. He was sitting up, yes, almost there—

He rolled flat onto his face and couldn't get back up.

"So, how'd that work out for you?" Grell cooed with syrupy sweetness.

"Fuck off," Ted mumbled into the sheets.

Grell helped roll him back over and tucked the blankets around him, fussing, "You're staying here until that nasty venom wears off."

"Yes, dear," Ted griped, smiling as Grell brought him up on his chest to cuddle. "Fine. I'll be good." He glanced out in the room. "Sorry, little guy. Gotta wait."

Although Ted couldn't be sure, he thought he heard a small, frustrated sigh.

"Hey, what was all that stuff you said before?" Ted asked.

"I say a lot of stuff." Grell ran his fingers through Ted's hair. "You'll have to be a bit more specific, darling."

"About me and the kid," Ted clarified.

"Ah, that."

"Yes, that!" Ted made a face. "Come on, Mr. Soul Expert. If a soul can't be bound to a living person, explain how it happened to me."

"The simplest explanation would be that you're not alive," Grell replied with a wry smile.

"Sorry. Last time I checked, very much with the living."

"And you don't recall any accidents?" Grell's hand moved over Ted's chest. "Stubbed your toe and fell off a cliff? Took a shower during a lightning storm? Pumped some gas while on your cell phone? Nothing at all?"

"No," Ted insisted, frowning as he watched Grell's hand pause over his heart. "What is it? I got a heartbeat, don't I?"

"Of course."

"Then why do you keep asking about accidents and shit?" Ted laughed nervously. "You're really starting to freak me out."

"Short of Great Azaethoth himself, I only know of two ways for souls to bind with the living," Grell said solemnly. "One involves a Silenced vessel, which you are not. The other, well, the living bit is quite optional."

"Okay?" Ted's brow furrowed. "What do you mean by 'optional'?"

"Death," Grell replied without hesitation.

Ted started to laugh, waiting for Grell to give in and tell him it was a joke. It didn't happen. He scoffed at Grell's flat expression, arguing passionately, "But I'm not dead!"

"Not right now," Grell pointed out. "At least, I'm pretty sure." He booped Ted's nose and watched him flinch. "No, right. Sorry, just checking. You're alive."

"I think I would remember if I freakin' died!" Ted snapped.

"Maybe you would," Grell said, gently taking Ted's hand and laying it over his own on Ted's chest. "But then again, maybe you wouldn't…."

Ted felt a rush of heat and a faint pulse. As the sensation grew, he realized it was his own. It thumped a little faster than what was probably normal, and he blamed Grell's touch and the strange conversation for its rapid pitter-patter.

"Listen," Grell implored, his golden eyes shining as he held Ted's hand firmly in place.

Ted tried, closing his eyes to focus on the rhythm.

Faster and faster it went, and then….

Another beat.

It was a second heartbeat thumping alongside his own. It was faint, weak, but definitely a unique rhythm.

"I don't understand," Ted whispered, his fingers tightening around Grell's. "What does this fuckin' mean…?"

"Something that I can't explain," Grell said quietly. "Some miraculous incident, certainly mired in tragedy, brought you and your little friend together. You died with him. Both of you died. At the same time. All right?"

"And… but… but… I'm… I'm still alive," Ted said, his stomach turning anxiously. "That's not possible! I'm not fuckin' dead!"

"I know," Grell soothed, "and that's because someone—or *something*—brought you back."

"What?"

"So," Grell said with a click of his tongue. "Now that we got all that weirdness out of the way— Is that gonna be a yes for dinner?"

CHAPTER 7.

"I THINK I'm gonna throw up," Ted whispered in horror.

"I'll hold your hair," Grell said with a friendly smile.

"You're being serious," Ted said, searching Grell's face for any sign that this was a terrible prank and finding none. "You really think I died and someone resurrected me?"

"I know they did," Grell said, nodding down to where their joined hands still rested on Ted's chest. "I've been around for a long time, love. I remember what real necromancy costs."

"Which is what?"

"Sacrifice," Grell replied. "Life for life."

Ted jerked his hand away, nauseated as he tried to sort out the full ramifications of what Grell was telling him. "Someone… died for me?"

"Only a tiny bit," Grell said, petting Ted's hair. "Someone gave part of their life for you."

"Isn't that what people do with ghouls?"

"No," Grell said. "A ghoul is a bookmark in a story that's already ended."

"And me?"

"Your story got a sequel."

"Fuck," Ted whispered shakily. "That's some heavy shit."

"Your parents into magic by chance? Perhaps any of your friends dabble in ancient forbidden spells?" Grell asked. "Any of your little ghost buddies decide to tell you the secrets of necromancy, eh?"

"No." Ted shook his head and loudly slurped on the swirly straw. "My life is so fucking boring. I work, I work some more, I come home, I work. Call my parents sometimes. Lots of gross and depressing shit in between. That's it."

"Really?"

"Up until coming here and shacking up with a hot king, yeah, not a whole lot going on," Ted said with a shy grin, trying to be braver than he felt.

"Mmm, so I take it you're going to accept my dinner invitation?" Grell preened. "Seeing as how your social calendar is so open and all."

"Yeah," Ted replied, biting his lower lip. "I mean, if you think you can spare the time while you're working so diligently on my murder case. Forty-six hours to go, right?"

Grell gasped dramatically. "I will have you know that I've been working very hard! So hard that I've already sent out a warrant for Visseract's arrest."

"No shit?" Ted frowned. "Wait, when the hell did you do that?"

"After the ghostie told us, before the spectacular fellatio." Grell smirked. "I sent the equivalent of a mental text message. Lovely little talent I learned from an Absola who needed help with a property dispute. We were having such a lovely time, and I didn't want to ruin the mood, darling."

"How very considerate of you."

"Mmhm. I told Vizier Ghulk to get on it at once, but Visseract must know we're onto him. The guilty little fiend is apparently off hiding somewhere," Grell said. "The rest of his clan conveniently doesn't know where he is either. Don't worry. We'll find him."

"So he killed Mire for his key to the pits? Or because Mire was gonna tell you what Visseract was up to with that god?"

"All good questions to ask him when we find him," Grell said. "My son was having visions of the world ending, all very contingent on your roommate being taken."

"Is it, uh, common for Asra to have visions like this?" Ted asked.

"No more than a mortal being able to chat up dead people. It's all a form of starsight, you see, a blessing from the gods. It's rare amongst the everlasting races, even more so for mortals."

"Don't suppose your son's visions gave anything else other than 'world ending bad, save Jay'?"

"No," Grell admitted. "The visions aren't always very clear, but somehow Silenced people are going to be used to end the world, specifically Jay. Visseract is helping Gronoch with this nasty little plan, and that makes him a traitor and probably a murderer. He will pay for his crimes, but not before telling me what he's up to. Keeping Jay safe remains an immediate priority. Whatever they want to use him for, they will not have him."

"Thanks," Ted said. "Kinda sucks not being able to help. He's a really good friend."

"Somehow this is all connected. Finding out the truth of Mire's death will hopefully shed some light into why Gronoch wants Silenced souls so terribly."

"Kunst was saying they wanted them to make slaves," Ted reminded him. "But you can't take souls out of Xenon, right?"

"No… not unless…." Grell paused to think. "It's not their souls they're after. Maybe it was something specific in the pits they were looking for."

"What all is down there?"

"Graves, ancient royal artifacts, some old books," Grell replied. "Nothing of any significance that I can think of. Nothing that a god should be after."

"Shouldn't we go down there and see?" Ted slurped at his drink. "Gronoch and Visseract didn't risk a war just to hang out and talk down there."

"Worth a look," Grell agreed. "But rest now. We can go exploring after dinner. It'll be fun!"

"Still set on wining and dining me, huh?" Ted grinned, laughing at Grell's stubborn pout.

"What?" Grell snapped their drinks away. "I can't have a little romance?"

"It's sweet," Ted said, his eyes starting to close as he fought back a yawn. "You're absolutely crazy, but it's still sweet. Mm, maybe later I'll find out about those two cocks."

"If you're lucky," Grell taunted, kissing Ted's cheek. "Now, *sleep*."

The moment Grell spoke those words, Ted passed right out. He could sense warmth, someone holding him, and he was completely at peace.

He was certainly dreaming again, because he could hear the roar of the ocean and feel sand beneath him. He was back at the beach, but he didn't know who he was with.

Ted could tell that he was upset, his stomach caught in the sensation of falling, and he was nauseated He was trying to find sunscreen, and he couldn't find it in his bag, but that wasn't why he was so upset.

There was something wrong….

He saw the little boy playing by the shore, but he was suddenly afraid. In a flash, the boy was gone, and all Ted could hear was someone screaming.

Ted woke up with a sharp gasp, his limbs jerking as if he was still falling.

Or sinking….

"Theodore?" Grell's voice was right beside him, his strong hands pulling him into a tight hold.

"Grell?" Ted was gasping, shocked to find that he was shaking all over.

"Bad dreams?" Grell asked, his face wrinkled with concern.

"I… I don't…. I don't know." Ted found that he could move without pain and surged up from the bed to embrace Grell. He smothered himself against his chest, panting, "I can't remember."

"I've got you, love," Grell soothed, stroking his back and kissing his hair.

Ted's pulse fluttered when Grell called him that: *love*. He should have been running straight for the hills. All of this was happening way too fast, but he couldn't stop himself from enjoying the rush. He'd tried finding happiness in all the normal ways and failed spectacularly; maybe a bit of abnormal was exactly what he needed.

Like a cat-monster king with bright eyes and a mouthful of sharp teeth who had given him the best blowjob ever.

"Nothing will harm you, not as long as I'm around," Grell continued. "I promise."

"Heh. You'll just eat them, right?" Ted tried to smile.

"Naturally. What do you do with your enemies?"

Ted laughed, pulling away with a smile. "Thanks. Sorry for... for all of that."

"Emotions don't frighten me," Grell promised, petting Ted's cheek and urging him to stay close. "Only people who don't cover their coughs and don't match their socks."

"Good to know. Mm, what time is it?"

"Almost four o'clock in the afternoon. Don't give me that look. You needed to rest. How's your leg?"

"Uh, good, I think?" Ted flexed his leg, reaching down to check the bandage. It disappeared when he touched it and revealed perfectly healed skin. "Yeah. Good. Thank you. So, anything else exciting going on other than only having thirty-somethin' fuckin' hours left?"

"Eh. Murder, drama, all about the same. Ghulk is still crying over almost getting eaten by those Vulgorans. Ah! Speaking of Vulgorans, our dear trusty ol' Humble Visseract has remained mysteriously absent."

"That screams fuckin' guilty."

"Probably." Grell stroked Ted's hair, kissing his lips softly and letting it linger.

Sighing deeply, Ted relaxed into the kiss. He should have been more focused on his pending trial, but he was definitely distracted. He was enjoying all the new affection, leaning into Grell's fingers and surprised at how hungry he was to be touched.

He'd been alone for so long, and he found himself chasing Grell's hand when he pulled away.

"How are you doing?" Grell asked, studying Ted's face carefully. "Really?"

It was a simple question Ted didn't get asked often.

Well, he did, but not with any real sincerity.

He was honestly not sure how to answer. He was so used to saying that he was fine, that he was okay, and that was always so far from the truth. His job was depressing, he saw awful things, and he had been so very lonely.

What he saw in his line of work haunted him in many ways, often physically, and there were traumas he couldn't shake. Most people went their whole lives only seeing a few loved ones who had died, and they were usually dressed and peacefully resting in a casket.

Ted had probably seen thousands, and there was nothing serene or pleasant about pulling someone off a toilet who'd expired a week previously. He had removed decedents from cramped hallways, living room floors, and even a department store dressing room once.

It had been years of constant death with no outlet, and his unusual ability certainly hadn't helped. Despite the horror, there were some sweet moments, but they were impossible to describe to another person without sounding insane:

The giggle of a family sending a leopard-print thong for their grandmother to wear beneath her demure pantsuit, the smile of a man being buried with his beloved taxidermied rooster, or the bittersweet honor of dressing a young child in his favorite superhero costume.

He got to hear that same grandma complain that she never wore any underwear a day in her life, and the man told him every state title and ribbon his rooster had won.

Even so, it was hard to find levity in these memories because they were so easily swallowed up in an endless stream of tearful ones.

Like how the child screamed and cried he didn't want to leave his parents behind, even if it meant he could be a superhero.

Ted tried to shut those thoughts down, but the damage was already done. Everything was washing over him like a tidal wave, and he was trapped. He didn't know what to say because his typical reply of "fine" or "okay" would be a blatant lie.

His agony reached up to curl around his ribs until he couldn't breathe, and he said the first thing that bubbled up.

"I'm… scared."

"What for?" Grell's brow creased, and he took hold of Ted's hand.

"The whole being on trial for murder thing?" Ted laughed nervously. "Uh, let's see. My entire religion being wrong? Still haven't even begun to unwrap that yet. Crazy fish monsters tried to kill us, and oh yeah, apparently I already fucking died at some point.

"I'm scared because nothing makes sense, and I have no fucking clue what's going on. I'm so fucking lost. I don't know what's gonna happen, and even on another damn world, I'm surrounded by death. I don't want this. I want…."

"What do you want?" Grell asked.

"I want to be happy," Ted replied helplessly. "Being here with you… that's, that's made me happy. And I'm kinda fuckin' scared of you too."

"Of me?" Grell looked startled. "Why, love?"

"Whatever this is, you and me," Ted said. "I'm not good at this shit. We just fuckin' met, and I don't know if this was just an amazing blowjob or what. I don't know what we're doing—"

"Theodore," Grell urged. "Listen to me, love. We still have time, and I promise you that you will be cleared of murder charges if it's the last thing I do. You will be a free man, I swear. And though I can't begin to understand how difficult it is finding out your little light god isn't real, I can help you learn about the old gods. I can teach you the ways of the Sages if you'd like. Hell, I'll teach you how to speak in godstongue if it will make you feel better."

"You really mean all that, don't you?" Ted whispered as his heart clenched, his anger fading in the wake of Grell's sincerity. "You'd really do all of that for me?"

"Yes," Grell promised. He cleared his throat and went on, "As for the amazing blowjob, I'm hoping it was the start of something great. I like you, all right? I'm not sure what the protocols are for a king dating a mortal, but sod it. I'll make some up."

"Dating?" Ted's face was getting hot.

"That's not such a bad idea, is it?" Grell smirked.

"Thought you weren't ready for a new relationship," Ted reminded him.

"I'm not prepared to take on another queen, but I think I can handle a boyfriend," Grell said carefully. "You know what I mean. Going steady, being exclusive, updating our status on social media?"

"Wow." Ted laughed without meaning to and kissed Grell firmly on his lips. "Mmmph. You really are insane."

"Quite a bit," Grell agreed. "As much fun as it would be to ruin your lush fuzzy body for any other lover and ship you back off to Aeon after the trial, I'm afraid that I would miss you."

"Well, we can't have that, can we?" Ted grinned.

"Certainly not," Grell snorted, raising Ted's hand to kiss it. "We will figure this all out together. The trial, your death, whether or not you can handle two cocks—"

"Yeah, I've got some questions about that—"

"And oh, I'll let you wear my varsity jacket. I'll even save you a spot at lunch."

"Okay, wait. How the hell do you know all this human stuff? You're like a pop culture trash compactor."

"I'll take that as a compliment, and it's because of television."

"You have fuckin' television?"

"Uh, duh." With a snap of Grell's fingers, a giant flatscreen appeared floating at the foot of the bed. "Don't tell anyone, but I'm stealing my cable."

"Hey! You even got Food Network!" Ted laughed as the channels magically flipped. He grinned from ear to ear and teased, "You seriously are crazy. But thank you. Really. For listening and for actually giving a shit, you know?"

"Giving a shit just happens to be one of my many immeasurable talents," Grell said proudly. "I'm also very good at Mario Kart, amigurumi crochet, and Battleship."

"I can't believe I agreed to date you," Ted groaned playfully.

"Don't worry. I'll write you letters in prison if we fail to exonerate you. Conjugal visits will be a must."

"Wow. I guess I've finally lost my mind."

"Does that mean you're ready for dinner?" Grell batted his eyes. "It's a tad early, but you definitely look like you need some—" He licked his lips ever so slowly. "—*sustenance*."

"Yes, please." The mere mention of food made Ted's stomach growl, and he didn't even mind the innuendo.

Another snap of Grell's fingers brought them into a cozy dining room. They were seated across from each other within arm's reach at an elaborately carved table next to a roaring fireplace. They were both wearing fresh suits, and Ted swore that somewhere between the snap and being seated that Grell had grabbed his butt.

Grell's ensemble was a loud purple-and-gray three-piece suit with a silk rose corsage on his lapel. Ted's suit was thankfully a much more modest outfit, simple and black with a dark green tie.

"You look lovely." Grell beamed and reached for his hand.

"You clean up pretty good too," Ted replied, smiling bashfully. He loved the flood of butterflies invading his chest and making every breath feel light. "So, what are we having?"

"That's up to you, love." Grell waved his fingers and empty plates appeared before them. "We can have whatever you'd like. I'm not picky."

"No?" Ted thought it over for a moment before he said, "How about a steak?"

"That's it? Just a steak?"

"I want a *really* big steak."

Very amused, Grell snapped his fingers and a giant sirloin strip appeared on Ted's plate. "Hope medium is okay."

"Perfect," Ted sighed, dreamily staring down at the steak. He noted that Grell had given himself filet mignon, a baked potato, and asparagus. "Shoulda known you'd be a filet guy."

"I like my meat very tender," Grell said with a wink.

"Can I have something to—"

With a quick snap, a full glass of red wine and a cup of ice water appeared.

"Thanks." Ted cut his steak, scrambling to think of something to say. He felt a little awkward after just pouring his heart out, and he didn't know what to talk about now.

"So," Grell said, easily breaking the brief silence, "tell me everything there is to know about you."

"Me?" Ted blinked. "Uh, hi, my name is Ted, I work with dead people, eh... I don't know. I feel like I've already said so much." He picked at the piece of steak he'd cut. "Where do I start?"

"We have all night." Grell picked up his wine and took a leisurely sip. "Not much else we can do until they find Visseract."

"No, we still gotta go to the library. Remember?"

"Yes, yes, I remember," Grell huffed. "After dinner, I promise we will do your little ghost friend's bidding and go to the library. But right now, I would like... well, as silly as it sounds, I would like to enjoy our meal."

Ted wanted to argue, but he found that he agreed. He hadn't been on a date in months, and he didn't want to rush through what could very well be his last meal as a free man. He made up his mind to enjoy this and ignore the ticking clock.

"Okay, deal. No trial stuff until after we've had dessert." He held up his fork. "I mean it. No more screwin' around. This is fuckin' serious, okay?"

"Deal." Grell grinned. "So. You have family, hmm? Tell me about them."

"Parents were normal, happy, Lucian," Ted replied, pausing to nibble at his steak. It was unbelievably delicious and rich, and he groaned softly. "Oh, that's good."

"I'm glad. Any brothers or sisters?"

"Just one. I have a younger brother. He's adopted. Literally dropped off on our doorstep. My parents were always super protective of him. Thought he was a gift from God."

"The Lord of Light, you mean."

"Yeah." Ted frowned at that. "And he's really not real? The Litany, all of that. It's just made up?"

"All religions are made up if you think about it," Grell replied thoughtfully. "The Sages have the advantage that their rituals and such were made up by actual gods. The Lord of Light was some bastard who popped out of nowhere, delivered his one little Litany for everyone to follow without question, and then he just buggers off."

"But he performed miracles," Ted argued. "He was the one true God who came to Earth to share the Litany with mankind—"

"Ah, he *claimed* to have performed miracles. He also said he was going to come back and visit mortals to bring them another Litany. Funny how no one has seen or heard from him in about fifteen hundred years."

"Well, no one's seen the gods hanging around either!"

"That's because your precious Lord of Light sucked up all the followers," Grell tutted. "Great Azaethoth got a bit depressed and decided to have himself a little nap. That's when the gods went into the dreaming. They might be sleeping, but they're still up there in Zebulon. Just because you aren't ready to accept it doesn't make it any less true."

"I'm trying, okay?" Ted scowled. "It's still kinda crazy that everything I believed in is apparently fuckin' fake, so I'm taking some fuckin' time to adjust." He took a sip of wine. "So, who was he really?"

"Who?"

"The Lord of Light!"

"I don't know. Maybe he's made up too. Some uppity mortals may have written the Litany themselves and just claimed they got it from a brand-new god no one had ever heard of."

"My parents are gonna be wrecked if they find out," Ted said glumly. "Following the Litany is everything to them. Like with my brother, Elliam, they really thought he was this holy gift—"

"Wait, wait. They thought he was a holy gift, and they named him 'Elliam'?" Grell scoffed. "What kind of name is that?"

"Your name is freakin' Thiazi!" Ted argued. "What kinda name is that?"

"It's Asran, and it means 'proud warrior,' thank you!" Grell laughed. "Come now. Elliam is a bit strange for a human, isn't it?"

"Ha!" Ted triumphantly chomped down on his next bite of steak. "Just wait until I tell you mine."

"Eh?" Grell paused. "Isn't it *Theodore*?"

"Tedward," Ted replied with a sly smile.

"Fuck off!" Grell stared and burst out laughing. "Come on. You're shitting me."

"Nope." Ted grinned. "My full name is Tedward Beauseph Sturm, and my brother is Elliam Jimantha Sturm."

"Your parents are sick individuals." Grell cackled. "Is that a rare Lucian tradition I didn't know about? Giving your children ridiculous names? By all the gods, those are awful."

"What about you, huh?" Ted countered. "What's your full name?"

"Thiazi desu Grell Tirana Diago Tazha Mondet," he replied dutifully.

"Holy fuck, that's a mouthful!" Ted exclaimed. "What the fuck does all that mean?"

"It's a family line," Grell explained. "Thiazi is the name my parents gave me."

"And the rest?"

"The surnames of the generations before mine, going all the way back to the Mondet revolution against the gods. We pass on names based on which parent carried the child. After all, they did all the real work, eh?"

"It's kinda beautiful," Ted admitted. "I mean, I'll never remember all that, but it's nice."

"Thank you, Tedward."

"Why don't people call you 'King Thiazi'?"

"We Asra are a bit funny about our names unless it's being used by a member of our own family. We refer to one another by our surnames to avoid appearing too familiar with others we aren't related to."

"But if you had a brother or something, wouldn't they be called Grell too? And your mom, right? Because she would have been a Grell."

"I didn't say it couldn't be confusing."

"Well, you got any siblings, Thiazi day-soup whatever your name is?"

"Only child I'm afraid. Ended up spoiled rotten."

"No shit." Ted laughed.

"The 'desu' part of my name actually means 'single child.' If my parents had had more children, I would be Thiazi *aesu* Grell because I would be the oldest out of many. My younger siblings would use *mesu*, *leusu*, and so on to indicate their order of birth."

"Is that the sort of personal stuff that's on your ear doodle-bobbers?"

"Indeed," Grell replied. "It's a good thing I didn't have any brothers or sisters, you know. I don't do well with sharing."

"I never would have thought."

"You get on with your little brother? Are you close?"

"We used to be." Ted paused to take another big bite of steak. "My parents got weird when he got older. Treated him like he was a bubble kid or something. Kept him cooped up in his room all the time."

"Why? Was he... eh... sickly?"

"No. I figured it was because he was found, you know?" Ted shrugged. "They were fucking obsessed with keeping him safe. Meanwhile, heh, I was out partying and gettin' into trouble...."

"When the cat's away overparenting, the rebellious older son will play?" Grell teased.

"Yeah, maybe I was a little jealous," Ted confessed. "I did try to kill him one time."

"Am I dining with an attempted murderer?" Grell raised his brows.

"Yeah, I guess you are." Ted grinned sheepishly.

"Certainly don't tell the court that. You're already on trial for one murder."

"It was an accident! You know, sort of. When he was, like, six, I may have tried to smother him with some stuffed animals."

"And how old were you, my darling little Psycho Sally?"

"Ten or eleven I think," Ted said. "I was unsuccessful, obviously."

"Good to know." Grell laughed, raising his glass in a toast.

"What about you?" Ted asked as he took another big bite of steak. "Mm, any fun family drama?"

"No, I'm afraid my family is quite boring and mostly dead."

"I'm sorry," Ted said earnestly. "You know, uh… about Vael."

"It's all right." Grell smiled, but there was still a hint of sadness. "We had a wonderful life together. My parents have been passed on for ages, and it's just me, my darling spawn, and a handful of cousins who like to keep too close at court."

"Do you actually like being king?" Ted asked, drinking his wine and neglecting the water entirely.

"Of course." Grell cackled. "I get to tell everyone what to do. Everyone always wants something. They're all whining about someone insulting somebody else's honor or this person owes some other person something. Ha, never a dull moment."

"You're being sarcastic," Ted accused.

"Mmm. I love how perceptive you are."

"Asshole," Ted sniped affectionately.

"How is everything? Need another steak, my gorgeous carnivore?"

"Shit," Ted wheezed. "I'll be doing good to finish this one. Everything is fucking awesome. This is the most fun I've had on a date in… fuck. Forever?"

"Good," Grell said, looking very pleased with himself. "I do have some exciting plans for dessert, if you're interested."

"Oh?" Ted knew immediately by the coy twinkle in Grell's eye that he meant something physical. His heart thudded as he innocently asked, "What kinda plans exactly? Am I gonna like 'em?"

"Considering how you destroyed that steak, I'm willing to bet you're a fan of big meat," Grell teased lewdly.

"I do enjoy some protein now and again," Ted flirted back. "I thought we were gonna go check out the library after dinner?"

"I'd rather check you out."

"Noted. We also still need to go to the pits, you know."

"Boring."

"You're ridiculous."

"Would you like to go for a little stroll?"

"Uh, where?"

"You haven't actually seen the city proper yet," Grell replied, reaching for Ted's hand. "Yes, my castle is beautiful, but so is my city. You told me, and I quote, no *trial stuff* until after dessert. I want to take you to my absolute favorite spot for dessert, and after that maybe the sort of dessert that doesn't require clothing."

"Sure," Ted said, squeezing his hand. "That sounds—"

The world shifted, and they were now standing in a giant marketplace.

"Ugh. Good. Sounds good."

There were dozens of stalls selling various wares, and all the buildings around them were constructed with a mix of the glowing lavender masonry like the castle and dull black brick. The smell was a thick cloud of frying food and sweet perfumes, with an undercurrent of dry musk that reminded Ted of going to the county fair.

Everywhere Ted looked, he saw fantastic and horrifying creatures. He saw lots of Asra, but there were no other humans here—or anything pretending to be human, anyway. He recognized one being as an Eldress with two small foals at its side, and there was a group of Vulgora haggling over some bolts of cloth.

The rest? He had no idea.

There were pale behemoths with tiny gossamer wings whose skin didn't seem to fit their bodies and hung off their bones in thick folds, and some slimy gremlins with giant heads sprouting fat manes of tentacles. He saw gaunt trolls who had huge tusks jutting out of their mouths and long pointed tails. The closest thing he saw to a human was a large monster with black skin and a hunchback whose face was painted up like a twisted clown.

"Shall we?" Grell offered his arm to Ted.

"Yeah, sure, but you know, just one tiny thing." Ted dropped his voice down to a frantic whisper as he hissed, "What the fuck am I looking at?"

"Right now, me."

"No! All of this!"

"A market. A place where people can come together to exchange goods and services."

Ted glared.

Grell laughed, patting Ted's shoulder. "Oh, the look on your face…." He gestured to the crowd. "You have met an Eldress before. They're the fourth race made by Great Azaethoth."

"And the fish-worm dudes are Vulgora?"

"Very good," Grell purred, walking into the market and keeping Ted close. "They're the second race Azaethoth created. All the beautiful big cats are Asra, of course. We were the first. Those pasty-looking giants with the little wings are Faedra, number five."

Ted made a face when he noticed none of the Faedra had eyes. Or noses. Just big mouths with—what else—crooked pointy teeth.

"The chaps with the tusks are the Absola, and the painted fellow is a Mostaistlis. They're six and seven respectively, the last races before Great Azaethoth made humans. Oh! And those goblins running around with tentacles are the Devarach. They were the third. Watch your pockets, they love to take things."

"So they're thieves?"

"Not quite. They believe in communal property. Everything belongs to everyone, so they can't steal what is already theirs."

As they moved through the market, all the creatures made way and bowed respectfully as they passed. Some of the smaller ones stared up at Ted in total amazement. One started to cry, quickly hiding behind its parent.

"Why is everybody looking at me all crazy?" Ted mumbled, not sure if he liked all of the attention.

"Most of them have never seen a human before," Grell explained. "Not many of my fine citizens ever venture over to Aeon."

"Is that why nobody looks human?"

"Not all of the everlasting can change their shape on their own, not without magic. Besides, there's no need for them to hide what they are. This is their home."

Ted tried to wave at a few of them, and he mostly got growls and hisses in reply. He didn't know if that was good or bad.

As they explored the market, Grell stopped often to chat with his people, checking in on those who had been sick or were in recovery following some injury. He congratulated a mother Eldress on the birth of her children, wished luck to a Faedra who was going to learn a new trade, and cautioned a fellow Asra about drinking too much.

They stopped at one of the vendors, a Faedra that was selling giant hunks of spun sugar wrapped around what looked like rock candy to Ted. The Faedra refused any payment, but Grell definitely snapped his fingers and made some coins appear on the counter as they left.

"You know, you're actually a pretty decent king," Ted noted.

"Don't sound so surprised." Grell smirked smugly, the world shifting again beneath their feet. "I'm an awesome king."

Ted now found himself on top of one of the tallest buildings, looking down on the beautiful city below. Behind them was the castle and the bridge, and the eerie forest surrounded everything outside the walls as far as Ted could see, except for a single break where a large spiky mountain range loomed.

"Wow." Ted took a bite of the spun sugar, and he nearly gagged when he tasted sweet alcohol. He swallowed it down, clearing his throat as he said, "This, uh, this is a nice view."

"I come here sometimes to think," Grell said, eating his spun sugar all the way down to the crunchy rock candy center. "Keeps me humble, relaxes me, reminds me of what I must protect."

"It's pretty badass," Ted said, "but maybe you should hang out here more often."

"Is that so?"

"Because you are so not fuckin' humble." Ted snickered.

"Nothing wrong with being confident," Grell teased. "I can't help that I'm amazing, and no one else notices."

"Well, I noticed." Ted smiled, leaning over to nudge Grell's side. "A few of your subjects down there might have too. Hard to avoid it with an ego as big as yours."

"You're rather amazing yourself, Tedward," Grell said with a little wink.

"Uh… thanks." Ted kept staring at Grell's golden eyes, and there was a fluttering rush of excitement as their hands brushed together.

"My pleasure," Grell said, taking Ted's hand and laying a soft kiss upon it.

Ted couldn't remember ever being so attracted to someone, and he already had some ideas in mind to explore this new desire. Grell had talked about a very special kind of dessert, and Ted was hungry for something other than sweets. He quickly finished his sugary treat, asking as casually as he could, "Now, about these two cocks…?"

"Oh?" Grell nibbled on a piece of crystal sugar. "Still curious about those?"

"Yeah, I wanna know—"

"If you can take both? With lots of lube and plenty of willpower, anything is possible."

"Now."

"Right now?" Grell pretended to be bashful. "We've barely finished our dessert, love. While I do admire the balls you have to order a king around—"

"Right now, Grell," Ted said firmly.

"Oh." Grell daintily wiped off his mouth and flashed a toothy grin. "Why yes, sir."

CHAPTER 8.

TED HAD no idea what he was in for, but he wanted it. He wanted Grell in a way he couldn't describe, and his desire was bolstered by the extreme situation he'd been thrown into.

Murder charges, his own death, and that the world he once thought was ruled by the Lord of Light was wrong.

He was out of his element, helpless, and he wanted to take back some kind of control. With Grell, he could have that. At least for a little while, he could grab the reins of his life, and what would happen would only be because he wanted it to.

And Grell was stupidly hot.

Not to mention funny, charming, and undeniably kind beneath his wicked snark.

As Ted found himself back in Grell's lavish bedroom, he let himself fully admire the king's handsome face. Though Grell was much shorter than Ted, his arms were thick and strong as they wrapped around him.

"We can do as much or as little as you'd like," Grell said, rubbing Ted's back and leaning up for a kiss.

"Mm. All of it. I want all of it." Ted kissed him back passionately, surrendering himself to Grell's tongue and hot lips.

"Come along, then," Grell said breathlessly, "and I'll take care of you."

Ted's head spun as Grell teleported them both into bed, and he grunted when Grell pushed him down onto his back. Grell was completely taking charge, and Ted loved it.

Their clothes magically melted away, and Ted moaned when Grell's hand slid down his stomach. He was already half-hard, turned on by Grell's dominant poise and his searing kiss. "Fuck...."

"All in good time, love," Grell teased, swiping his tongue across Ted's lower lip. "Mmm...."

"I'm sorry," Ted said suddenly, his nerves bubbling away when Grell's hand dipped between his legs. "If I'm not better, I mean. Like I told you before, it's been a while, and... uh... I don't usually do it like this."

"Love," Grell soothed, "I've not done this in centuries. I'm sure you will be fantastic. If you prefer, I'll gladly switch—"

"No," Ted said, bashful in his eagerness. "I want you like this. Please. But can... can I see, uh, what you're working with?"

"Of course," Grell replied, rolling over onto his side and bending his knee. His cock appeared human at first glance, thick and uncut, but Ted could see two slick heads peeking out from the edge of his foreskin.

"Can I...." Ted started to reach out, but he hesitated.

"Go right ahead, love," Grell urged. "They don't bite."

Ted burst out laughing. "Fuck, I'm sorry. I just, well, with everything else around here and all these crazy monsters? I wouldn't be surprised."

Grell chuckled. "It's quite all right."

Ted kissed Grell, still chuckling and letting his hand slide down Grell's broad chest. He swept over Grell's stomach and finally reached his destination. He grabbed hold of Grell's cocks, unable to wrap his fingers around his full girth. "Wow."

"Uh-huh," Grell said with a cheeky grin.

Ted wanted to keep kissing, but he had to see. He watched as Grell's foreskin drew back as he got harder, two thick shafts now leaking in his hand.

He stroked one and then the other, marveling at their size and heat. His cheeks were burning at the idea of taking just one of these monsters, and thinking about both made his loins clench with lust. He didn't know if he could, but hell, he really wanted to try.

The cocks seemed to be about the same size, though one was seated a bit farther back beneath its twin. Ted kept touching and playing, watching them leak and glisten in the low light. "Fuck, you're so wet...."

"Mmm, normal for Asra," Grell said, reaching down to grab hold of Ted's and give him a firm squeeze. "Mm, and so are you, love. Eager for me, are you?"

"Yes." Ted rocked into Grell's hand and gave one of his cocks a responding stroke. "I'm... mm... I'm ready. I wanna do this. I want you."

Smiling warmly, Grell kissed Ted and promised him, "Then prepare to have your mind blown, love."

Ted watched Grell slide down his body and grunted in surprise as he spread his legs wide. He felt a surge of heat from the firm way Grell positioned him, and he tucked his arms up behind his head.

Grell stroked Ted's muscular thighs, dragging his fingers down the underside of them and cupping Ted's butt. "You have the most spectacular body, love." Grell bowed his head, running his long tongue from the tip of Ted's cock, over his balls, and right to his hole. "Mmmph, and your ass is absolutely perfect."

"You're not so bad yourself," Ted teased. His grin dropped when Grell's tongue lapped at his hole, slick and hot, and he groaned, "Oh fuck."

Grell licked all around the tight muscle, clearly enjoying himself and taking his time. His hands stroked Ted's thighs with such reverence, and the tip of his tongue started to push inside.

"Ohh... fuck...." Ted groaned, his entire vocabulary reduced to that single word as Grell's tongue slid in. There was no pain, no burn, only a faint hint of pressure and a tugging sensation as his body opened up.

It had been so long since someone had prepped him, and certainly no one had ever done it with a giant tongue. Grell had to be some sort of magic, because nothing had ever felt like this. Ted was worried he was already going to come, and he tried to breathe his way through the tension building between his legs.

Grell seemed to somehow sense his looming orgasm and took that as his cue to start fucking Ted with his tongue. He pushed it impossibly deeper, a never-ending thrust of slick muscle that felt better than any cock or toy ever had.

"Fuck, fuck, ohhh fuck!" Ted moaned, delirious from the new and exciting pleasure. He could actually feel Grell's tongue twirling around his prostate, pounding into him relentlessly and making his legs shake. "Grell! Fuck! I'm, I'm right there!"

He'd meant it as a warning, but Grell accepted it as encouragement. His tongue thickened, stabbing into Ted's prostate with merciless precision as it thrust into his wet hole.

"F-uckkk!" Ted whimpered, his voice cracking as his climax crashed into him. He watched his cock spurt and then slowly ooze a thick load across his stomach, amazed that he was able to come just from Grell's fantastic tongue.

It didn't want to end, his body still buzzing on the tipping point of insanity as he continued to spill, and Grell's tongue refused to stop. All Ted could do was tremble and take it, groaning a long string of nonsense.

"Oh, so good, it's so fuckin', fuck, fuck-fuck-fuck, oh, my, fuck, oh my *fuck*, I can't, it's just, ohhh...."

"Mmmm," Grell moaned, low and deep, finally releasing Ted from his orgasmic prison as he pulled his tongue free. He rose back up with a very satisfied smile, his tongue flopping out of his mouth to lap up Ted's come. "Absolutely delicious, love."

"You too," Ted said, his mind completely fried. He was further amazed that he was still hard, and he gasped softly, "Grell, you're fuckin' amazing."

"So are you, love," Grell said, smacking his lips once he'd finished cleaning Ted up. "Mmph. Definitely need more of that."

"You can totally have it whenever you want." Ted laughed. His laughter was cut short when Grell's fingers pushed inside his hole. He was so loose and wet now, and he easily got lost in Grell's exploring fingers. "Fuck... what did you do to me?"

"Got you ready for me," Grell said roughly, canting his head down for a deep kiss. "Mmm... you feel so perfect, love."

"Come on," Ted urged, bucking up into Grell's hand. He was overwhelmed with the lust surging through his body, greedy and desperate for something to fill him up. "Just give 'em to me."

"Patience," Grell scolded affectionately, settling between Ted's legs and lifting them up. "We're going to take this slow—"

"Grell," Ted grunted, grabbing one of Grell's cocks and giving him a firm squeeze. "Now."

"You're so bossy." Grell snickered, absolutely delighted, and rewarded Ted with a harsh bite on his shoulder. He stayed latched there and rolled his hips forward.

"Fuck!" Ted gasped from the flash of pain, loving the grip of Grell's teeth and groaning as one of his thick cocks started to push in.

Even with Grell's amorous prep, Ted was expecting some discomfort. There was absolutely none, and he only felt fabulous pleasure as before. He could feel his body stretching, gloriously full as Grell buried himself completely within him.

Releasing Ted's shoulder, Grell turned his head to nuzzle his neck. "Oh, my love," he purred, "you feel amazing... you're so hot and tight... I'm going to make you come all night long."

"Grell," Ted whispered, not even recognizing his own voice. He sounded exhausted and desperate, and he reached up to grip Grell's broad shoulders.

This is what he wanted: someone inside of him and making him fall apart. Finally receiving it just the way he wanted made him feel so vulnerable and fragile, and there must have been something about his expression that alerted Grell to this fresh wave of emotion.

"I've got you," Grell murmured, his golden eyes shining bright. "I'm going to take care of you, love. All I want is to make you feel good... all you have to do is let me... all I want is you, just like this."

Tears welling up in his eyes, Ted tried to speak, but all that came out was a low moan as Grell started to move. Only short thrusts at first, but soon they were deep and hard and Ted couldn't believe how he was sobbing.

Nothing could possibly compare to Grell fucking him, leaving Ted a blubbering mess of sensation and bliss. Every thrust was positively perfect, filling him beyond anything he'd ever had before, and he was stunned when Grell suddenly got even bigger.

He could feel the tension twisting up in his body as Grell's cock swelled inside of him, pushing impossibly deeper and making him ache in his very core. He thought briefly that Grell had slipped in his other cock, but that one he could feel rubbing between his cheeks. He didn't understand what was happening except it was fantastic, and he dragged his nails up Grell's shoulders with a groan.

"Oh fuck, that, that, keep fuckin' doin' that!" Ted pleaded, crying out when Grell gave him a fierce slam. He thought his stomach might have moved, and he threw his head back on the pillows. "Fuck... Grell!"

Grell was letting out low growls and greedy groans, sounding more animal than man as he pounded Ted's tight ass. He was exuberant and quite vocal, whispering the filthiest things in Ted's ear. "My love, I'm going to fuck you until you can't even move...."

"Yes," Ted whimpered.

"I'm going to pump your sweet little body with my come until you're dripping. I want to hear you screaming my name while I'm filling you up...."

"Yes, fuck, yes!" Ted groaned as Grell grabbed his legs and forced them against his chest, starting to hammer away at him with a new intensity. All Ted could do was hang on and moan, the new angle making his head spin and his entire body buzz with pleasure.

He was going to come, he could feel it building, and Grell showed no signs of stopping. He grabbed the back of Grell's neck and dragged him into a hot kiss. "Come on… come on, Your fuckin' Highness… make me fuckin' bust!"

Snarling ferociously, Grell bared his jagged teeth and fucked Ted until he was screaming. Grell was absolutely unhinged, and his teeth snapped down on Ted's shoulder, biting hard.

Ted howled excitedly and immediately came—fuck, how, he was only half-hard and yet he was coming—and his stomach dropped as if he was falling. It was the most beautiful feeling, and Grell hadn't stopped slamming into him.

His orgasm was still going, and Ted wrapped his arms around Grell's neck to anchor himself. He groaned as Grell's load filled him up, leaving him throbbing and still climaxing until he couldn't breathe. It was too much, too good, and he was crying.

Grell's lips pressed all over his face, kissing him sweetly as he gushed, "Oh, my love…. Ted… you were perfect."

Ted's legs fell down around Grell's waist, and he kept clinging to Grell's neck. He could feel Grell pulsing inside of him, and thick come was gushing out from his hole. The final tremors of his mind-shattering orgasm were fading, and he was still shaking and sweating.

"Holy fuck," Ted whispered, gazing up at Grell in amazement. He didn't know what else to say. No one had ever made him feel like this, and he kissed Grell with everything he had. He put what he couldn't find the words to express into that kiss, sliding his hands through Grell's hair.

Grell's returning kiss was just as passionate, his thick arms curling beneath Ted's back to hold him close. He was smiling, appearing so youthful and happy, breathless as he said, "So, I think that went well, eh?"

Ted laughed, wiping at his eyes with the heel of his hand. "You fuckin' smartass. That was… that was great. It was amazing."

"You were pretty lovely too," Grell teased, settling down on Ted's chest and kissing the tip of his nose. "Mmm… need a moment?"

"A moment for what?" Ted asked dumbly.

"For the rest of me," Grell replied with an innocent smile.

Ted realized he could still feel Grell's other cock rubbing against him, hard and hot, and his stomach clenched.

But it wasn't with trepidation—no, it was from excitement.

"We can stop," Grell soothed, clearly misreading Ted. "Asra make love for hours, you see, but we—"

"I want it," Ted insisted. "I wanna go again." He was already scooting back to get up on his knees. He rolled over to present his ass to Grell, his face burning up as he urged, "Like this, come on."

"Oh, by Great Azaethoth's giant dangling gonads," Grell whispered, his hands greedily squeezing Ted's ass and spreading his cheeks. "You look positively divine like this, my love."

Ted smothered his face in his hands, arching himself up. He could feel Grell's come oozing out of him—fuck, it was so thick—and he whispered, "Just, uh, go slow, okay?"

"I will," Grell assured him, shifting closer and pushing the tip of his second cock inside.

Ted gasped as he was penetrated again, amazed at how soft and wet his hole was. There was no resistance, and his body eagerly swallowed up every thick inch of Grell's cock. It was a little weird to feel himself being stuffed with one cock while the other was sliding limply against his tailbone, but he didn't mind.

Already he was thinking about whether Grell could stuff both inside of him, and his own cock flexed with interest. Fuck, just the very thought was overwhelming, and he had to remember to breathe or else he feared he might pass out.

It didn't take long for that other cock to stiffen up again, but now Ted's attention was solely focused on the one inside of him. There was impossible pressure and a new depth in this position, and he groaned loudly as Grell began to leisurely thrust.

"You're so beautiful," Grell praised, running his palms up Ted's hips and stroking the broad muscles of his back. "Do you like this? Do you feel good?"

"Yes," Ted grunted, parting his legs and backing up on Grell with a happy moan. "Feels so fuckin' good…."

"Just relax," Grell murmured. "I've got you." He rolled forward, slow and gentle, pulling out almost completely before plunging back into Ted's hole.

Ted melted beneath every tender thrust, relaxing and dragging a pillow over to rest his head on. He loved this completely. He could give himself over, and Grell was more than glad to take care of him. It was so good, so very good, and he couldn't remember a time when anyone had ever worshipped his body like this.

Although the brutal pace from before had been fun, this slower and more intimate rhythm was positively heavenly.

Or would that be Zebulon-ly, he wondered with a blissful smile.

Whatever he called it, he knew he'd never experienced such bliss. He could feel a lick of fire moving down his spine, and the urge for release was building once more. He gasped more urgently, and he moaned when Grell moved faster.

Soon the force of Grell's hips pressed Ted flat against the bed, and Grell teased his fangs along the back of Ted's neck. Ted shivered, squeezing his pillow and moaning pitifully, savoring the sound of their bodies slapping together.

Grell slammed in deep, holding himself inside and rolling his hips in wide circles. "Oh, my love… your little body is going to make me come again… you're so damn good, I can hardly stand it."

"Grell…." Ted was rendered speechless, all of the pressure inside of him winding up tight and making him cry out.

"Come, love," Grell growled. "Let me take you with me… come on…."

Ted didn't know how it was happening, but each delicious grind was sending him closer to another climax. His muscles were weird and heavy, and he didn't think he could….

Grell's cock moved inside him with impossible dexterity, and there was new pressure against his prostate. His mouth opened to moan, but all he could do was suck in oxygen and try not to scream.

Another twitch of Grell's cock and he was coming again, suddenly wailing into his pillows.

Ted's orgasm continued to rock every inch of his body, and he shook all over. He didn't think he could form a single word, his muscles turning to goo, and he let out a desperate moan when he felt Grell stuttering and coming inside of him.

For a moment, they were totally in sync. Every throb of Grell's cock pulsing in his ass made Ted ache, and he swore their hearts were beating as one. The ecstasy left him whimpering, his skin numb and tingling down to the tips of his fingers.

Grell's unrelenting stamina finally seemed to falter, and he collapsed lazily against Ted's back, kissing the bite marks he'd left behind on his shoulder. "Mm…. Tedward of Aeon, you continue to be spectacular."

Ted gave him a thumbs-up.

Grell laughed, snuggling close and nuzzling Ted with a very satisfied sigh. "Need a breather, love?"

"Uh-huh," Ted said, amazed that he had even been able to say that. His body was heavy and tired, but so very warm and content. No one had ever left him feeling so ruined and equally revered. He groaned when Grell pulled out, then rolled over onto his side to face him.

Grell pressed their lips together in a brief kiss, asking sincerely, "Are you all right, love? Did I hurt you?"

"No," Ted said quickly, clearing his throat and trying to get his mouth working properly again. "I'm so good. So fucking good." He stretched his shoulders back and winced when the bite burned a little. "Might be feeling that later, though."

"I'll heal you," Grell promised, "but right now, I'm enjoying looking at you. Marked, I mean. As if you're mine."

"I am yours," Ted said, meeting Grell's eyes with a little smile. "Dating, right? We're a thing now." He stretched again and groaned at the lingering ache in his bones. "Pretty sure after what we just did, more than a piece of me is yours, because you just fuckin' owned me."

"Good," Grell said with a very pleased grin. They kissed again, reaching out their arms to embrace and cuddle. "Oh, very good, because I shall like to do that again soon."

"Very soon?"

"Oh, very much so."

Ted was still trying to sort out his thoughts from what had just happened, but he couldn't resist a big smile. Grell's eager appetite was infectious, and he snickered. "Fuck, I've created a monster."

"Guilty," Grell laughed gleefully.

"Oh, you just wait," Ted taunted. "Let me get my shit together over here and we're gonna talk about both of those cocks going in my—"

"Your Highness!" An Asra suddenly appeared right beside the bed.

Ted jumped, embarrassed and cursing. "Fuck! I hate that shit so much!"

"What is it?" Grell demanded, pulling the blankets over Ted with a snap of his fingers and glaring at the Asra. "I said that I didn't want to be disturbed. As you can see, we've been working *very hard* on the prisoner's defense."

"Vizier Ghulk wishes to speak with you," the Asra said worriedly. "Says he has urgent news for the trial, and he must see you at once!"

"Fine." Grell grunted. "Tell him to meet me in court in ten minutes."

"Right away, Your Highness," the Asra confirmed, bowing his head and vanishing.

"This should be fun," Grell said grumpily.

"So much for round two of dessert," Ted mumbled. "Or was it three?"

"Oh, don't you worry, love," Grell assured him. "Round three is still guaranteed."

"You sure about that?" Ted grinned, pushing himself up for a kiss. "Mmmph. As much as I am dying for some more of that dick—"

"Don't you mean dicks?" Grell snickered.

"Yeah, them too. As much as I want them, you swore we'd get back to the case as soon as dessert was over."

"Are you sure that was me?" Grell frowned. "Mm, doesn't sound like me."

"Yes."

"Hmmph. Well, as soon as you're a free man, Tedward of Aeon, I am going to spend entire *days* satisfying every juicy inch of your body."

"Promise?"

"Pinkie promise."

CHAPTER 9.

GHULK LOOKED like he was practically shaking with excitement when Ted and Grell teleported into court before him. Ted wrinkled his nose when he saw that Mire's corpse was still here and starting to swell.

Probably why it was just the three of them in there now, he mused to himself. No one else wanted to deal with the stench.

He and Grell had gotten dressed, but even with magic it hadn't been easy. They'd barely been able to keep their hands off each other and almost ended up back in bed. Definitely would have been nicer than standing here staring at Ghulk, but Ted knew they still had a case to solve. The hours were flying by in a wonderful rush of excitement and passion, but soon they were going to run out.

Ghulk's hooves clapped against the floor as he bowed down, exclaiming, "Your Highness! Thank you so much for meeting me! I have news about Humble Visseract!"

"Did he write a signed confession and throw himself in the dungeon?" Grell asked wistfully.

"What?" Ghulk was aghast, shaking his giant head. "No, Your Highness! I think I've discovered his motives for murdering your beloved cousin! I've been listening to rumors from court, and he learned that you had given Mire your key—"

"Yes, to the pits," Grell said briskly. "We already know that."

"Uh...." Ghulk was alarmed. "You do?"

"Uh-huh," Ted chimed in.

"Well... hmm." Ghulk tittered for a moment and suddenly jumped. "Ha! Well, I've got more news, Your Highness! Did you know he was in league with Gronoch, the god of healing and attrition?"

"Yup," Grell said, emphasizing the *P* with a loud pop of his lips. He crossed his arms, clearly unimpressed. "Next you're going to tell me that this means war because Visseract met with Gronoch down in the pits, aren't you?"

Ghulk's milky eyes widened, and his head dropped with a disappointed huff. "Yes, Your Highness."

Ted grinned, pleased that his information from Kunst was coming in handy. Making Ghulk look like an idiot was an unexpected bonus.

"Too bad." Grell winked at Ted. "Our handsome and deliciously thick suspect has already graciously pointed out that since we don't know exactly where they met and considering most of the pits are technically outside of Xenon, there is no solid evidence of the treaty having been violated. So, no declaring war on Zebulon, I'm afraid."

Smiling bashfully, Ted allowed himself to feel a small tickle of pride.

"But Your Highness!" Ghulk pleaded.

"I can't believe that I missed out on prime post-coitus cuddling time for this." Grell groaned. "Please shut up."

Shutting up appeared to be the last thing on Ghulk's mind, and he continued to argue with Grell. Ted wandered a few feet away to give them some space. He found himself drawn to Mire's swelling corpse and was pleasantly surprised to see that decomposition was unchanged from what he knew outside of Xenon.

Somehow that was comforting.

Mire's eyes had dehydrated and sunk into his skull, and his belly had puffed up as his corpse prepared to putrefy. A sparkle by Mire's ear caught Ted's attention, something catching the light that he thought maybe he'd noticed before—

There was a small tug on Ted's arm, and he knew the touch immediately. "Hey, little buddy."

Another insistent tug.

Ted looked around quickly. He saw the shadow of the little boy hovering in the corner, and he was waving urgently.

The library.

He didn't know how he knew, but he did. He turned back to where Grell and Ghulk were still arguing, clearing his throat. "Hey, uh, Your Highness? We need to go."

"What is it?" Grell asked, holding up his palm in Ghulk's face to quiet him. "What's wrong?"

"Little buddy is telling me to come on," Ted replied.

"Good enough for me!" Grell said, clearly tired of Ghulk's flapping mouth. "Now, while I appreciate your efforts to assist in finding Humble Visseract, try harder. Because you suck. Take care, Ghulk!"

Leaving Ghulk pouting behind them, Grell marched over to take Ted's hand and started walking. Their first step together landed on the library floor as Grell seamlessly teleported them over.

"Let's see what your little friend is up to, eh?" Grell looked around curiously. "Can you see him?"

"Not yet, but I'm pretty sure he's here somewhere," Ted said, starting to walk up to one of the aisles of books. "Ghulk seems really eager to help, huh?"

"He's one of the many who doesn't like Visseract. He also didn't like my cousin, either."

"Fuck, does anybody get along here?"

"No, it's government." Grell slid his hand along the books. "No one actually likes each other. We just pretend to occasionally."

"Sounds like my world." Ted snorted, glancing back at Grell. He watched as the king gazed over his books with a fond smile, prompting him to ask, "You and Vael hung out here a lot?"

"It was his favorite place in the castle. We'd spend days in here reading together. It's why I hung his picture over there. I figured... this is where he'd want to be remembered."

Ted reached back for Grell's hand.

Grell squeezed, asking politely, "Do you like to read, Ted?"

"Not really," Ted confessed. "It's hard for me to sit down and read somethin'. Can't focus. Probably why I couldn't handle school. Too many fuckin' books."

"Oh." Grell quickly tried to hide his disappointment.

"Maybe, uh, you could read to me instead?" Ted offered. "I love listening to you talk, and you could read all your favorites to me. Guarantee they're all gonna be brand-new."

"Thank you," Grell said with a warm smile. "I would like that very much."

"Fuck, you're gorgeous when you smile like that," Ted said softly, unable to resist leaning in for a kiss. He worried only after their lips touched that this might be inappropriate, but Grell kissed him back just as sweetly.

"Mmm... come along," Grell urged. "We have work to do." He reached down and smacked Ted's ass.

"Ow, fuck!" Ted blushed and rubbed his butt, breaking away to keep exploring. There was a small tug at his elbow, and he turned back around, catching a glimpse of the little boy rushing around Grell.

Ted followed, using the opportunity to pinch Grell's hip as he slipped by. He tried to keep up with the shadowy little figure, finding himself in a dark corner of the library. There were more scrolls than books here, and a long gilded one dropped at Ted's feet.

"What is it you're trying to show me, little buddy?" Ted picked up the scroll and unrolled it, flinching when little shards of metal spilled out. "Shit!"

They'd been carefully wrapped up in the scroll and now littered the floor.

Grell snapped his fingers, and all of the pieces rose up into the air for his inspection. He turned them this way and that, slowly bringing them together like the pieces of a puzzle to create a small luminous purple band.

"Hey, is that one of your ear thingies?" Ted said, squinting at the detailed designs.

"Yes. It's someone's mating band. It starts off as one large piece, specially forged for the couple, and then it's split in half during the wedding ceremony. One for each of them."

"Can you tell who it belonged to?"

"No," Grell said, turning the band to show a crack where a few fragments were still missing. "I can't read it. The bit I need is gone, of course." He scowled. "Some great help your little friend was."

"Hey, he knows what he's doing!" Ted argued. "I mean, I think he does." He rubbed his forehead. "If he wanted us to find this damn thing, it has to be important."

"Hmmph."

"Well, I don't see you coming up with anything!" Ted snapped, looking back at the band. The purple color was so damned familiar, and he swore he was having déjà vu.

"I'm sorry, I've been a little busy banging your brains out for the last few hours!" Grell growled. "I'm trying to think!"

"Think harder! And hey, I still really wanna fuckin' cuddle later!"

"Me too!" Grell bit back.

"Down," a soft voice whispered. "You have to go down…."

Ted turned when he heard the voice, trying to figure out where it was coming from. "Little buddy? Is that you?"

"Oh, him again." Grell rolled his eyes. "Maybe he'll show us a picture of someone's foot and tell us here's the killer! Very helpful, he is."

"Shush," Ted hissed, moving out to the sitting area with the giant chairs. He could see the little boy hovering behind one, and he took a knee. "Hey there, little dude. What's up? What are you trying to tell me?"

"You have to go down," the little boy whispered, peering around the chair. "Down in the pits. You have to see why."

"The pits," Ted repeated his words out loud. "We have to go down into the pits to see why."

"Why what?" Grell frowned.

"Why Mire was killed maybe? Why Visseract was down there? Maybe all of it." Ted stood up. "Can we go there?"

"We can, but…."

"What is it?"

"You're going to see things that you may not understand and perhaps will even upset you," Grell cautioned. "I realize that you're quite familiar with human funeral rites, but we Asra practice things much differently than your kind."

"What the hell does that mean?" Ted gulped.

"Come," Grell said, offering his hand, "and I'll show you."

Ted trusted Grell, but his nerves were on edge as he took his hand. Something pulled in his chest as the world moved around them, and the hand he was holding turned into a giant paw.

Grell had resumed his monstrous cat body, and they were now standing in a massive cave.

No, not a cave, Ted realized as he looked around in awe.

It was a mausoleum.

There were large slots in the walls, from the smooth floor all the way up to the high ceiling above them. Everything had been carved into the very rock, and the slots held bodies in varying stages of decomposition. The majority of them were skeletal and mummified, but some were juicy and actively putrefying.

Ted didn't see any caskets or vaults. The bodies had been tucked into the slots and left there to rot. Although only a few seemed fresh, the smell of decay was quite overwhelming.

"The pits are where we bring our dead now," Grell explained somberly. "Just as a king must rule, he must also serve his people and protect their remains."

"Protect them from what?" Ted asked, remembering to make himself grin to keep from throwing up.

"Grave robbers," a familiar and snotty voice replied. "The graveyards of the Asra were often ransacked by humans when they still lived on Aeon. There are also records of other members of the everlasting races such as the Faedra or the Vulgora who would desecrate their burial sites."

"And even other Asra," Grell added bitterly, stalking over to where the voice was coming from. He swung his paw, batting over a small blue orb. "Ah, Professor Kunst. So good to see you again."

The orb rolled up to Ted's feet, and he picked it up. "Ah, hey, dude."

"It's about time you two came down here," Kunst complained. "I've been waiting here for hours!"

"If I shake you, can you tell me my future?" Ted grinned, tempted to give the glowing orb a good jolt. "Or are you just gonna say 'don't count on it'?"

"I will certainly not!" Kunst snarled. "I am not some cheap plastic prognosticator! I am a living soul bound to this infernal ball until the binding is severed, and don't you dare even think about—"

There was a soft groan from one of the slots, and Ted saw one of the bodies move.

"The fuck?"

"It's nothing to worry about," Grell said, padding back to Ted's side. "Pay no attention to it."

"Grell, that body moved." Ted clung to Kunst's orb. "Are they… are they not all dead? Do you entomb people while they're fuckin' alive?"

"My dear Tedward," Grell soothed, "let me explain. Of all the everlasting races created by the gods, we Asra live the longest. We were meant to serve gods, after all. We can live for thousands of years, and that lifespan is a burden for some.

"When an Asra is ready to pass on, we hold a funeral for them, and their body is brought here so that they may sleep as the gods do. Burial sites for Asra have always been secret places, their locations only given to our kings, who are charged with guarding them."

"But they're not dead," Ted said bluntly. "They're not sleeping like the gods or whatever, they're dying."

"Once the funeral is conducted, they're dead," Grell insisted. "In the eyes of the Asran people, they've passed on."

"But they're not really dead."

"Okay, by human standards, perhaps they're still a tiny bit alive until they pass on in their little dreaming," Grell conceded with an exasperated sigh, "but to us, they're very much dead."

"Fuck," Ted whispered as he glanced over the slots. He wondered how many of the Asra had been alive when they were brought down here, and he was struggling not to let his unease show.

"Even a single millennium is a long time to live," Kunst offered. "The world changes, and yet, they stay the same. Sometimes it's just too much."

"I just… I can't imagine…."

"You don't have to understand it to respect it," Kunst said quietly. "This is what the Asra do."

"No, I know. You're right. I know that. It was just, uh, very surprising." Ted glanced up to Grell. "This is what you were afraid to show me?"

"Yes," Grell mumbled and twitched his tail.

"It's okay." Ted petted Grell's shoulder. "Look, I've seen a lot of weird and crazy stuff. Death is like that. It can be gross and scary, but… it can also be beautiful."

Grell perked up.

"You do this for all your people when they die?" Ted asked. "You bring them here and take care of them?"

"Yes," Grell replied. "One day when I'm too tired to carry them, my son will take my place."

"See, that's beautiful," Ted insisted. "It's a family thing. That's really cool." He was honestly trying not to be creeped out, especially when his eyes drifted back to the body he'd seen move before. "So, uh, why would people wanna rob Asran graves?"

"The bones," both Grell and Kunst replied at the same time.

"Oh, go ahead," Grell scoffed. "Please. I'll let the dead human tell the other human all about it."

"Thank you, Your Highness," Kunst said, managing to sound quite huffy despite being trapped in the orb and ignoring Grell's obvious sarcasm. "There was a time before the gods went into the dreaming when all of Great Azaethoth's children lived on Aeon together."

"The Asra were already in Xenon," Grell interjected. "At least, you know, most of us."

"Yes," Kunst griped. "The Asra were up in Xenon, the Vulgora lived in the oceans, the Faedra in the forest, and so on. Often enough, they all lived quite peacefully with humans. That is, until the gods left. Without the great deities there to protect them, humans hunted all the everlasting races for their various parts."

"Parts?" Ted echoed.

"They killed the Eldress for their horns, the Faedra for their wings, the Asra for their bones. All of the everlasting people who didn't flee to Xenon were being tracked down by humans. They were outnumbered, trapped, and slaughtered."

"There are some who were able to hide themselves," Grell added. "Although they're functionally extinct from Aeon, the everlasting people live on through their descendants."

"Descendants? Like what, their kids, living among humans?" Ted scratched his head. "Think I would remember someone who looked like they were half fish monster."

"Some of the everlasting bred with humans and produced very human-looking offspring," Grell explained. "Perhaps that Olympian runner all over the news is a truly fantastic human athlete, or perhaps somewhere in his tree there was a spot of monster-shagging with an Eldress.

"An old lady who has an almost magical way with plants? Maybe she's a very gifted gardener, or maybe her great-grandpa got it on with a Faedra. Fantastic lover? Obviously an Asra."

Blushing and rubbing his neck, Ted confessed, "Maybe it's just me being an ignorant Lucian, but I've never heard of any of this stuff."

"The rise of the Lucian faith is what made everything worse." Kunst grunted in disgust. "The Litany claimed the everlasting races were demons and abominations that had to be destroyed because they offended the Lord of Light, and the hunts only intensified."

"While still desecrating our corpses for pieces," Grell snapped bitterly.

"Fuck, that's horrible," Ted murmured. "Like people killing elephants because they think their ivory would give them big dicks or something."

"Except our anatomical bits actually do possess magical properties," Grell said with a weary smile. "Asra were easy targets because of how we bury our dead, and countless graves were ravaged...." He trailed off, turning his head to look down toward the end of the mausoleum.

There was a large archway, presumably leading into another cave.

"Grell?" Ted frowned. "What's wrong?"

"Come on!" Grell suddenly took off, bolting across the room and through the archway.

"The fuck!" Ted tucked Kunst's orb under his arm and ran after Grell, struggling to keep up. They passed through more cavernous mausoleums, and Ted noticed that the bodies were getting older and more decayed as they went.

By the time he caught up to Grell, the bones around him had apparently turned to dust.

No, not dust.

They were gone.

Ted stared in horror at a whole room of empty slots. There were cracks in the walls where the graves had been violently emptied, and Grell had collapsed in front of a small cluster of them.

"Oh no," Kunst whispered brokenly.

"Grell," Ted gasped. "I'm so, so fucking sorry." He didn't dare approach, not yet, warily watching Grell tremble in rage.

"My queen," Grell spat angrily. "They took him. They took my fucking queen. And my parents, and my fuckin' grandparents. All the ancient ones! They're all fucking gone!" He rose back up, his tail lashing. "I'm going to find Visseract and eat him while he's still fucking alive! I will tear out his entrails and make them his fuckin' out-trails!"

"Uh, so, he's having a moment," Ted whispered to Kunst, backing away as Grell continued to rage. "Can you tell me why anyone would want Asran bones? What do they do exactly?"

"They can be used to change one's form, to shape-shift as they do," Kunst replied quickly. "They can also help someone travel between worlds, create portals, and astral project."

"Astral what now?"

"It's when your soul leaves your body," Kunst explained. "Those who have mastered the ability can leave their body at any time and travel great distances."

"And why would Gronoch and Visseract want to do any of that stuff?"

"I don't know," Kunst said, huffing in frustration. "I know what I heard, and this doesn't make any sense. I know they were talking about using Silenced souls to make slaves, but I don't understand how they would do that or why they would need the bones. Gods can already move between worlds, and Silenced people can't perform any kind of magic."

"Even with special kitty-monster bones?"

"Yes. Some may be able to use small trinkets and charms that are already charged with magic, but nothing like this."

"Well, fuck."

Grell bowed his head against one of the empty slots, howling mournfully. His anger was fading away, and all that was left was his obvious pain.

Hating to see him like this, Ted set down Kunst's orb and hurried over. He kneeled beside Grell and wrapped his arms around his neck, peppering his fur with kisses. "Hey, I'm here."

Grell tensed briefly, but then he relaxed, soon melting in Ted's embrace. "I've failed my people. I failed my own damn family."

"What are you talking about?" Ted shook his head. "You didn't do this!"

"It's my job to protect these graves," Grell argued. "I should have known something like this could happen."

"No," Ted countered stubbornly. "This isn't your fault. You couldn't have known what Visseract was going to do! Listen to me, we're gonna find him, and you're gonna eat the crap out of him, okay?"

Grell managed to look surprised, asking, "You really believe that, don't you?"

"Yes!" Ted hugged Grell close. "Together, we fought off a bunch of fuckin' fish people. We talked to that crazy cat lady out in the woods!" He paused, something scratching in the back of his mind.

The crazy cat lady in the woods—*Silas.*

"For the record," Grell teased halfheartedly, "I'm the one who fought off the fish people. You were a bit busy being passed out at the time, although I appreciated your unspoken moral support."

"Remember." The little boy's voice was nagging in Ted's ear, and a small hand pulled on his arm. "You have to remember!"

Ted could hear the ocean, screaming, and then....

The purple bead—he remembered where he'd seen it before. *Twice.*

"What is it?" Grell asked, his lips drawing back in a concerned pout. "Ted? Are you feeling all right?"

"Silas," Ted said urgently. "Old cat lady who lives down in the cave! We have to go see Silas right now."

"What the hell for?" Grell snapped grumpily. "I'm a bit preoccupied dealing with a very personal and very deep emotional collapse. I need to sit around in my pajamas and eat ice cream. Can we go see her later?"

"The ear thingie!" Ted exclaimed. "The broken bead we found! I've seen it before! The missing piece is on Mire's corpse! And I know who has the other half!"

"Well, fuck me, who?"

"It's her! It's Silas!"

"Oh shit."

CHAPTER 10.

KUNST THREATENED to find a way to free himself of the orb and haunt them both forever if they left him in the pits, and so Ted carried him along as Grell ported them back to court.

The only person there was Mire.

Grell took on his human form and called the guards to summon Vizier Ghulk immediately. He bared his teeth when they told him a few moments later that they were having trouble locating Ghulk but were still actively trying to find him.

"Hmmph," Grell huffed. "When you want that stupid slime pony around, he's nowhere to be found. When you don't want him, he's the biggest dick sore in all of Xenon."

"It's fine," Ted soothed, reaching down to massage Grell's shoulders. "We'll get him to take us to Silas, and maybe she can explain why Mire's half of the purple mating bead thing was hidden in some scroll in the library."

"And you're certain it's Mire's?"

"Still got the broken one we found in the library?"

"Here," Grell said, snapping his fingers.

It magically appeared floating above Ted's hand. Another snap retrieved the broken shard from Mire's corpse, and it clicked right into place with the rest of the bead.

"See?" Ted gasped. "It totally fucking fits. This is great. This is awesome. This…. What does this mean?"

"That my slimy little cousin was married to Thulogian Silas," Grell said, scrubbing his hands over his face.

"How did you not know that? Isn't that a thing you should know?"

"I don't know!" Grell threw up his arms in frustration. "I don't seem to recall receiving an invitation to the rehearsal!"

"They wed in secret ages ago," Kunst drawled. "Everyone knows that."

"Hey, wait!" Ted snapped, glaring down at Kunst's orb. "No, not everybody knows that! What are you talking about?"

"Mire was supposed to marry someone from the Vulgoran clan, but the negotiations kept being postponed," Kunst replied impatiently.

"Now that I do know," Grell piped up. "Asra aren't big on arranged marriages, but the Vulgorans are simply mad for them."

"Can a Vulgoran and an Asra... uh...?" Ted made a circle with his fingers and thumb, using the index finger of his other hand to thrust suggestively into the opening. "You know."

"With enough imagination, anything is possible," Grell declared, "but it's very unlikely that any offspring would have been produced. The Vulgorans wanted a link to the royal family, and who knows why Mire ever agreed to it."

"Especially if he was already married to Silas." Ted turned around and eyed Kunst. "And how do you know all of this, huh?"

"Because I've been wandering around the castle for weeks!" Kunst exclaimed. "Being stabbed to death is a great way to create a restless spirit!"

"Didn't you say you died saving the world or something?"

"I did!" Kunst argued passionately. "I sacrificed myself as part of an ancient ritual—"

"Glamour magic," Grell said suddenly, kneeling close to Mire's corpse. His hand had been hovering over him, and he drew it back with a scowl.

"Like, that stuff people use to cover zits?" Ted asked.

"Yes, but much more powerful," Grell replied. "Glamour can be imbued in charms and jewelry to completely transform a person's appearance. Mire must have been using it to hide his mating bead. When he died, the enchantment faded."

"And the killer went all smashy-smashy on it to destroy any evidence that Mire was already married?"

"So it would seem."

"Your Highness!" Ghulk's voice called out, his hooves clopping clumsily across the floor as he rushed inside. "You needed to see me?"

"We need you to take us back to see Silas," Grell commanded. "Right now."

"Uh, of course," Ghulk said, his milky eyes wide with surprise. "As you wish, Your Highness."

Back out into the forest they went with Ghulk leading the way. Grell was quiet, tense, and his eyes didn't seem as bright as usual. Ted carried Kunst as before, tucking the orb under his arm while they walked along.

Up in the night sky, Ted could see the bridge glowing and fading. It was still beautiful, but now his heart thudded with dread. This mystery was getting more twisted by the minute, and all he could do was keep pushing forward.

But he didn't have to do it alone.

Grell had reached for his hand, giving him a strained smile.

Ted couldn't begin to imagine the stress Grell was going through, and he squeezed his hand. "You know, if she's tied up in this somehow, maybe she knows what happened to the bones?"

"Perhaps," Grell said with a short laugh. "I'm not expecting much, to be honest."

Up ahead, Ghulk had already disappeared down into the hole. There was a long pause, and he shouted, "Your Highness! Oh no! Please! Come quick!"

"Wait here," Grell snarled, instantly transforming into his cat form and leaping down the hole after Ghulk.

"No! Fuck that!" Ted grunted. "Wait up!"

"Maybe we should just wait—" Kunst tried to protest.

"Shut up!" Ted bolted down the hole, trying to be more careful than his first trip here. It was completely dark, and he tried to hold up Kunst like a flashlight, complaining, "What the hell? Why is it so dark—"

His foot slipped in something slick, and he fell, trying to catch himself on his hands. He groaned, looking up to watch Kunst's orb bounce and roll along the ground.

It came to a stop next to....

The open mouth of an Asra, its eyes frozen in death and dull in the orb's dim light.

"Oh, gross! Get me away, get me away from it!" Kunst howled, his orb twitching helplessly as he tried to roll out of a sticky puddle of blood. "Ugh!"

The torches lit with a snap, Grell human again and offering his hands to help Ted up. "Are you okay, love?"

"I'm... I'm...." Ted stared at the body, recognizing it now as Silas Thulogian. "Shit!"

"She's dead," Ghulk whispered brokenly, collapsing down on his front legs and resting his large head against her shoulder. "Oh, Thulogian, my dear Thulogian... oh no."

"Looks like you're facing another set of murder charges," Grell mumbled, gesturing to the blood smeared on Ted's legs from where he'd slipped.

"Oh, for fuck's sake!" Ted groaned. He pointed accusingly at Ghulk, snapping, "What about him? He's over there touching her!"

"Technically, you were the first," Kunst piped up. "And Asran law is very clear—"

"Shut up!"

"Sorry, my love." Grell grimaced. "The law must stand."

"Fuck me," Ted groaned.

"Later, love."

"Another murder charge? Come the fuck on!" Ted wanted to tear out his hair. He groaned in frustration and looked back to Silas's body. "Okay. It's fine. Just another fuckin' murder. No big deal. A big cat monster person has been stabbed to death again. Cool. No weapon left behind. Right, got it, awesome. And... and... what the fuck, why is Ghulk eating her foot?"

"Drop the corpse, Ghulk!" Grell snarled.

"I'm sorry, Your Highness!" Ghulk howled, quickly retreating from Silas's body.

"She is an Asra," Grell roared, his small human form about to burst as he struggled to control his transformation. "She will be fucking entombed with her people! Not fuckin' served for dinner!"

"I loved her!" Ghulk snapped back. He stood up, baring his horrible teeth as he continued to rage. "I loved her more than anything in this world! Mire treated her like a burden, ordering her to live down in this hole so no one would know he was already mated!"

"The fuck is going on?" Ted demanded, still horrified. "If you love her so damn much, why were you trying to fuckin' eat her?"

"The Eldress used to eat their dead!" Kunst called out helpfully. "They were consumed by their loved ones after they died, and later began to use embalming to discourage the practice!"

Ted held his face in his hands.

"You had a thing for Thulogian Silas?" Grell asked briskly, trying to keep the conversation on track. "And you knew about the marriage?"

"Yes!" Ghulk sobbed. "We were friends! The best of friends! She was always so kind to me! Why do you think I was the only one who could come see her without being attacked?"

"You realize you've just made yourself our new top suspect for murdering Mire," Grell pointed out.

"I don't care!" Ghulk bowed his head with a mournful howl. "I wish I had… I wish I had killed him. I wish I could raise him up and kill him again for how he treated her! But I just know that wretched Visseract got to him first! This is awful!"

"I guess Visseract thought she might spill the beans?" Ted scratched his chin thoughtfully. "But if Visseract was gonna give her what she wanted, that Kindress thing, why would she rat?"

"It doesn't make much sense, does it?" Grell mused. "Hmmph." He looked over at Kunst. "What say you, Professor? Anything useful to add?"

"Oh, hmm, hmm, I'm not sure," Kunst quipped. "It's hard to think"—his voice rose to a hysterical shout—"*when I'm smothered up against a corpse!*"

"Big fuckin' baby," Ted grumbled, carefully stepping over the blood to pick up the orb. He figured his clothes were already ruined and wiped the orb off on his shirt. "There! Happy?"

"Better, thank you," Kunst said haughtily. "Hmmph. Well, whoever hid the mating bauble didn't want anyone to know that Mire and Silas were mates."

"Yeah, thanks, Captain Obvious," Ted snarked. "That still doesn't help us."

"It's late, I'm tired, I would like to go to bed," Grell growled. His eyes snapped to Ghulk, commanding, "You! Go back to the castle. Tell the rest of the court what's happened, and don't you dare nibble on Silas's body."

"Yes, Your Highness," Ghulk said, cowering obediently.

"You," Grell said, grabbing Kunst and waving his hand over the orb. He let go, and the glowing ball was now hovering on its own. "I'm sending you to the library."

"To search for clues? Perform research?" Kunst asked eagerly. "I'll be glad to do anything I can to help—"

"No, because you're annoying me, and you make my head hurt," Grell grunted. "And you, Tedward of Aeon." He took Ted's hand. "You're coming with me. Brace yourself."

"For what?"

"Just in case you get cut in half when we teleport."

"Wait, what—"

As Grell pulled Ted forward, the cave vanished, and he found himself back at the pool full of glowing eels. He was grateful to find his body intact and wearing some modest swimming trunks for this visit, although Grell had chosen to go nude as he dove into the water.

Ted sat down on the edge of the pool, waiting for Grell to surface. "Well, I'm glad I made it here in one piece. Uh, you okay?"

"Not really, no," Grell replied bluntly. "I now have two murders to solve, the sacred bones of my queen and family to find, and I've got the worst fucking headache."

"*We* have two murders to solve," Ted corrected, "since I keep getting myself charged hanging around you and all that shit."

"Hmmph."

Ted watched Grell duck under the water and swim for a bit, and he was not sure what to say now. The silence wasn't awkward, but he still felt the need to break it. He could tell Grell was upset, and he didn't know how to comfort him.

"Hey," Ted said, waiting for Grell to surface, "we're going to find your queen's bones. And everybody else's. We're gonna figure this shit out."

"And if we don't?" Grell asked, paddling over to stand in front of Ted. "What am I supposed to tell my son when he comes home from Aeon? Oops, lost your mommy's bones, sorry about that."

"You tell him the truth," Ted urged. "There's a fucking god out there stealing them. You didn't lose them. It wasn't like, oh, huh, did I leave those in my other pants? No, they were taken!"

Grell grunted, turning away and scowling.

"You know," Ted said hesitantly, reaching out with his legs to gently draw Grell in. "There is other stuff you could do."

"Other stuff?" Grell quirked a brow but let himself get pulled up between Ted's thighs. He hugged Ted's hips, looking up at him expectantly.

"Humans do all kinds of stuff when they're trying to have a funeral without a body," Ted explained carefully. "They might use an empty casket, just to help visualize the loss. Sometimes they might bury stuff that the person owned, stuff that was special to them."

"Like what?" Grell asked quietly. He didn't seem offended, only curious.

"Well, it all depends," Ted replied. "It could be photos, letters, personal things. Some families might bring an outfit, and we'll place it in the casket like there was someone in there. One wife brought some dirty socks because it was the last thing she remembered him wearing."

"I don't think my queen's old crunchy socks are much of a suitable replacement for his body."

"Not a replacement," Ted said sincerely. "This is a promise. It's a promise that you're going to keep trying to find his bones, and I'm going to help you." He blinked, caught off guard by the way Grell was staring at him now. "What?"

"Are you sure you're human?" Grell asked, his strong hands sliding up Ted's back.

"Pretty sure."

"Because you're really quite amazing," Grell said with a smile. "You're thoughtful, considerate, and I'm afraid I must confess I'm becoming more than a little fond of you."

"I... I really like you too," Ted confessed, his face quickly warming up. "I wanna help you, like you're trying to help me. I'm just... uh...." He was lost in Grell's bright eyes and left speechless.

Grell held him tight, easily lifting him off the edge of the pool and bringing him down into the water with him. He guided Ted's legs around his waist, holding him there and kissing him.

It was sweet, unhurried, and Ted wanted to kiss Grell like this for hours. They were floating lazily through the pool, the glowing eels sliding by them as the massive bridge made the night sky twinkle and shine.

Ted petted Grell's hair and his broad shoulders, groaning quietly from the inevitable passion starting to brew between them once more.

"Grell," he murmured, loving how hot and wet his lips were from kissing.

"When my hand is on your ass, feel free to call me Thiazi," Grell said, giving Ted's bottom a firm squeeze.

"Okay, Thiazi!" Ted laughed, snagging another deep kiss. He suddenly had to turn his head away so he wouldn't yawn directly into Grell's mouth. "Ah, fuck, sorry."

"Don't be," Grell said with a grin. "Mmm, it's been a long day, love. I'll ravage your tight little body tomorrow, hmm?"

"Is this before or after my trial?"

"Why not both?"

"We have until midnight tomorrow, right?" Ted tried to smile with confidence. "We could probably make that work. And hey, you still owe me some prime cuddling, right?"

"That I do." A snap of Grell's fingers took them back to bed, warm and dry and dressed in matching rainbow unicorn onesies.

Ted's hood was pulled up over his head, and he reached up to feel the floppy ears and horn. "Oh my God. You're fuckin' ridiculous."

"What?" Grell blinked. "Isn't this something human couples do?"

"Yeah, it's just…." Ted started laughing again, grinning at the sight of the powerful Asran king wearing sparkly unicorn pajamas. He tugged at Grell's hood, pulling it up for him. "There."

"Better?"

"Much." Ted kept snickering to himself, curling up on Grell's chest and hugging him close. Grell's arm curled around his shoulders and held him there, and Ted couldn't believe how light he felt.

Even though he'd just acquired new murder charges not even an hour ago, he was happy. He had no idea how long this bliss would last, but he was going to hang on to it as hard as he could.

"I've settled on a schedule for us for tomorrow," Grell said with a smug little grin.

"Oh? Do tell."

"First thing, primal hot sex," Grell replied seriously. "At least three positions, and I plan to make you come each time. Then we'll have breakfast. We'll make sure Ghulk didn't eat Silas's body, and we start questioning everyone."

"What about lunch?" Ted smiled.

"Yes, we'll break for lunch," Grell agreed. "We'll need our strength, because I guarantee my idiotic court will have no information at all to give us. It will not be an easy day, and dinner will probably be late."

"That's okay," Ted mumbled sleepily. "Maybe we could try talking to the fish people first. Mire was all tangled up with them, and we were attacked by 'em. There's gotta be somethin' goin' on there. If they won't talk, you can just eat 'em."

"Wonderful idea, my gorgeous little detective," Grell said with a chuckle. He kissed the top of Ted's head, playfully batting the horn as he said, "Now, let's get some sleep."

"Good night, Thiazi." Ted sighed, his eyes already closing.

"Good night, Ted."

Ted was soon asleep, and his dreams were quiet for a while. He dreamed of nothing but darkness and the sound of the ocean. It was relaxing at first, but soon the noise became a roar that he couldn't escape, and he woke up with a start.

His heart was pounding, and he looked all around bewilderedly. He was alone, no sign of Grell, but the little boy was there. "Little buddy?"

The little boy was standing next to an Asra with silver stripes and a purple bead hanging by her ear. He was petting her, saying quietly, "Silas has to talk to you before she goes."

"Thulogian Silas," Ted murmured, recognizing the Asra now. "Hey! Tell me who killed you! What happened?"

Silas said nothing, shaking her head and starting to walk away.

"Follow her," the boy said urgently, grabbing for Ted's hand and dragging him out of bed. "Come on!"

Ted hurried to keep up, chasing after the boy and the departing Asra as they vanished through the wall. The harder he ran, the farther away Silas became, and there was no way to reach her. The hallway in front of him grew longer and longer, and there was nothing he could do.

"Fuck! Come on!"

As Ted continued to pound his feet against the floor, the stones began to give way. He fell, dropping down into a giant body of water.

It was salty, warm… the ocean.

He tried to swim to the surface, but something was pulling him down. He was getting so tired, so very weak, and he knew then he was drowning. He couldn't stop breathing in the salty water, and his lungs were on fire.

There was something in his arms now, warm and small, and flashes of light danced in front of his face. He tried to focus on them when he realized he was seeing pictures.

Mire with the fish people, going over potions and bottles.

Silas and Mire, holding each other and crying.

Mire confronting Visseract and a human man in the pits—no, not a human, Gronoch.

It was coming at him faster and faster, so quickly that he couldn't understand everything he was seeing. He tried to take one last breath, and he heard himself shout. No, he was screaming.

A name….

What was the name?

"Ted?"

No, that was his name. What was it….

"Ted!" Grell snapped worriedly, shaking him awake. "Ted! What's wrong, love?"

"Ah, fuck!" Ted bolted up, panting and wheezing, checking all over himself frantically. "Wet, why am I wet?"

"You're sweating like a Vulgoran during a purity test," Grell said, snapping his fingers and putting Ted in a fresh shirt and boxer shorts. "There, is that better, love?"

"Thanks," Ted muttered, running his trembling fingers through his hair, still damp with sweat. "Fuck. I'm sorry, I…."

"It's fine. I can get you another onesie."

"I was having a dream. A really, really supremely fucked-up dream." Ted heard Grell's fingers snap and found a glass of whiskey in his hand. "Fuck, thank you."

"Relax, love," Grell purred gently. "You're safe. Nothing is going to harm you."

"In the dream, I was drowning," Ted said, taking a big gulp and hissing at the burn. "I was trying to find Silas, and then I was in the fucking ocean… oh fuck."

"What's the matter?"

"I saw it," Ted said shakily as the visions washed back over him with a new clarity. "I saw what Silas was trying to show me. Mire was trying to make a deal with the Vulgorans for fertility magic—"

"Well, they do have lots of holes."

"He wanted it for Silas," Ted went on, ignoring his comment. "She couldn't have kids. Carry them, make them, whatever. No one else knew. That's why he kept their marriage a secret, so he could barter his position to the Vulgorans. Not even her bestie Ghulk knew.

"Mire saw Visseract and Gronoch hiding in the pits, heard them talking about making slaves with the bones. He ran, told Silas what he saw. Wanted her to come tell you because he didn't trust anyone else, and then… then he was killed."

"Can't see who killed him?"

"No, but Silas threatened to spill the beans if Visseract didn't give her what she wanted so she could bring Mire back," Ted went on quickly as he tried to sort through the visions. "They kept going somewhere together. Somewhere with water…. Shit. I'm missing something. I'm still fucking missing something!"

"Calm down," Grell soothed. "Was it about Graham? Who's Graham?"

"Huh?"

"You were screaming that name," Grell explained. "It's what woke me up. I was starting to get a bit jealous, to be honest."

"Oh fuck," Ted gasped, reaching up to cradle his head. Just like that, it all clicked into place. "I remember…."

"What, my love?"

"I know where to find Visseract, and I…." Ted tried to swallow down the lump in his throat. "I remember how I died."

CHAPTER 11.

"How?" Grell asked, reaching for Ted and drawing him close. "Talk to me, love."

"The beach." Ted took another big sip of whiskey, silently grateful it kept refilling. "Me and my old boyfriend had gone to the beach. That's when he proposed, and I turned him down. We got into a big fight.

"But there was this boy. His name was Graham. He kept wanting to play. He was there with his parents, and he just wanted to play with us. Oh God." Ted's chest clenched in pain, and he looked up with tears in his eyes.

Graham was standing at the foot of the bed, and for the first time, Ted could see his face. He had brown eyes and a fluffy mop of dark hair. He wasn't wearing a scarf, Ted now realized.

He had a striped beach towel draped around his neck.

"He came to ask me to play, to take him out in the waves," Ted said, his voice dropping to a whisper. "I was still mad at my boyfriend. I was upset. I was looking for sunscreen, couldn't find it, and when Graham asked me again, I snapped at him.

"He was so upset. I felt like a complete fucking tool, and by the time I calmed down... it was too late." Ted closed his eyes. "Everyone was screaming, screaming for Graham. He went into the water on his own. God, where were his parents? I can't... I can't remember...."

"It's okay," Grell murmured, stroking a strong hand across Ted's back. "Just keep talking, love. Go on."

"The water," Ted said, sniffing noisily and trying to stay focused. "I went into the water to get him. It was all my fuckin' fault. If I hadn't been such a jerk to him, maybe he wouldn't have tried to go on his own. I kept swimming, kept diving….

"And I found him. I found him, and I held on as tightly as I could… but the current. Fuck, we were caught in something, and it just kept pulling us out, deeper and deeper…." Ted was crying, reaching out to take Graham's hands.

"But you never let go," Graham said with a sad smile. "You kept holding on to me."

"I kept thinking that they'd find us," Ted cried quietly. "They'd dive down, they'd see us and save us both…."

"They never did, did they?" Grell asked somberly, stroking Ted's hair.

"I drowned." Ted couldn't believe he'd said it out loud. "I drowned trying to save Graham, and… and he died too." He squeezed Graham's hands as hard as he could. "I'm sorry, little buddy. I'm so sorry."

"It's okay," Graham said. "I'm not mad at you, Ted. I'm okay. I know you were trying to save me. When I died, at least I wasn't alone." He smiled, bright and happy. "You were with me."

"Fuck." Ted sniffled weakly, knocking back the whiskey and trying to calm himself. "That's why you've been trying to help me? To show me stuff?"

"You couldn't save me, but maybe I can help save you," Graham said cheerfully. His image faded a little, and Ted couldn't feel his hand any longer. "I saw a fish man take the bead from the dead kitty while you were sleeping. I knew it was important, I just knew it!"

"Fish man?" Ted paused. "You saw a fish man take the bead?"

"Visseract?" Grell asked quietly. "That fish man?"

"I don't know," Graham said, his image returning more vividly before fading away again. "I couldn't see his face… I'm sorry… I…."

"Hey, hey, it's okay, little buddy," Ted soothed. "You okay? Getting sleepy?"

"Yeah." Graham vanished completely, but Ted could still feel his presence. "Mm. Sorry."

"Is he all right?" Grell asked, nearly interrupting Graham because he couldn't hear him.

"He's okay," Ted said earnestly. "Sorry, I know it's weird having to listen to a one-sided conversation and all, but uh, yeah, he's good. Manifesting like this can take a lot outta a spirit. I've seen it happen before. They just kinda run outta juice, but he might perk back up in a bit."

"Does he know what wonderful little person hid the bead away?"

"No, couldn't see his face. Why would Visseract or any fish dudes want to hide the bead?"

"Mire was trying to barter himself for marriage when he was already hitched," Grell replied. "The Vulgorans might have been trying to save some face. It would be quite embarrassing for them if it got out that Mire was about to swindle them out of fertility magic for that wife everyone else seemed to know about except for them."

"Big ol' scandal of people-eating proportions?"

"Precisely," Grell confirmed. "What I want to know is why take the damn thing to the library? Why didn't our fishy little culprit just run off with it?"

"More monsters came." Graham's voice sounded far away. "The fish man had to run. Hid it there."

"Okay," Ted said, turning to Grell to relay the information. "Graham says that other people were coming, and fish dude had to scoot. I guess he got scared and stashed it there." He shrugged. "Maybe he thought he could come back and get it later."

"This would explain why those Vulgorans attacked us," Grell mused. "If Visseract found out we were going to see Silas, he might have thought she would confess the truth of her marriage to Mire."

"Well, shit. Sounds like Visseract is our fuckin' dude." Ted let out a long sigh of relief, looking back toward where he had seen Graham last. There was one more thing he had to know. "Hey, little dude. I really appreciate all of your help, and, uh, I hate to ask because I know you're really tired, but…." He took a deep breath. "Do you know who brought me back?"

"No," Graham replied softly. "I don't remember. We were in the ocean, and then I was with you. We were driving back to your apartment, and you took the crazy road because you were upset…. That's it."

"After the beach trip," Ted recalled. "Yeah, I took the long way back because I didn't wanna go home. Fuckin' hell."

"What did he say?" Grell asked.

"He doesn't know who brought me back either."

"Damn." Grell frowned, taking Ted's hand in his and pressing a kiss to it. "I wish there was some sort of card for this situation, love. 'Sorry you drowned' with a picture of a puppy or something."

"You're sweet." Ted managed a smile and gulped another mouthful of whiskey before setting the glass aside. "I'll be okay. I mean, now I know, right? I know who Graham is, I know what happened."

"And your family never mentioned, ahem, your demise?" Grell asked politely.

"No. I remember them being upset about me and my guy breaking up, but pretty sure they don't fuckin' know I died. I guess it happened right there at the beach."

"What about the former boyfriend? Any ideas?"

"Haven't spoken to him in a long time, but I'm sure he would have said something about fuckin' necromancy. His damn uncle is a cop. He's a good boy, you know? Woulda freaked him out."

"Well, I'm quite grateful to your mysterious rescuer, whoever or whatever it was," Grell said quietly, cradling Ted's hand against his cheek. "You're here."

"With you," Ted said with a warm smile. He paused. "I mean, yeah, the double dose of murder charges I could do without, but the rest is pretty cool."

Grell laughed. "We'll get through that, love. We still have until midnight tonight, and well…." His brow furrowed up. "And not that I'm trying to downplay this sudden revelation of your death and sweet bonding with Casper over there, but did I hear you correctly before? You know where Visseract is?"

"Shit!" Ted had been so caught up that he had honestly forgotten about that part of his vision. He bolted out of bed, exclaiming, "Yes! I know where to find that slimy son of a bitch! We gotta go! We gotta go right now!"

Grell grunted as he got to his feet, changing out of his unicorn onesie and into a new emerald suit with a snap. Another click of his fingers gave Ted a fresh T-shirt and jeans. "So that's a no on breakfast?"

"Yes," Ted said, shifting anxiously in his new shoes. "We need to go wherever there's an ocean here. It's a beach with black sand and some super wicked-looking giant rocks. You got an ocean? Some kinda water?"

"We do," Grell replied. "I'll tell the guards to prepare to move and meet us there at once." He closed his eyes briefly. "There. Done. Are you ready?"

"Let's fuckin' go get this bastard," Ted confirmed, pulling Grell in for a firm kiss. The world moved around them, and he could suddenly hear waves crashing.

The sound reminded him so much of his dream that he shuddered and jerked, staring out at a long beach. The sand was as black as it was in the vision and glittered beneath the eternally dark sky, shining in the light cast from the bridge off in the distance.

The water went on as far as he could see, with sporadic bright spots, perhaps from more of those glowing eels swimming around. Behind them, the beach rose up to meet a large collection of rocks. It was the jagged foot of a mountain, rising high into the sky like a fistful of daggers.

"Are you okay?" Grell asked, drawing Ted close in a comforting embrace. "Being here?"

"Here?" Ted didn't mind the closeness, but the cause for Grell's concern didn't register at first. "I've never been here before."

"I meant being by an ocean after, well, your recent discovery of an ocean-affiliated death?"

"That. Right." Ted bowed his head until their brows met and took a deep breath. Though he was touched by Grell's concern, he honestly didn't know how he felt. "No fuckin' clue."

"We don't have to do this now if you're not comfortable," Grell assured him, brushing a hand over his cheek. "We could wait and send the guards in first if you'd prefer."

"No," Ted said firmly, though he let himself lean into Grell's palm and take the offered comfort. "I need to do this. Graham and Silas want me to see something. I just… I just have this feeling."

"Then where to, love?"

"Uh…." Ted turned away from the ocean, and he looked up at the rocky foothills. There was one part of the mountain that seemed darker than all the rest. As soon as he saw it, he knew that's where they had to go.

"A cave," he said. "There's a cave up there. That's where Visseract is. Silas is sure of it."

"How the hell did she know where to go?" Grell asked with an incredulous huff.

"I don't fuckin' know! She called 1-800-Find-Fish-Man!"

"You and I both know that joke is beneath you. This is what happens when you skip the most important meal of the day." Grell shrugged off his human form and crouched down once he was fully transformed. "Come along, then."

"What? You can't just poof us up there?"

"No. The same energy field in the forest exists here. So, unless you want me to wing it and risk cutting your gorgeous body in half, climb up and hang on."

Moving as gracefully as he could, Ted eased himself up onto Grell's back. He leaned forward and hugged his neck awkwardly. "You know, I did plan to ride you, but this isn't quite what I had in mind."

"You'll have plenty of chances later," Grell teased. "Now, I was serious about hanging on. Here we go!"

Ted grunted as Grell leaped up the side of the rocks, scaling them with inhuman speed and dexterity. He could feel the huge muscles of Grell's shoulders and back flexing beneath him, and he did his best to dig in and hold on tight.

"Gotta tell me where I'm going, love," Grell reminded him as he went higher. "Kind of a big mountain."

"Right! Uh...." Ted closed his eyes and tried to focus. "It's... eh...."

"Higher," Graham's voice urged. "Around that ledge up there... that's where the darkness is...."

"Yeah, what he said!"

"Can't hear your little dead friend, love!" Grell groaned.

"Sorry!" Ted grimaced. "Go a little higher, and it's around that ledge up there!"

Claws scrambling against the mountainside, Grell fought his way to the ledge and pulled himself up with a loud wheeze. "Ugh. I've been watching far too much television. I'm out of shape."

In front of them now was a large opening that led into a dark cave. The sound of the ocean seemed louder up here as it echoed off the stone, and it filled Ted with undeniable dread.

"Think you're in the right kinda shape to fight a murdering fish dude?" Ted asked as he slid off Grell's back and stood beside him as they both peered into the cave.

"And still fuck you stupid after," Grell huffed, his tail flicking sharply. "Hmmph."

"So, are we waiting for the guards or...?"

"I'm thinking."

"About what?"

"What could possibly be down there and how I'd be much happier facing whatever it is had I been able to enjoy a nice hot breakfast."

"Ah, come on!" Ted scratched behind Grell's ears. "My big, tough kitty monster! You can totally take whatever we run into. We got this, right?"

Grell did not look amused. "You know what else would have been good this morning? Sex! Hot primal sex would have been good."

"Was that supposed to be before or after breakfast?" Ted drawled. "I can't keep track of your bitching."

"Easy enough to catch up. Reach down here between my legs and it'll give you a hell of a place to start."

Ted started laughing, unable to resist Grell's sly grin. It made his heart feel light, and he could push his worries aside for a few precious moments.

"There's that smile," Grell purred, wrapping his tail around Ted's waist for a gentle squeeze. "Even without breakfast and steaming sex, I suppose this morning hasn't been entirely wasted just to see that."

"We are about to finally confront Visseract and make me a free man, yeah?" Ted grinned bashfully. "It ain't been wasted yet."

"I meant that I still got to spend it with you, even though I wasn't inside of you."

"Creep." Ted reached up to cradle the sides of Grell's face and planted a kiss firmly on his wet nose.

"What was that for?" Grell blinked.

"For the smile." Ted clapped his hands together. "So. We ready?"

"Just stay behind me, love." Grell walked forward and lifted his head. Immediately, the cave lit up from little cracks in the rock so they could travel safely.

Ted stayed a few steps behind Grell, being mindful of his tail as they went along. He couldn't shake his weird feeling of unease, but he knew this was where they were supposed to be.

He could sense that they were descending, going deeper into the mountain with every step, and the cave soon opened up into a mammoth cavern. Grell's lights were so high above their head now that they looked like stars, and Ted couldn't see shit.

Stumbling, he caught himself on Grell's tail. "Fuck, sorry!" He blushed as it curled around him, helping him stand. "Thanks."

"Stay close and be careful," Grell said quietly, skillfully padding over the rocky floor. "I can smell something…. We're getting close."

Ted caught a whiff, something faint but familiar. He knew that scent. "Death."

The end of the cavern shuttered into a small grotto, and Grell created more lights so they could see better. There was a small camp set up here, and a large collapsed figure was stretched out across a pallet.

It was the corpse of Humble Visseract, discolored with foamy purge crusted around his mouth. There was a bottle in his hand, empty, and three broken vials at the end of his tail. A rolled-up scroll was neatly resting by his head.

"Oh, what the fuck!" Ted groaned. He stomped his feet, crossing his arms and refusing to come any closer. "Nope, nope, nope! I'm not going anywhere near that fuckin' dead dude! Not getting charged for this one too!"

"Damn." Grell moved forward and sniffed at the bottle in Visseract's hand. He hissed and drew back, saying, "Poison. Eldress milk." He batted at the scroll, using his paws to open it up.

"What is it?"

"My sincerest apologies for all the trouble," Grell began to read out loud, "but consider this my confession. I murdered Mire and Silas both for conspiring against my clan and threatening our honor. They plotted to cheat us out of our sacred magic, blah, blah, blah, I'm a murdering twat, blah, blah, blah, I chose to die by my own hand, blah, blah." He lifted his paw, and the scroll rolled back up. "Bloody hell."

"Does it mean I'm fuckin' innocent now?" Ted asked bluntly. "Because I'll take that for two hundred, Alex."

"No sign of the bones," Grell said, a hint of disappointment hunching his shoulders, "but these vials are interesting." He leaned down to get a whiff and hissed, "These are the tears!"

"Wait, as in, the Tears of Big Head Honcho God?"

"Yes," Grell replied urgently. "These vials were filled with the tears of Great Azaethoth himself."

"What does that smell like?"

"Imagine a really very old book, but you know it could put your insides on your outsides if you messed with it."

"Got it."

"This means Silas was right about the Kindress being involved," Grell said, snorting and rubbing at his nose. "Someone, most likely that fiend Gronoch, must have found where the tears are kept and intended to use them against the Kindress."

"Like, do what we say or we'll sprinkle your daddy's tears on you?"

"Something like that."

The entire cavern lit up, and a pack of Asra were filtering in behind them.

"Ah, the cavalry has arrived!" Grell chirped, turning around to greet them. "Thank you all for coming, and no, we don't validate parking."

Ted recognized one as the guard who was constantly barging in, and he watched as he bowed down before Grell.

"Your Highness," the guard with the worst timing in the world said, "we came as quickly as we could! We followed the beacon you left us, but…." He managed to look embarrassed.

"Let me guess," Grell mused, his tail swishing. "You were afraid that you were going to portal in here and find me and the prisoner in the swing of carnal passions again?"

"Uh… yes, Your Highness." The guard cringed. "I was concerned that was a possibility."

"Very possible, thank you for your discretion."

"I thought it best if we took the long way from the beach and made sure that now was an appropriate time to…." His eyes found Visseract, and he gasped. "Humble Visseract is dead?"

"Looks that way," Grell replied. "You're welcome to poke him with a stick if you'd like to make sure…." He squinted. "What is your name?"

"Haveras Mozzie, Your Highness."

"Well, Mozzie, I suppose we are to assume he took his own life after murdering Silas and Mire, based on the little love note he left us."

Mozzie looked at Ted. "Does this mean the prisoner is free?"

"Not quite, though the trial tonight will most certainly find him innocent now," Grell said, tilting his head thoughtfully. "I suppose we'll have to find a new prosecutor since this one is dead and all."

"Right away, Your Highness," Mozzie said. "Shall we let the Vulgorans know that their heir is dead?"

"Go on," Grell huffed, waving a paw.

While Grell continued to give out orders to the guards, Ted crept a little closer to the body. He didn't know why, but something just wasn't sitting right with him. All of this seemed wrong.

He crouched down, peering at Visseract's clawed hand holding the bottle. Not all of his fingers were fully wrapped around it, and upon further inspection, it seemed as if it had been wedged in his hand. Even the way he was stretched out on the pallet was off. Ted could see purplish discolorations on Visseract's body, but it was on the side facing up and not the one he was lying on.

"What's wrong, love?" Grell asked, padding over to Ted's side. "Thought you'd be cheering. You're going to be a free man as soon as I can rouse the court."

"This isn't right," Ted said quietly. "I don't think this is a suicide."

"What's the matter?"

"I don't know what the rate of rigor mortis is for fish people, but I'm pretty sure that bottle was placed in his hand after he was already dead," Ted replied. "With humans, two things can happen after death. They either go limp until rigor starts to set in on its own a few hours later, or they're already in what we call instant rigor.

"They go rigid immediately. We see it with people who die really suddenly and usually real bad. Like, when someone shoots themselves and their hand will be frozen like they're still pulling the trigger, bad."

"And our dear Visseract here?"

"Well, if he went into instant rigor, his hand should be clamped all around that bottle, and it's not," Ted said. "If he went all limp after he died, it should have just fallen out of his hand with the way he's stretched out. And that's the other thing.

"The discolorations you see? We call that livor mortis. After someone dies, all their blood starts to settle because of gravity. Somebody is on their back, it'll settle there and turn it that same purple color. They die on their face, blood goes there and makes their face purple, get it?"

"But all of Visseract's purple bits are upright," Grell pointed out, eyeing the corpse with a frown.

"Exactly," Ted said. "It's like he died laying on that side, hung out for a while, and someone came back and moved him to set all of this up. That kinda discoloration can take hours to show up. He might have already been dead when Silas was killed. And I mean, come on, that suicide note is totally bogus."

"While that may be true, it does mean you'll be found innocent of all murder charges," Grell said with a short huff. "If I had to guess, Gronoch came through here and finished Visseract off to hide his mess. He already got what he came for, right?"

"The bones?"

"Mmhm. Now he's just tying up loose ends, and I have no interest in telling my court that a god was here," Grell went on. "Three deaths have been enough of a headache. Don't want to worry about a damn war too."

"So that's it?" Ted huffed. "We let a god get away with murder? A god who might be using Head Honcho God's tears to do bad stuff with that star baby?"

"Or we go to war against Zebulon," Grell replied impatiently.

"Didn't you guys beat their butts before? You won your big rebellion, right?" Ted was trying to keep his voice down, and he threw his hands up in frustration. "Come on!"

"Barely," Grell said with a somber smile. "Sorry if I'm not thirsting to drag my people into a bloody battle against the gods. I'm more worried about entombing two of them."

"It's time for that now?"

"The case is closed," Grell said with a shrug of his broad shoulders.

"Don't we have to wait for the court to make their super official ruling?" Ted smirked.

"Justice has been served because I say it's been served, and oh, wait, I'm king. Now the dead can go to rest, thank you, you cheeky little ass. That's my decision as king of the Asra and Xenon."

"Yes, your Most Royal Highness."

Grell rolled his eyes. "Without my son here, it's going to be a righteous pain in the ass."

"You know, I could help you," Ted offered, glancing back to see the Asra porting in and out. The crowd here was growing, and he could see some of the Vulgorans beginning to arrive.

"I can imagine many helpful things for you to do," Grell said with his usual snark. "Rub my back, alphabetize my audio cassettes, braid my hair all pretty, or perhaps another scorching round of coitus?"

"I do kinda move bodies for a living," Ted said dryly.

"And then what would you suggest, Tedward of Aeon?" Grell batted his eyes.

"We take a quick little trip back to my work in the land of Aeon for some of my equipment and I help you out?" Ted suggested. He nodded to the ever-growing crowd. "Looks like it's gonna get real cozy in here soon."

Grell seemed to be thinking it over, and he made a sour face when one of the Vulgorans started screaming and flailing its tail at the sight of Visseract's body. "Ugh, and very noisy it seems. Yes, fuck it, let's go."

CHAPTER 12.

THE WORLD turned, Ted's stomach lurched, and they were standing in the middle of downtown Archersville. It was early morning, traffic was bustling by, horns were honking, and no one seemed to have noticed that two men had magically appeared out of thin air.

The sun hurt his eyes, and Ted squinted as he waited for them to adjust. He missed the soft twilight of Xenon immediately, not to mention how much quieter it was there.

"Damn, it's bright here," Grell complained, snapping his fingers and creating a pair of slick red-tinted shades to put on. They matched the crimson-and-black velvet suit he was now wearing. "Mm, much better. Where to, love?"

"It's two blocks down and then over by the post office—" Everything moved again, and Ted now found himself standing in the lobby of the funeral home he worked in.

Kitty was here, frozen in place by the front desk and reaching to pick up the phone that was actively ringing. Two older men were walking out of a visitation room but were also still as statues.

"What the hell did you do?" Ted demanded.

"I'm the damn king of the Asra." Grell rolled his eyes. "I stopped time here for a minute. Nifty trick I picked up from a Faedra in a game of cards. They're all fine, I promise, but it's probably best they don't know we're borrowing their things, eh?"

"Right," Ted said, reaching out to touch Kitty's arm. She was warm, but it was still bothering him to see her so motionless.

They hadn't been close, but he would miss their late-night chats when they were out on removals. He didn't miss them enough to hurry back here to his miserable job anytime soon, and it gave him pause when he realized there really wasn't anything here that he would miss that badly.

It wasn't just the job that had been miserable—Ted's entire life had been dismal. His only real friend was his roommate, he saw such terrible things, ghosts bothered him constantly, and he'd been so very lonely.

Xenon had seemed strange when he'd first arrived, but he was already longing to return. It was quiet there, and he missed the soft purple glow. He liked being with Grell more than he was ready to admit, and he couldn't imagine coming back to Archersville now. The city was too bright, too busy, and there wasn't anything here left for him.

The world of Xenon, on the other hand, was full of promise, potential, and....

"Are we gonna get going, or am I just going to stand here and stare at you?" Grell asked. "Not that I mind looking at you, but I enjoy it much more when you're naked."

A very sarcastic and perverted kitty-monster king, who Ted would rather be with than spend another moment here.

"On it." Ted took off into the back of the funeral home to the garage. He grabbed two oversized body bags, a portable stretcher, and a box of gloves. Arms full, he turned back to Grell. "Okay, we're good!"

Grell put his hand on Ted's shoulder, and Ted was certain he was going to throw up from the intense vertigo that came with portaling. Back at court, Ted dropped the supplies and took a deep breath. Breathing in the smell of Mire definitely didn't help his nausea.

"Ugh, okay, no more of that for a little while, please."

"Sorry," Grell said, offering a sympathetic smile. "Well, what now, Mr. Funeral Home Man?"

"I guess you don't care about gloves, huh?" Ted smirked as he slid a pair on.

"Nope."

"Okay, then." Ted unzipped the thick body bag, explaining, "We're each gonna get on either side of him. You roll him to you so I can stuff the bag under him. And then I roll him to me so you can pull it out halfway, and just like that, he's in the bag."

"Or option B," Grell said, snapping his fingers and magically stuffing Mire into the body bag.

"That works too." Ted grabbed the zipper and sealed it up. He was careful to avoid the dried blood on the floor and stood up, saying, "Okay. To the pits?"

"Sure your little stomach can take it?" Grell teased.

"Eat a dick. Let's go."

Getting Mire into his new slot was going to be especially difficult because it was at least six feet off the ground, his body probably weighed at least a ton, and Grell cheerfully explained that the actual entombment had to be performed by hand.

No magic.

Grell turned into his cat form, shrank down to fit inside the hole, and dragged the end of the body bag up using his teeth, with Ted struggling to help push up from below and praying to any god that might be listening that Grell didn't drop Mire on top of him.

Grell kept shrinking and pulling until they were able to position Mire all the way into the slot. Even at such a diminutive size, Grell's strength was incredible. He then simply crawled back out, resumed his normal size, and removed the body bag with a snap of his fingers.

Going to retrieve Silas was easier, definitely less messy, and her slot in the pit wall was right on the bottom. Grell was quiet as they worked, pushing her into her final resting place with only a small sigh. He looked down to the archway that led into the older section of the pits, but he said nothing.

"You should come work for the funeral home," Ted teased, trying to lighten the mood as he took off his gloves. "Being able to snap somebody down a spiral staircase would make my life so much fuckin' easier."

Grell made the gloves disappear with a twitch of his nose and smiled, but it was clear his heart wasn't in it.

"You okay?" Ted asked, reaching up to stroke Grell's furry shoulder.

"I was thinking about what you said," Grell said. "About putting something in the grave as a promise."

"Yeah?" Ted stepped a little closer. "Did you think of somethin'?"

"I did," Grell said, shifting into his human form. There was a small music box in his hands, and he held it close to his chest.

"That was Vael's?" Ted was certain by the way Grell cradled it that it was special.

"Yes," Grell replied, his brow furrowed.

"We can go right now if you want," Ted offered. He suddenly worried that he had overstepped and amended, "Or you can just go by yourself, you know. I can stay here... watch Mire drip."

"I'd like for you to come with me." Grell looked up at Ted. "Please."

"Yeah, totally."

Ted followed Grell down into the pits to the empty slots. He didn't know what to say, standing back as Grell reverently placed the music box in Vael's empty crypt. Anything Ted could think of sounded so hollow and meaningless, and he figured Grell probably wouldn't want to hear it anyway.

Much to his surprise, Grell suddenly turned around and embraced him, smothering his face into Ted's broad chest. Ted held him tightly, kissing the top of his head. "Hey, I got you."

"Thank you," Grell said quietly. "For everything."

"Thank you too," Ted replied. "You know, for everything."

"My pleasure."

"So." Ted shifted a little, rubbing his hands over Grell's back. "Still got time for some of that hot primal sex before we go to court tonight?"

Grell laughed at that, peering up at Ted with a sly grin. "We've just buried two bodies, and I've laid a promise in my dead husband's empty grave to find his bones, and you're thinking about sex?"

"Uh," Ted stammered, blushing immediately. "Yes?"

"Oh, how I adore you," Grell growled, surging up to claim a passionate kiss.

Ted fell backward, half expecting to land on the stone floor. Instead, he found himself flat on his back in Grell's bed and their lips still locked together.

Grell was kissing him harshly, nearly breaking skin when his teeth grazed Ted's lower lip.

"Fuck," Ted panted, sliding his hands through Grell's hair and wrapping his legs around his waist. He was already getting hard, and he could feel Grell's stiffening cocks pressing against his own.

They had taken their time before, but Grell didn't seem like he wanted to wait. Neither did Ted, to be honest. He wanted Grell inside of him, and he wanted him now.

Ted was soon tearing at his own clothes, trying to get everything between them out of the way. He wanted skin on skin, the taste of Grell's tongue, and he wanted to be stuffed completely full.

Grell was on the same page, making their clothing vanish with a quick snap and sliding his hands down Ted's bare body. "By all the gods, you're so beautiful."

"Yeah?" Ted was learning to love how Grell could make him blush so easily, grinning up at him. "Probably look even more beautiful full of some dick. What do you think?"

"Beauty *and* brains," Grell gushed. "How did I ever get so lucky?"

"Your son is an asshole," Ted replied with a laugh.

"True," Grell said wistfully, leaning in for a deep kiss. "Mmm, I'll be sure to write him a very touching thank-you card when he returns."

"I'll sign it too!" Ted wrapped his arms around Grell's neck, trying to use his grip to flip their positions. It was awkward, and

Grell didn't budge, leaving Ted to gripe, "Hey, come on, work with me here."

"What are you trying to do?"

"Uh, trying to get on top?"

"Oh?" Grell grinned, rolling onto his back and pulling Ted on top of him. He smirked up at him, sliding his hands up his legs and grabbing his hips. "And now that you're there, what are you planning to do?"

"I really do wanna ride you, you know," Ted said with a bright smile, rolling his ass down and enjoying the little groans Grell made in reply. Being so much bigger than Grell was a little awkward, but Grell didn't seem to mind at all. "This is good?"

"Oh, most definitely," Grell agreed, one of his cocks magically slick as it pushed up against Ted's hole. He squeezed Ted's thighs, gazing at him hungrily. "Take whatever you want, love. I'm yours."

"I'm takin' it all," Ted promised, grunting as the tip of Grell's cock caught, and he began to lower himself down. He breathed through the stretch, willing his body to open up.

Grell wasn't moving, staying still and letting Ted control the pace. He stroked Ted's thighs, encouraging him, "There you go, love... just like that...."

Ted grunted, working a few more inches in before he had to stop and regroup. He lifted his hips, grinding back down on what he'd already taken. He moved slowly, not sure if Grell was even halfway in yet, but it still felt really good.

He was determined to take it all, groaning low as his ass stretched to accommodate Grell's thick girth. He kept rolling his hips, tilting his head back and moaning in triumph as he finally sat flush in Grell's lap, his cock fully seated inside of him.

"Perfect," Grell praised, caressing Ted's stomach and hips. His voice was strained, hoarse with lust, as he growled, "Absolutely perfect."

Panting hard, Ted fucked himself down on Grell's cock. He flexed his strong legs to power his slams, letting himself moan out loud with each thrust. There was no pain, only the hot tension of incredible pressure as he rode the king hard.

Grell arched his body up to force himself deeper, groaning pleasurably as Ted moved with him.

"Fuck, fuck!" Ted gasped, his hands pitching forward to brace himself on Grell's chest. He had to slow down again, struggling to keep up the pace with Grell pushing into him like that. It felt like Grell was getting bigger, and he could barely stand it.

He shifted his weight, trying a new angle to keep moving. He was so full, so tight, but he didn't want to stop. He planted his hips all the way down in Grell's lap and started grinding, his legs soon trembling. "Ah, f-fuck... it's so good... you feel so fuckin' good...."

Grell sat up, grabbing on to Ted's sides and pressing a searing kiss to his lips. "Just like that, love... nice and slow, there you go...."

Ted wrapped his arms around Grell's neck, loving the new intimacy of this position. Their chests were pressed flush together, and Ted's legs curled around Grell's back as he pressed forward. "Mmph.... Grell...."

"Thiazi," he urged, smothering hot kisses against Ted's throat. "Call me Thiazi, love."

"Mmm, Thiazi," Ted murmured, groaning as Grell started to thrust up into him. He was bouncing in Grell's lap, speared on his thick cock over and over, his head falling back as he let himself go completely. "Ohhh, fuck.... *Thiazi*!"

Grell held on to him tight, urging him down on his dick faster and faster, his strong hands keeping him right where he wanted him. It was hot, perfect, and Ted couldn't stop moaning. He was too lost in the moment to be self-conscious about how vocal he was being. It was just too damn good, and he had to let it out.

"Fuck, fuck, fuck! Thiazi!" he cried, amazed at the strength behind Grell's hips as he pounded up into him. "God, yes! Fuck! Right there, like that, just like that! You feel fuckin' amazing! I love your fuckin' cock, fuck!"

"Gonna come for me, love?" Grell growled fiercely, baring his teeth in a possessive snarl.

"Yes!" Ted moaned, already feeling the heat of his climax starting to creep over him. Grell was swelling inside of him, impossibly thicker and reaching new depths, and Ted couldn't move. He gasped, frozen in place by the intense ache. "Fuck, fuck, oh, fuck!"

"I've got you," Grell purred, taking over and rutting up into Ted with a new surge of energy. He lifted Ted's legs and fucked up into him, thrusting so hard that the bed beneath them was shaking.

Clinging to Grell's shoulders, Ted gritted his teeth and let out a howl of pleasure as he came. He was hot all over, and his thighs trembled as his cock pulsed between them. Every slam of Grell's hips forced out another gush of come, and Ted couldn't stop climaxing.

Even as Grell came inside of him and left him completely stuffed, Ted was still riding out the crest of an incredible orgasm. He went limp in Grell's strong embrace, sobbing softly against his shoulder. The pleasure was bordering on painful, finally beginning to fade as Grell stilled his hips.

Grell rubbed Ted's back, nuzzling into his hair and against his cheek. "Mmm, good, my love?"

"Mmmmm...," Ted mumbled, unsure if he could even raise his head. He was exhausted and more than a bit sticky, but he was utterly and completely satisfied. "So good.... Mmph."

"Very." Grell kissed Ted's neck. "Feel like we both needed that, eh? I know I did." He gently eased Ted onto his back, setting him by the pillows and snuggling up against his side.

Ted fought to catch his breath, grinning blissfully as his normal motor functions started to come back on line. "Fuck... yeah. That was great. So fucking great."

Grell beamed proudly, trailing his fingers down Ted's chest. "Consider me subscribed, love. I've become very fond of doing naughty things to your body."

Laughing, Ted rolled over to claim a kiss. "Mmm, I'm becomin' very fond of you doin' 'em to me."

Grell held the kiss for a long moment. "I'll have to go do some kingly things here soon. A new prosecutor needs to be appointed before the trial tonight."

"And then what?" Ted asked quietly, a stone dropping down into his gut.

"We hold the trial at midnight, present Humble Visseract's confession, they find you innocent, and then you'll be cleared of all charges," Grell said. "Free to do as you'd like."

"And us?" Ted hated how easily his insecurities came creeping in, and his heart skipped several beats when Grell took hold of his hand.

"I'm hoping you'd like to stay here and keep doing me," Grell said sincerely.

"Yeah?" Ted immediately perked up. "You'd let me stay here? With you?"

"Where else?" Grell smiled warmly. "I suppose if you want to return to Aeon, I could visit you there. Bright, horrible place that it is, I would go there to see you."

"I don't know…." Ted paused, trying to collect his thoughts. "I don't know if I wanna go back."

"Then don't."

"You're not gonna try to tell me I should go back for my job? For my family?"

"Your job makes you miserable," Grell said dryly. "Especially with your gift. It's eating you up inside. Don't even try to deny it. Fuck your job. And your family? Meh. We can always visit them if you'd like."

"We?" Ted echoed shyly.

"Well, of course!" Grell smirked. "I'm very good with meeting parents, trust me. I've watched every romantic comedy made by man. I know just what to do. They'll love me."

Ted laughed at that, shaking his head. "Fuck, you're ridiculous."

"This and many other things," Grell teased. He kissed Ted's hand, adding, "I do mean it, love. About us being together. I want you to stay here in Xenon with me."

"Yeah?" Ted gulped, his chest filling with a sudden warmth. "I could, uh, yeah, I could hang here for a little while. I would really, really like that."

"Good," Grell said, capturing Ted's lips in another deep kiss.

Ted sighed, easily caught back up in Grell's tongue and groaning when Grell crawled back on top of him. He didn't have to go home to his lonely, depressing life. He could stay here, date a king, and be happy.

It was a dream come true.

Granted, he could have never dreamed up a king who had two cocks and a wicked libido to match, but he wasn't complaining.

Especially when that second cock was slipping inside of him to start gently thrusting and promising the delivery of another mind-shattering orgasm.

Ted hugged Grell's shoulders, trading heated kisses and breathless pants, spreading his legs wide. He moaned with every deep thrust, arching his body to meet Grell's hips as he took him again to the edge of madness and pleasure.

He could be happy here, Ted knew. There were hardly any ghosts to bother him, no staircases to tangle with, and he had the undivided attention of an amazing man. Grell was funny, charming, and Ted simply couldn't get enough of him.

Ted had never been so wanted or desired, and he didn't want to ever lose this feeling. Not ever.

He wasn't afraid of the future, knowing he would have Grell at his side. He still didn't know who had brought him back from the dead or why, but none of that seemed to matter now. When he was in Grell's arms, nothing else mattered.

Grell worshipped Ted's body until he was falling apart again, working him through a divine orgasm and kissing all the sweet sounds out of his mouth. Ted moaned happily as Grell filled him again, rocking both of them through the shudders of their blissful ends until Ted was positively exhausted.

"Wow," Ted breathed, stretching out on the bed with a big grin. "That was, uh, really good."

"Yes, it was," Grell agreed, panting quietly.

"Still gotta go do your kingly duties?" Ted asked, rolling on his side with a contented grunt.

"Meh," Grell scoffed. "Everyone is probably busy tripping over themselves trying to figure out a way to profit from Visseract's death. It can wait a little longer."

"Just can't stand to leave me, huh?" Ted teased smugly.

"Mm, keep thinking you might disappear if I let you out of my sight." Grell reached out to pet Ted's hair, lightly fluffing it with his fingers. "I'll deal with those vultures later."

"Can't put it off forever."

"Sure I can. I'm king!" Grell cackled, smooching Ted's lips and sliding his hand down his hip. "I can do whatever I want, love."

"Feels like you're trying to do me again," Ted said, groaning when Grell's hand slipped between his cheeks and stroked his wet hole. "Yup, definitely feels like it."

"Your suspicion is correct," Grell said gleefully. "I think it's time we talked about you taking both of my cocks... if you're interested."

"Both of them?" Ted's face heated up. "As in, at the same time?"

"Uh-huh."

"Oh fuck."

"Oh yes." Grell smiled wickedly. "I can promise you that it will be an intense pleasure beyond anything you can possibly imagine."

"Yeah, uh, okay. Sign me the fuck up." Ted pulled Grell into a greedy kiss, hooking his leg over his hips and ready to get going again.

"Pssst...."

"Huh?" Ted lifted his head, hearing a familiar little voice nearby. "Graham?"

"I'm sorry," Graham whispered urgently. "I know you're busy putting your mouth on your friend's mouth, but...."

"Hey, it's okay. One second." Ted sat up, quickly pulling the blankets over him and Grell.

"Ah, your little friend came to say hello?" Grell huffed, sounding a bit annoyed.

"Yeah, sorry," Ted said with a sheepish grin. He looked to the side of the bed and spied a familiar little shadow. "Hey, little buddy. What's up?"

"Kunst won't let me stay in the library," Graham said sadly. "He says he's too busy for me. Can I watch TV with you guys?" His shadow seemed to shrink in on itself. "Or are you busy too?"

"No, we're not busy," Ted promised, glancing back imploringly at Grell. "We can totally hang out and watch some cartoons or somethin', right?"

"First time I've ever been cockblocked by a pint-sized ghost," Grell mumbled under his breath. He cleared his throat, saying, "It's fine. Really. How about we have a nice cuddle and we watch some nasty reality television before dinner?"

"It can't be that nasty," Ted said firmly, settling back down in Grell's arms and resting his head on his chest. He smiled when he saw Graham's shadow creeping up onto the bed behind him. "Got innocent eyes over here watching, remember."

"Fine," Grell fussed, snapping his fingers to rapidly flip through the channels. "Here, how about this? Big angry chef, small children cooking?"

"Yeah? What do you think, little buddy?" Ted asked. "Cool with you?"

"This is good," Graham said eagerly. "I like this one!"

"Awesome," Ted said, smiling as he cuddled in close. He looked up at Grell, quietly mouthing, "Thank you."

"Eh, it's no problem," Grell replied casually, wrapping his arm around Ted. "It's not like anyone's ever died of blue balls before, right? Pretty sure they haven't, anyway. Ah, well, you'll just have to think of something to make it up to me, hmm?"

"Yeah, yeah." Ted chuckled heartily, rolling his eyes. "I'll get right on it."

Ted couldn't think of a more perfect way to spend the day. It was a seamless blend of his old life and the new, all of the people he cared about snuggled together here with him watching television. The pressure of the trial was lifted as his innocence was now secured, and he could finally relax. Even though he suspected this little adventure wasn't quite over yet, he was content to enjoy this moment.

After all the insanity he'd struggled through over these past few days, Ted figured he was due a break.

Just a few moments of peace, quiet, and….

"Hey, Ted?" Graham sounded shy.

"What is it, little dude?"

"What's 'blue balls'?"

"Uh…."

Well, shit.

CHAPTER 13.

THE AWKWARDNESS of trying to explain to a little dead boy the meaning behind that particular phrase was something Ted would not soon forget. Between Grell's poor attempts to stifle his cackling and Graham's gasping disgust when all was revealed, Ted wasn't sure if he could recall a more embarrassing moment.

Once that mystery had been solved for young Graham, they all got settled back down to keep watching television. Ted didn't mean to, but he was soon dozing off before the next episode rolled on. His sleep was a bit restless, his mind buzzing over the other big mystery that was still unsolved.

Who really killed Visseract?

He was positive that it wasn't a suicide, but he didn't know what else to do. Grell clearly wanted to put this behind them and move on, and they were all out of options, suspects, and evidence. Unless Kunst had managed to find something of use in the library, the case was going to be closed.

He couldn't really blame Grell for not wanting to fight a god or go start a big war, but this didn't feel like justice at all.

What was the whole point of seeing Silas's visions? Was there something else Ted was supposed to have seen? What had he missed? Was there more to this Kindress thing and the tears?

He didn't know, and his sleep didn't bring any answers.

When Ted woke up, he was still snuggled in Grell's arms, but he didn't sense Graham. He lifted his head, looked around for a moment, and smiled when Grell's hand slid down to his butt.

Grell's eyes were still closed, but he was smiling.

"Are you pretending to be asleep?" Ted asked playfully.

Grell's hand squeezed down.

"Hey!" Ted laughed, wiggling and smacking at Grell's arm. "Wake up!"

"Huh? Hmm?" Grell opened his eyes, looking around in mock confusion. "What's happening?"

"You being a giant perv," Ted said with a snicker.

"Me?" Grell blinked innocently while giving Ted's ass another thorough grope. "Never."

"Mmm, good morning to you too. Or afternoon. Evening? Whatever." Ted grinned as they kissed, leisurely tangling their bodies back together. He could feel Grell's cocks grinding against his own, making him gasp softly.

"Is the little one around?" Grell asked urgently.

"Graham? No, I don't think so."

"Good," Grell said, rolling Ted onto his back with a wicked grin. "Because I know exactly what I want for breakfast, and it is not child-appropriate."

"Breakfast?" Ted scoffed, groaning as Grell spread his legs. "Thought we were gonna have dinner?"

"I just woke up. Therefore, this is now breakfast," Grell informed him with a wink, slinking down Ted's thick body and leaving little bites and kisses in his wake.

Ted relaxed against the pillows, watching Grell pet and tease his way toward his cock. He groaned as Grell's hot mouth took him down in one swift thrust, and he arched his back when his amazing tongue spiraled around his shaft. "Ah… fuck…. Thiazi…."

Grell started to suck, his hands greedily stroking Ted's thighs. He moaned quietly, clearly enjoying himself as he absolutely devoured every inch of Ted's cock.

"Ah, mmm, fuck," Ted panted, his hips shakily rising up. He threw one of his legs up on Grell's shoulder, groaning when Grell grabbed his ass and pulled him closer, encouraging him to move.

Ted braced himself against the headboard, thrusting up into Grell's mouth. He started off slow, moaning as Grell's tongue twisted around his cock and squeezed. He was soon moving faster, fucking Grell's throat and grunting loudly.

Grell took it all, his fingers digging into Ted's ass as he growled hungrily.

"Thiazi!" Ted was already so close, and he was unable to resist Grell's oral finesse for another second. He felt his orgasm down in his very core, his hips jerking forward as he came hard. "God, yes! Yesss, fuck!"

The added suction of Grell swallowing it all down made Ted shiver, his legs limp as Grell continued to ravage him with his tongue and lips. His climax continued to pulse until he was trembling all over, gasping brokenly, "Oh f-fuck...."

Grell pulled off with a noisy slurp, running his tongue over Ted's cock one last time as he declared, "Ah, delicious."

"Yeah...?" Ted grinned dopily. "You're welcome to it any fuckin' time you want."

"Mmm, I'll remember you said that," Grell teased, crawling back up over Ted to claim a fierce kiss.

Ted loved how Grell held him, and the sensation of his weight pinning him against the bed was so good. He let himself be pliant, relaxed, and wrapped his legs around Grell's waist with a happy sigh.

"We're not getting up for dinner, are we?" Ted asked, biting his lower lip when Grell's hard cocks grazed his hip.

"That depends on what you're hungry for," Grell teased, playfully nipping at Ted's jaw.

"Mmmph, fuck." Ted slid his fingers through Grell's hair, groaning as he started getting hard again. He couldn't explain the warmth overtaking him, but it had to be from Grell's magical touch.

"Maybe something... meaty?" Grell wagged his brows salaciously.

"Yeah." Ted grinned, giving Grell's hair a little tug. "Definitely thick and meaty."

Grell snickered, kissing Ted firmly as he lined himself up. "Oh, you just hold on, love. I've got just the thing."

The head of Grell's cock was right there, so very close to where Ted wanted him, and he could feel himself getting wet, *fuck*, and Grell was just about to slip inside—

"Your Highness!" an all-too-familiar voice called out.

"Oh, for fuck's sake!" Grell turned his head to snarl at Mozzie. "What the fuck is so fucking important that you decided to just come barging in? Huh? Did somebody else die?"

"Uh, n-no, Your Highness," Mozzie stammered.

"Did anything explode?"

"No, Your Highness."

"Have my people decided to rise up and dethrone me?"

"No, Your Highness!"

"Then *fuck off*!" Grell roared furiously.

"But, but, but…!" Mozzie cowered, trembling as he tried to explain, "Your occult advisor is insisting on seeing you! He says he has urgent news about the case, Your Highness!"

"My what now?" Grell scowled.

"You have an occult advisor?" Ted asked, scrubbing a hand across his face.

"Apparently I do," Grell scoffed in surprise. He narrowed his eyes at the guard, demanding, "And who is my occult advisor exactly?"

"Uh, uh, it's uh, Professor Emil Kunst," Mozzie said nervously. "He said, he said you left him in charge of wrapping up the investigation, and he's been working out of the library?"

"What in the actual fuck?" Ted burst out laughing.

"That undead little shit," Grell mumbled.

"He said he needs to see you at once, Your Highness," Mozzie said, backing away quickly. "So sorry to have disturbed you, so very sorry—"

"Just go," Grell groaned angrily.

"Right away, Your Highness!" Mozzie vanished as fast as he could.

Whining loudly, Grell flopped down on top of Ted. "Oh, does anyone in the whole universe suffer as I do?"

"Poor baby," Ted soothed, rubbing Grell's back and laughing. "I know, I know. It's so hard being king all the time, huh?"

"It really is!" Grell chirped, lifting his head to smooch Ted's lips. "Hmmph. I suppose the mood has been lost now, eh?"

"Not entirely," Ted said, grinning slyly and rolling his hips up against Grell's. "Still pretty hungry, if you catch my drift."

"Oh, you delicious little minx," Grell purred happily. "Just lay back and relax, love. I'll make sure to leave you very, very satisfied."

And satisfied Ted was, two more times before they finally decided to get out of bed and face the world. Grell took Ted out into the pools to clean up and dressed them both in fresh clothes afterward.

"You know, I'm still looking forward to takin' both those bad boys of yours when we ain't being rushed," Ted teased, adjusting his new jeans with a smirk.

"Oh, it will be my pleasure," Grell assured him, "and well worth the wait."

"We ready to go see your new occult advisor?"

"I'm positively *dripping* with excitement," Grell drawled. "This will be the absolute last time I ever do anything nice for a damn ghost."

A snap of Grell's fingers took them to the library, and Ted almost didn't recognize it. There were books and papers strewn everywhere, texts left in haphazard stacks all over the floor, and scrolls unrolled over the chairs.

Grell's fury was palpable, and Ted quickly called out, "Hey, uh, Kunst? What the fuck happened in here?"

"About time you two showed up!" Kunst snapped, his orb floating out from between the shelves and hovering before them.

"What in the fucking *fuck* did you do to my library?" Grell snarled.

"Since you two have been busy doing whatever it is you've been doing," Kunst huffed, "I've been hard at work!"

"Didn't you hear?" Ted snorted. "The case is closed. Visseract offed himself after killing Mire and Silas."

"Oh, please," Kunst sneered. "Don't insult my intelligence. Neither of you believe that awful setup, do you?"

"And how do you know it was a setup?"

"As the newly appointed royal occult advisor, I had the guards take me to the crime scene before the body was removed," Kunst said proudly.

"You're really something else, aren't you?" Grell was trying not to look impressed. "Didn't happen to mention to them that you appointed yourself?"

"Look," Kunst said urgently, "now that we're all on the same page, there is something you must know. The broken vials? I believe I have identified the substance within."

"And?" Grell grunted.

"I believe those vials held Great Azaethoth's Tears," Kunst said triumphantly, his orb flickering brightly.

"Whoopie-do!" Grell threw his hands up in frustration. "We already figured that!"

"But, ah, *who* were they for?"

"Huh?" Ted stared. "What do you mean?"

"Three vials," Kunst replied. "For three conspirators, yes? One was for Thulogian Silas to buy her silence, and one was for Humble Visseract, who we already know was actively working with Gronoch."

"Right," Ted confirmed. "So?"

"There's a third," Kunst said impatiently. "Who is the third vial for?"

Ted and Grell exchanged the same confused stare.

"There's a third person still out there!" Kunst snapped. "Someone else was working with Visseract and Gronoch! Gronoch wouldn't have any reason to keep a vial of tears around if he already had access to the source, much less shatter it so wastefully."

"But then who would?" Ted countered. "Why go to all the trouble of getting the damn tears just to smash 'em up like that? Kinda seems like a big 'fuck you' if the tears are as powerful as you guys are saying."

"Yes, their magic is great, but they're nothing but a rat turd in a sandstorm compared to the power they could extort from the Kindress," Grell pointed out. "Tears can't resurrect someone, but the Kindress could."

"Silas wanted the tears to make the Kindress bring back Mire," Ted recalled. "Visseract probably wanted a never-ending supply of fish food or one of those little pirate chests that has the bobbing lid or something."

"While this is very fascinating," Grell drawled, "we're left with more questions than answers."

"True," Kunst admitted, "but it does indicate a third suspect that we've yet to identify!"

"Enough of this," Grell growled. "As soon as the clock strikes midnight, the trial is starting. As far as I'm concerned, this case is closed. I've already buried my dead and cut my losses. It's over."

"But Your Highness—"

"I'm king, and I said it's done!" Grell warned.

"Look, Kunst," Ted said quickly, trying to intervene, "just let it go. All this shit with Gronoch could start a war, okay? You get that, don't you?"

"Yes!" Kunst hissed stubbornly. "And I'm trying to prevent a war on Aeon! Do you have any idea what will happen if Gronoch is successful?"

"He'll... do some weird stuff... with bones?"

"He wants to wake Salgumel!" Kunst barked. "The God of Dreams and Sleep! The one whose cults have all gone mad for centuries trying to wake him because he's gone absolutely insane in the dreaming! Gronoch is following right in Tollmathan's footsteps. I guarantee it!"

"And that's... bad?" Ted said slowly.

"Very bad!" Kunst lurched his orb forward and bopped Ted in the forehead.

"Quit that or it's back down to the pits with you!" Grell scolded, smacking Kunst's orb back. "Now listen here! Whatever the gods are planning, my son is on it."

"The prince?" Kunst spat.

"Yes, I know, he's a little prick," Grell huffed, "but his visions are never wrong. He's our trump card. Whatever Gronoch is planning is not going to work without ol' what's his name—"

"Jay," Ted said.

"Right! Him!" Grell brushed off his hands and shrugged. "Nothing to worry about as long as my boy keeps an eye on Jay."

"Who the hell is Jay?" Kunst demanded.

"Silenced boy, gonna keep him safe to save the world or something," Grell explained quickly. "All very complicated."

"My roommate," Ted explained. "Apparently, if anything happens to him, the world is gonna end."

"And he's Silenced?" Kunst suddenly flew away and nudged an old scroll toward them. "It all makes sense!"

"What does?"

"What I overheard!" Kunst said impatiently. "It's not Silenced souls that Gronoch is after! He wants living bodies!" His orb flickered. "That's why the bridge is so dim! Something is keeping Silenced souls from passing to Xenon! Some sort of stasis to make them into weapons, and he needs the bones for it!"

"But why?" Ted groaned, getting frustrated. "Why does he need to astral projectile them or whatever?"

"I suppose that's the million-dollar question," Grell drawled. "How about we let Kunst here think on that for a while, and we'll catch up later when he actually has something useful to share, eh?"

"I shall not give up, Your Highness!" Kunst declared. "I already have a theory, very sound, but perhaps if you or Ted could spare just a bit of time to assist me?"

"How about we go out for dinner?" Grell asked, taking Ted's hand and kissing it sweetly.

"Go out?" Ted blushed. "Like, what, on another date?"

"Exactly so. We're dating. People who are dating go out on dates!"

"This cannot seriously be happening right now," Kunst whined in annoyance. "The fate of Aeon hangs in the balance, and you two are... are... *hooking up?*"

"Yup. Tell us your theory when it's more than a theory. Can't talk now, bye-bye," Grell quipped, reaching up and tapping Kunst's orb.

Kunst floated in circles, shook violently, but didn't make a sound.

"What did you do?" Ted snorted with laughter.

"Hit his mute button," Grell replied with a wink. "Now tell me, love. Where is one place in the world you've always wanted to go? Anywhere at all."

"Uh." Ted didn't know what to say. He was embarrassed that his tastes might seem too pedestrian, but there was only one place that came to mind. "There's this restaurant called the Angus Barn right outside of Archersville that's really nice? Steaks as big as your fuckin' head."

"A steakhouse?" Grell wrinkled his nose. "I offer you the world... and you want to go to a damn steakhouse? Are there crushed peanut shells on the floor?"

"Hey, I've always wanted to go," Ted said, blushing and crossing his arms stubbornly. "Look, it probably seems stupid to a king and all your fuckin' fancy stuff—"

"If that's what you want," Grell soothed, "then that's what you shall have."

"Really?" Ted glowered.

"I was just surprised."

"You're such a snobby douche, you know that?"

"I'm well aware, but I adore you, and I want you to be happy," Grell insisted, hugging Ted's waist and pulling him close. "That's what matters most, love."

"Thank you," Ted said, slowly unfolding his arms and draping them over Grell's shoulders. "That means a lot to me, actually."

Kunst's orb bounced up and down on the floor by their feet, trying to get their attention.

Grell kicked him across the room and, without missing a beat, asked politely, "Shall we?"

"Shit, is he okay?"

"He's fine. He's dead. Ready?"

"Yes," Ted replied, trying not to snicker too loudly. "I'm fuckin' ready."

Grell kissed him with a greedy little chuckle.

Ted heard a snap, and when he pulled back, he was sitting across from Grell at a candlelit table in the wine cellar of the Angus Barn. The walls were pale brick and lined with hundreds of bottles, the lights dim, and there was a roaring fireplace beside them.

"Holy fuck." Ted looked all around in awe. "We're in the wine cellar. This, this is their exclusive private dining room! Like, there's a waiting list to get down here!"

"Fuck the list," Grell said proudly, waving for a waiter to start pouring them each a glass of wine. "Nothing's too good for my boo."

"Thank you," Ted said, grinning from ear to ear. "I'm sure there are many laws against abusing magic like this—"

"Pffft."

"—and it's downright romantic that you did this for me." Ted raised his glass in a toast. "To you, King Thiazi Grell desu Etcetera."

"Thank you, Tedward Whatever Your Name Was," Grell replied, clicking his glass lightly to Ted's, "for making this old king very, very happy."

Sipping his wine, Ted felt his cheeks warm up, and it wasn't from the alcohol.

"Should pop in and visit my son," Grell teased. "I'm feeling the urge to be a grateful father all of a sudden."

"Shit. Me too." Ted laughed. "I'll buy him all the fuckin' catnip he wants." He fiddled with the stem of his glass. "I've never dated anyone who had a kid before."

"Or who happened to be a charming Asra?" Grell smirked.

"Or was quite this full of themselves," Ted added with a grin.

"Or has two cocks that he can use to leave your mortal body quivering with pleasure?" Grell batted his eyes sweetly.

"Or was a king." Ted gulped back the wine. "Lotta firsts for me, you know?"

"Well," Grell said thoughtfully, "let's see. I've never dated anyone with starsight before. Never anyone who had died, that's definitely new. And I've never dated anyone who makes me feel quite the way you do."

Ted honestly didn't know what to say, but his heart was pounding so hard that he swore he could feel that second mysterious beat.

"You're funny, you're sweet, and you happen to be one of the most compassionate creatures I've ever met," Grell went on sincerely. "Being with you... I feel whole again."

Ted grabbed Grell's hand, still unsure of what to say. All he could do was smile like a fool and drink in the wonderful praise.

The way Grell was looking at him made him feel...

Loved.

After a few moments, he smirked and eyed Grell expectantly.

"Oh, right," Grell said suddenly. "And you have the sweetest little hole this side of Xenon and Aeon too." He winked lecherously. "Better?"

"Was worried you were gettin' soft on me," Ted teased.

"For you, Tedward, I only get hard," Grell promised.

Naturally, that was the moment their waiter returned to take their order. He smiled politely but was definitely trying to hold back a laugh. "Are you gentlemen ready to order?"

"After you, love," Grell said, grinning and peering at Ted over the top of his menu.

Ted cleared his throat, awkwardly scanning the entrees. He looked back up at the waiter, challenging, "What's the biggest steak you got?"

"Ah, that's my man," Grell sighed dreamily.

The Angus Barn's largest steak was a forty-two-ounce monstrosity of a bone-in ribeye called the Tomahawk Chop, and Ted ate every last bite.

Grell drank all the wine.

After declining dessert, Ted was whisked back to Xenon and snuggled up in Grell's bed. Grell had to run a quick errand and left Ted with an aching stomach and debating the wisdom of eating a steak bigger than his head.

When Grell returned, his posh suit turned back into his colorful unicorn onesie as he slid into bed beside Ted. He patted Ted's aching belly, cooing, "Aw, my poor little darling. Sicky tummy?"

"I regret nothing," Ted said stubbornly.

Snickering, Grell leaned in for a kiss.

Ted's clothes were transformed into his own matching unicorn onesie. His tummy was grateful for the extra room, but he was confused. "Everything okay?"

"Finally got the court corralled," Grell replied, rubbing Ted's stomach soothingly. "They'll be dragging their tentacles and claws and assorted bits together for your trial tomorrow morning. The Vulgorans requested a postponement so they can have a funeral for Humble Visseract tonight."

"Well, damn." Ted was relieved. Trying to stand trial with an aching stomach hadn't been appealing. He relaxed, cuddling up on Grell's chest. "Who's the new prosecutor?"

"That idiot Ghulk."

"Goody. Still think I'll be found innocent?"

"Of course. Or I'll just eat Ghulk."

"You're so sweet."

"Like cotton candy," Grell confirmed with a grin. "Except I don't get stuck in your dental work."

"Yeah, you get stuck in other places." Ted laughed, but he was suddenly bashful when Grell looked at him, waiting for him to elaborate. "You know, like in my heart kinda places. Or like in my thoughts! I dunno!" He groaned. "I'm shutting up now."

"Ah, you're so very romantic, Tedward."

"You shut up too. Let's go to sleep."

"I can think of other enticing places to get stuck in."

"Go to sleep. I'm already full-up on meat for tonight."

"Ouch!"

Ted couldn't help but laugh, snuggling in just a bit closer. "Seriously," he breathed, "thank you for taking me out. It was fuckin' great. Maybe tomorrow after my trial…."

"Yes?"

"We can work on you getting stuck in some good places. Maybe even, you know, at the same time."

"Oh, my love." Grell was beaming. "I do so adore you. You're definitely sitting next to me at lunch now."

Ted laughed again.

Grell smiled and kissed his brow. "Sleep sweetly, Tedward of Aeon."

"Sweet dreams, King Grell of Xenon."

CHAPTER 14.

TED WOKE up in Grell's arms, warm and happy. He stretched his legs, burying his face into Grell's chest with a contented sigh. He hadn't heard one ghost, not a single phone ringing, and it had been years since he'd slept so well. No matter what happened today, he knew he could keep this.

The happiness, the sense of peace, and his beautiful king.

"Good morning," Grell purred, shifting beneath Ted as he stirred. "Mmm... don't you look lovely."

Ted was certain his hair was a mess, but he grinned anyway. "Good morning. Time for breakfast, going to trial with the court, and then steamy sex before lunch?"

"You read my mind," Grell said. "That's a perfectly wonderful idea."

They stayed in bed for a few more minutes before Grell summoned them a luscious breakfast. They ate in bed, enjoying the comfortable silence between bites of food. Even though his trial was coming up soon, Ted wasn't worried.

For better or worse, the trial was going to declare him innocent. All of this would be over, and he could enjoy his budding romance with Grell in peace.

He could sense Graham nearby, feel his little hand touch his shoulder, but he didn't speak. The gesture seemed comforting, and Ted took it as a wish of luck for what was about to happen.

When breakfast was done, Grell got them dressed and took Ted's hands to press little kisses all over them. "Are you ready, love?"

"Ready as I can be," Ted said with a forced smile. "Let's get this shit over with, okay?"

"Agreed," Grell said, keeping hold of one of Ted's hands as he ported them to court.

The room was full of monsters of all shapes and sizes, and Ted fidgeted. It was still unnerving to see so many of them together like this.

Kunst was waiting for them, hovering nearby, and he zipped right over to Grell with an insistent wiggle.

"Ah, right," Grell said, tapping the orb. "Unmuted."

"Thank you, Your Highness," Kunst said with obvious annoyance. "I trust your little date went well?"

"Oh, it was wonderful," Grell replied with syrupy sweetness. "How was being a silent bowling ball all night?"

"Surprisingly productive."

"Good."

Kunst huffed expectantly. "Despite the lack of assistance, ahem, I was able to make some headway, and I think you will be very pleased. Would you like to hear my theory about the bones?"

"Not particularly, no."

"We'll talk about it later," Ted said with an encouraging smile. "After the trial?"

"Fine." It was apparently possible for floating blue orbs to pout.

Grell transformed into his Asra body and took his place in his large throne, clicking his teeth loudly for silence. He gestured for Ted to stand next to him before addressing the crowd, "We're here today to rule on the deaths of Sergan Mire and Thulogian Silas.

"The prisoner says that he is innocent, I am serving as defense for him, and Vizier Ghulk will handle the responsibility of prosecution."

"I'm ready, Your Highness!" Ghulk exclaimed, trotting up to kneel in front of Grell.

"Very well," Grell replied briskly. "Begin."

"I will show the court that Ted of Aeon conspired to murder our beloved Asran brethren and Humble Visseract because he is a power-hungry mortal who seeks to take the throne for himself!" Ghulk declared to the crowd.

"What?" Ted scoffed.

"Just let him talk," Grell said with a shrug. "Don't worry. It's all going to be rubbish."

"He needed a way to gain power," Ghulk went on dramatically. "Look at him! A puny mortal with barely a scrap of magic! Of course he would want the throne! And how else could he do it except murder two Asra!"

Ted scrubbed his hands over his face.

"This way, he could take advantage of Asran law and get himself engaged to the king!" Ghulk declared.

"Wait, what now?" Ted's hands dropped.

Grell looked furious, and the crowd was murmuring with excitement.

"He helped the king move both bodies of the fallen Asra into the pits! All part of his nefarious plan!" Ghulk sounded almost hysterical with glee. "Now he is engaged to the king!"

"Are we fucking engaged?" Ted hissed.

"Technically, but it didn't seem worth mentioning," Grell hissed back.

"Strongly disagree!" Ted's stomach tightened. He wished he could strangle Grell.

"Only members of the royal family handle the dead," Kunst added helpfully. "As soon as you entombed those bodies, you became engaged. It's an ancient Asran tradition for—"

"Shut up!" Ted groaned.

"I'm sure he now plots to kill our beloved king," Ghulk said with a loud huff. "As soon as they're wed, he will strike! He will take the throne and become the first mortal ruler of the Asra!"

"Aren't you gonna, you know, defend me?" Ted demanded, glaring haughtily at Grell.

"Ah, right." Grell leaned forward, saying sternly to the court, "That is simply not true."

"And?" Ted urged.

"I'm working on it, be patient," Grell muttered. "I didn't expect him to actually have anything!"

"For the love of fuck," Ted grunted, stepping up to face Ghulk. "I didn't kill anyone! You all know Mire was already dead before I got here! I landed in his fucking blood!"

"Blood you spilled, treacherous human!" Ghulk accused.

"Do you realize how fucking insane that sounds?" Ted clenched his hands into fists. "Come on! You're all super smart people-creatures! Most of you saw me fall! I didn't do this!"

"But you do admit to being romantically involved with the king?" Ghulk sneered.

"Uh… that's… well…." Ted stood up straight. "That's none of your fuckin' business."

"See?" Ghulk laughed, smacking his hooves on the floor. "He doesn't deny it!"

"Is this engagement thing fuckin' legit?" Ted whirled around to face Grell. "Like, for real?"

"Tiny bit," Grell replied. "I certainly wasn't going to enforce it—"

"You asshole!" Ted barked. "I wouldn't have helped you if I knew it meant I had to marry you!"

Grell scowled.

"You should have told me! 'Oh, by the way, this means we're gonna get married!' See how fuckin' easy that was?"

"Eh," Grell grunted. "I'm not sure I got it all. Could you do it one more time?"

"Fuckin' prick!" Ted bared his teeth. "You ever maybe think this is exactly why I wouldn't wanna be your queen?"

"You ever maybe think that you're more attractive with your mouth shut?"

"Uncalled for!" Kunst chimed in.

"Fuck both of you!" Ted snarled, throwing his hands up.

"I was trying to help!" Kunst protested.

"Help less!"

"This is ridiculous," Ghulk yelled, stomping his hoof. "I demand justice to be carried out for my beloved Silas! I'll never be able to hear her sweet voice or call out to her again!" He reared up

at Ted. "Tedward of Aeon killed them both and then forced Humble
Visseract to commit suicide! Let this be over!"

"Call out?" Ted froze.

"I always called out to my beloved!" Ghulk sneered.
"Always!"

"Holy fuck," Ted gasped, his eyes wide and reaching out for
Grell's shoulder. "It's him."

"What?" Grell blinked. "Him who?"

"Ghulk!" Ted pointed. "He did it! He killed Silas! He always
calls out to her! He has to let her know that he's coming so she
doesn't attack!"

"Shut up," Ghulk warned. "You're the murderer here! Not me!"

"But not the last time!" Ted went on defiantly. "He didn't call
out to her when we went there about the bead because he knew she
was already fuckin' dead! And nobody except me fuckin' talks to
dead people around here!"

"Shut up! Shut up!" Ghulk screamed. "Shut your wretched
little mouth, human!"

"Silence," Grell roared at Ghulk, his tail lashing impatiently.
He nodded at Ted, urging, "Keep going, love."

"You're the third person Gronoch promised the tears to!" Ted
exclaimed, his mind buzzing with excitement as all the pieces came
together. "You got in good with him after you killed Mire, and you
actually thought Silas was gonna be all on your weird horse dick,
but she still loved him! She was gonna use her share of the tears to
bring him back!

"And oh, did that piss you off. You couldn't stand the idea of
her rejecting you! After everything you did for her? After loving
her for so long? You just couldn't take being trapped in the friend
zone anymore! That's why you killed her, and then you killed
Visseract!"

"No!" Ghulk shrieked. "Lies! Horrible lies! I would have no
reason to kill Humble Visseract!"

"Oh yeah?" Ted challenged. "But I bet your boss would, huh?
Visseract was getting sloppy, sending his guys after me and Grell?

You had to make it all go away, so you fuckin' iced him and set it all up like a suicide. Hell, that's why you smashed up all those tears, because your big god boss promised to give you some more and you assholes wanted us to close the case!"

The guards were closing in around Ghulk, and he was shaking all over. His cloudy eyes began to leak milky fluid, and his hooves were clattering along the floor as he looked for an escape.

"You're a fucking murderer, dude!" Ted declared. "Not me! Case fucking dismissed!"

"If you want to see your precious bones again, you'll let me go!" Ghulk screamed frantically.

"What?" Grell croaked.

"Let me go, and I'll tell you where the bones are!" Ghulk shrieked.

"I know…." It was Graham, his little hand taking Ted's and tugging. "I know where they are."

Ted squeezed back, scoffing without hesitation, "Fuck off, zombie-corn. You're going down for this. We don't need you."

"Tedward—" Grell began to growl.

"Do you trust me?" Ted asked urgently.

Grell's golden eyes widened, uncertain, but he soon settled back down. "Yes, my queen," he whispered softly. "With everything that I am."

Hearing those words sent a shiver through Ted that he would address later, and he turned back to Ghulk. "You're done, dude."

Grell rose up from the throne, triumphantly declaring, "I hereby rule to convict Vizier Ghulk of these crimes and release the human prisoner! What says the court?"

"Aye!" the crowd roared in reply, and the Asran guards descended upon Ghulk with unnatural speed to start dragging him away.

Relief flooded over Ted. It was finally all over. He was a free man again, free to do as he pleased. He could sense that Grell was smiling at him, and he already had a pretty good idea of exactly what he wanted to do.

"No!" Ghulk screamed. "No! No, you will not get away with this! Gronoch will come for me! He will come for me, you'll see! Once the gods have awakened Salgumel and taken Aeon, I will make sure they come back here for you, King Grell!"

"Blah, blah, blah," Grell jeered, swishing his tail with a short laugh. "The gods are more than welcome to try. I'll be sure to send down a pack of Uno cards so you have something to do while you're waiting for your little rescue. Enjoy rotting in a dungeon for the rest of eternity."

The crowd laughed and cheered, tentacles and claws waving as Ghulk was forcibly removed from the court.

"Now," Grell said, turning to Ted, "someone said something about trusting them regarding the earthly remains of my most precious loved ones?"

"Yeah," Ted said, giving Graham's hand a little squeeze. "I've got this."

"Court's dismissed!" Grell commanded.

"Uh, Your Highness?" Kunst sounded like he was cringing. "Though congratulations are due for winning Ted's freedom and solving the case, there's still the matter of the engagement to settle?"

The dispersing court began to crowd around the throne again, all of their eyes eagerly watching them.

"Shut up, bubble boy," Ted said with a grunt, his cheeks heating up fast.

"The engagement has been offered," Kunst said stubbornly. "Technically, though you've already accepted it by assisting Grell with the entombment, you have to give a formal answer to the court—"

"He has until the next full moon to give a formal answer, twat," Grell snapped. "Let it go." He shook his head at the members of court. "Shove off, you gossip-gobbling slags! We've got some very important business to attend to!"

Through portals or magical doorways, everyone left the court until only Grell, Ted, and Kunst remained.

Well, and Graham, of course.

"We need to go," Graham urged, pulling Ted forward.

Ted stumbled, letting Graham guide him around the throne to the back of the platform it sat upon. "Where are we going?"

"Right here!" Graham appeared, his little hands pointing down to the floor. "Here!"

Kneeling down, Ted hesitantly reached for the tile floor. He expected to touch firm stone, but his fingers slipped right through and he felt something cool and smooth. He grabbed it, lifting up a large jawbone.

"Holy shit," Grell gasped, slipping into his human form and joining Ted on the floor. They took turns reaching down into the hidden space, pulling out bone after bone. "They've been down here this whole time?"

"Guess they needed a sneaky place to stash them?" Ted suggested, laughing triumphantly as the pile of bones began to grow. "Fuck, this is great! Graham, how did you find these?"

"Exploring," Graham said with a smile. "Found them while the horsey man was yelling."

"Thank you, Graham," Ted said, smiling brightly.

"Thanks from me too," Grell said, his expression somber as he lifted up a large skull and petted it reverently. "My most sincere thanks, little one."

"Is that Vael?" Ted asked politely.

"My father," Grell replied, glancing around the pile. "I'm afraid there's only enough bones here for two skeletons. Maybe part of a third... and none of them are Vael's."

"I'm sorry," Ted said, reaching out to squeeze Grell's shoulder. "We'll keep looking, okay? Maybe Ghulk and those other fuckheads had more hiding spots."

"Maybe," Grell said, gently placing the skull with the other bones. "I'll need to figure out who is who and what is what and return them to the pits."

"You want some help?" Ted scoffed. "Or is that going to land me buying a house with you or somethin'?"

"I'm sorry I didn't say anything about the damn engagement," Grell said with an agitated groan. "It's an antiquated tradition, and I wasn't thinking much of it at the time. I definitely didn't think you'd be of a mind to accept it, considering how well it went the last time someone proposed to you."

"Yeah, I died," Ted said flatly.

"And you ended up single, ahem."

"That too."

"An engagement doesn't mean there has to be a wedding right away," Kunst chirped helpfully. "Although there's been no record of an Asran engagement being refused—"

"Mute time," Grell threatened, reaching up to bop Kunst's orb.

"Hey, hey!" Kunst flew out of the way. "Look, you want to keep the Asran traditions going, and you two are obviously getting along very well, why not just accept the engagement and put off the wedding for a few hundred years?"

"Uh, because I'll be dead?" Ted snarled, standing up hastily, his cheeks burning.

"Enough," Grell growled, snapping with both hands.

Kunst and the bones vanished, and a drink appeared in Grell's hand that he immediately began to chug.

"Hey," Ted complained, holding out his empty hand.

Grell was still drinking but snapped his fingers one more time to give Ted a glass.

"Here's to freedom," Ted said, raising his drink and taking a swig. "So." He stared thoughtfully at Grell. "Were you going to tell me about the whole getting married thing?"

"Planned to," Grell said with a wince. "Thought we'd have a good laugh about it… in a few months when you were already well and madly in love with me."

"That was your fuckin' plan?"

"Didn't say it was a good one," Grell replied, strolling over to sit back down on the throne. "And I didn't think Ghulk was going to bring it up in the middle of your damn trial."

Ted followed him, nursing his never-ending drink. "Why'd you call me queen, then?" he asked. "Why?"

"You asked me if I trusted you," Grell replied. "And I do. Not just with my heart, but with something even greater: the well-being of my people, their future, and laying the dead back to rest as intended.

"In that moment, I had to make a decision that would not only affect our future, but my people, my entire race. It would have been easy to make that decision based on how much I like sticking it in you, but... I didn't.

"I'd be lying if it wasn't a factor, but I do know you, Tedward of Aeon. I know how you care for the dead, despite the stain they've left on your soul. The same compassion you gave to me when we entombed Silas and Mire was the same when I buried a music box where my beloved should be.

"You were giving me a choice to not only help me, but to help the dead. That depth, that sort of passion... makes you worthy of being a queen."

Ted's mouth opened and closed a few times as he staggered a little closer to Grell and took his hand. "That's... uh... a pretty good reason."

"I'm not asking you to marry me," Grell said softly, "but perhaps I'm asking you... to give the idea a chance. Give us a chance and see what happens. I know, in my soul, that you'd make a fantastic queen."

Grell was looking at him with such sincerity that Ted could feel his breath catching in his chest. He couldn't tear his eyes away for a second, and his fingers tightened around his glass.

"Ew," Graham complained. "You guys are gonna make kissy faces again, aren't you?"

"Yup, time to go, kiddo," Ted replied.

"Grosssss!"

"What was that?" Grell frowned.

"Nothing." Ted hid a smile, waiting for Graham's presence to fade. "Just... give me a second."

"Oh, of course."

"Well," Ted said after a leisurely pause, swigging back his drink and throwing the glass behind him as he sat down into Grell's lap, "I will tell you that I'm not saying yes."

"Oh?" Grell said, a quick snap of his fingers taking care of the mess and making his own drink disappear. His hands were now free to roam Ted's thighs. "This feels like a bit of yes to something."

"It's a yes that I care about you a lot, I want to keep dating, and I'd like to celebrate being cleared of all murder charges by riding your dicks on this throne," Ted said very matter-of-factly.

"All very good things," Grell said, his palms making their way up Ted's hips. "I like where this is going."

"But I'm not gonna marry you," Ted said firmly. "I'm not gonna be one of those dumb princess chicks who marries the prince dude after, like, two days of knowing him."

"I'm a king. Does that make any difference?"

"Nope," Ted said, leaning in for a kiss. He rolled his hips down slowly, grinning when he felt how hard Grell already was. "I think I'm gonna settle on a very solid maybe. Maybe I'll let you put a ring on it and marry you one day, but that ain't today."

"That's still not a no," Grell gleefully pointed out, twirling his fingers and making Ted's clothes vanish.

"True," Ted said, his hips continuing to move and grinning when Grell's clothes faded away, leaving bare flesh beneath him to grind on. "How about... waiting-to-be-permanently-engaged?"

"Doesn't exactly roll off the tongue, does it?" Grell chided playfully. "Not quite something to put on a card, you know? Please come to our 'Waiting-To-Be-Permanently-Engaged Party.' Meh."

"Shut up."

"I'm also not a fan of the 'permanent' bit. Feel like I can win you over if I try really hard and think good thoughts."

"Shut up and kiss me," Ted pleaded with a loud groan.

"Yes, my queen," Grell said, dragging Ted in for a hungry kiss.

Ted didn't even bother denouncing the new nickname, letting himself fall into the hot press of Grell's lips. It seemed so natural now, holding each other, touching and caressing all over. The thrill of fucking Grell right here on his throne was not lost on Ted, and it honestly made this so much hotter.

Grell's cocks were pressing up against Ted's ass, and Ted could feel himself getting wet, his hole magically probed and stretched with a wave of Grell's hand. It was easy for Grell's first cock to slide inside Ted's body, Ted eagerly accepting it with a heated moan. It was deliciously thick, and Ted couldn't stop himself from slamming down a few times to savor the hot stretch.

The pressure was amazing and made him ache, already so full. He could keep going just like this and easily make himself come, but he wasn't done yet. He wanted all of Grell inside him, and he was determined to take both of his cocks.

The second one, well, that was going to take a bit more work.

As soon as Grell tried to push inside, there was a flash of pain that made Ted hiss. He grunted, trying to readjust himself and push down, but the resistance was still too much. Grell slipped a finger in alongside his first cock and tried to work Ted open before going again, but the burn was still intolerable even with his magic.

"Can't you make me wetter?" Ted griped.

"Your ass is like Niagara Falls right now!" Grell shot back. "Just hold on! You're too damn tight, and I don't want to hurt you!"

"Hold the fuck on!" Ted declared, reaching back and stubbornly grabbing Grell's second cock away from him. He pushed the tip up against his hole and began to sink down. The burn was still there, hot and almost blinding, but Ted was not going to give up. He groaned, gritting his teeth and willing his body to open up.

Slowly, yes, it breached him. The burn lingered, but he refused to stop. He groaned as he pushed down a little more, his body fighting against the new intrusion and fireworks lighting up under his skin from the intensity. There, fuck, the head was inside him, and he could hardly believe that he'd finally done it.

"Ted," Grell gasped, his fingers squeezing down on his thighs. "Oh... fuck...."

"Yeaaaah, you're damn right," Ted panted, letting out another fierce moan as his hole relaxed enough for a few more inches to slip in. He'd never tried to take on so much before, and he could feel a surge of adrenaline rushing through his whole body, leaving him tingling as his cock leaked between them.

He began to move his hips in short bursts, grunting and moaning until he was finally able to take both thick cocks totally inside of him. He was so full, so full that he ached down in his core and trying to move wasn't an option. The slightest movement sent a cascade of sensation to all of his nerves, and it was totally overwhelming. He sat very still, daring to lean in for a kiss. "Thiazi... I...."

"Oh, Tedward," Grell soothed, kissing him softly. "If a mouse farts in here, I'm going to come, because right now your stuffed little ass is the most fantastic thing I've ever felt."

Ted couldn't help but laugh, protesting, "I had this whole plan of seducing you and fucking your brains out, you know. Not going quite how I planned it."

"Things rarely do in my experience," Grell said quietly. "I mean, I never expected that I might be falling in love with you."

"Thiazi," Ted murmured, shifting his hips and moaning loudly, his own cock throbbing from all the stimulation. "You'd better not be fucking around with me."

"Never," Grell purred, seizing Ted in a passionate kiss and rolling his hips up to drive both of his cocks into him.

Ted threw his head back with a sob, his thighs trembling as Grell fucked him right into sheer madness. It was too much too fast, and he moaned desperately as he suddenly came, his cock firing off several hot squirts between their grinding bodies.

Once wouldn't be enough, it never was for Grell, and he continued to thrust up into Ted's ass with ferocious strength. His magical skill kept the pain of overstimulation at bay, and Ted only felt the most intense pleasure. The pain was gone now, leaving him with a blinding bliss that had him smiling deliriously and moaning for more.

Grell buried his face into Ted's neck, dragging his sharp teeth over his throat with a loud snarl. He groped Ted's ass and thighs as he continued to fuck him, daring to bite down and moaning excitedly, "Ah, Ted... my love...."

"Thiazi!" Ted cried, clinging to Grell's thick shoulders. The sensation of Grell's teeth pressing into his skin created a flash of white-hot pain followed by intense suction that made Ted shudder. Fuck, it was going to be the mother of all hickeys, but he didn't even care. He wanted more, grabbing a handful of Grell's hair and holding him there, pleading, "Please, come on, come on, please!"

Grell growled, biting down harder in reply. His hips were losing speed, holding Ted down on his cocks as he grinded up into him before thrusting deeply again.

This slower, harder pace was making Ted melt, every nerve in his entire body winding up tight in anticipation of climax. He couldn't believe Grell could fuck like this, pushing him to his absolute physical limits and then shoving him right over the edge. He groaned as he came again, bouncing up and down in Grell's lap to soak up every ounce of pleasure.

Grell sped back up, pounding Ted as he panted, "There, my love. Mmm, look at you. You're so beautiful riding me... mmm, now come on. I'm gonna come, I'm coming!" He let out a sound that didn't even seem human, a deep primal roar that seemed to make the entire room vibrate. He licked the bite on Ted's neck, pulling him against his chest. "Oh, Ted... mmph."

Ted's orgasm didn't stop until Grell was finally done thrusting, and he was absolutely exhausted. He let Grell cradle him close, groaning low as he was overcome by the heat of two thick loads continuing to fill him up.

They kissed, long and slow, and Ted threw his arms around Grell's shoulders. His heart was thumping so fast that he could feel the other pulse—the beat of his mysterious savior—but all that mattered right now was being here in Grell's embrace.

"Did you mean it?"

"What, love?" Grell asked, peering up at Ted.

"About falling in love with me?" Ted asked, terrified of the answer but knowing that he had to hear it. He needed it to be real, and calling him "love" wasn't enough.

"Well," Grell purred, leaning up for another kiss. "What else can I say…?"

"Guilty?"

"Absolutely."

CHAPTER 15.

"ARE YOU two decent?" Kunst asked, his orb hesitantly peeking around the corner at one of the court's many doorways.

"Hang on!" Ted called back. He grinned at Grell, asking, "Don't suppose you could wiggle those magic fingers of yours and fix us up?"

"Oh, I suppose," Grell huffed, rolling his eyes dramatically. "It pains me to cover your naked flesh because I do so enjoy looking at it, but if you're insisting...."

"I am."

With a quick snap, Grell was fully dressed in a lush purple jacquard suit with a black dress shirt. He gave Ted a pair of jeans, snug ones, and a black V-neck shirt. Any sign of their debaucherous fun on the throne was out of sight, and Grell shouted, "Much against my will, yes, we are now decent."

Kunst floated over in a huff, snapping, "Now, I need to talk to you both about the situation with the bones!"

"Which situation is that?" Grell asked, clearly bored. "That they're still missing or the other thing?"

"The other thing!" Kunst's orb shuddered with obvious annoyance. "I believe I know why Gronoch wanted such a large volume of Asran bones. If he was merely looking to create some kind of mindless Silenced slaves, he wouldn't need so much. A tiny pinch of those ancient Asran bones would be enough to remove the souls from hundreds of mortals."

"So what is he trying to do?" Ted frowned.

"Gronoch might be trying to remove the soul of a god," Kunst replied with a gasp. "Can you imagine?"

"Uh… not really. Why is that a bad thing?"

"He could be removing the god's soul to create a sort of ghoul," Kunst explained hurriedly. "With the god's soul removed, perhaps he could use one of the Silenced mortals' souls to take it over and serve him."

"So, a Silenced person would be driving around in a god's body?"

"Even if it was possible to force a god to astral project," Grell drawled as he rose up from the throne, "a mortal soul cannot be bound to an immortal vessel."

"What about another immortal soul?" Ted frowned, snagging Grell's spot and sitting down on the throne. "Is that, like, a thing?"

"Theoretically? Perhaps Gronoch was looking to upgrade to a more powerful god's body?" Kunst suggested, his orb pulsing thoughtfully.

"That still doesn't explain why he needs Silenced mortals," Grell argued. "Somehow, the fate of Aeon hinges on Ted's little roommate being taken. My son's visions aren't always succinct, but that much he was absolutely sure of."

"As true as that may be, my conclusion remains the same," Kunst said. "There is no other purpose for so many bones except to forcibly remove a god's soul from their body."

"What the fuck is he doing on the throne?" a new voice sneered angrily.

Ted looked up to see a very familiar naked young man glaring at him. He blinked a few times to make sure this was a real person and not a ghostly illusion of some kind, grunting, "Hi."

"Oh, look, speak of the devil! It's my spawn," Grell said cheerfully. "How good of you to pop in and say hello. Don't you have a human you're supposed to be guarding?"

"He's fine," the young man snarled as he stalked closer. "Left him with Starkiller and Azaethoth the Lesser."

"Star-what now?" Ted asked.

"A mortal with the power to kill a god," Grell replied. "Very strong, big eyebrows, thought we went over this."

"Hey," the young man snapped impatiently. "Wanna explain why the fuckin' cat kicker is sitting there?"

"Hey, I got a name!" Ted growled, standing up and advancing toward the being formerly known as Mr. Twigs. "And I never fuckin' kicked you! You kept tripping me, you little fuzzy psycho!"

"Fuck you!"

"Hey, fuck you!"

"All right, all right!" Grell roared, holding his hands up for silence. "Now, everyone play nice for five damn seconds. Daddy is getting a headache. Ted, this is my son, Asta. Asta, this is—"

"Ted, Kicker of Cats," Asta cut in nastily. "We've met, Daddy."

"I never—" Ted growled.

"Darling child, light of my life, fruit of my loins," Grell began sweetly. He bared his teeth. "Shut it."

Asta growled but didn't speak.

"A lot has changed since you've been in Aeon," Grell said as he came to stand beside Ted. "I'm happy to announce that me and Tedward here are going steady."

"Going what? You mean, you… you two…?" Asta looked horrified. "Oh, fucking gross! I'm going to vomit."

Ted smirked, proudly wrapping his arm around Grell's shoulders. "Hell yeah. It's been great. We're gettin' along good, havin' ourselves a swell fuckin' time."

"For the love of Great Azaethoth," Asta whined, "please tell me you're not doin' it."

"Every day," Ted replied, enjoying how pale Asta grew. "Sometimes twice."

"I'm seriously gonna spew."

"Come on." Grell swatted at Ted, trying not to laugh. "Easy, love."

"I have fucking underwear older than him!" Asta complained. "This is beyond sick! He's… he's just so…! Ulgh!"

"Look, I'll spare you the sticky details of our sordid love affair," Grell soothed. "I do really have something important to talk to you about. We've had some interesting developments, and I believe they're connected to your vision."

"World ending, Jay being turned into a weapon?" Asta still appeared nauseated. "That one?"

"Well, it's certainly not about that time you said the Backstreet Boys were getting back together."

"Ha, shows what you know!" Asra protested, holding his head up high. "I just finished up following them for the entire East Coast of their reunion tour!"

"Wait, so you left Jay with strangers, went to go see some fuckin' concerts, and then you came back here?" Ted scoffed. "Some great protector!"

"It was only for, like, three shows! Back off, Cat Kicker. Jay is fine."

"What the hell are you doing back here?"

"Ulgh," Asta groaned dramatically. "Because Jay went to freakin' Starkiller to find out what happened to you. He was all, 'Wahhh, Ted is missing, and I think my cat did it!'"

"But you did!"

"Ahem, play nice, children," Grell scolded. "Now, Asta, please listen. Humble Visseract and Vizier Ghulk were conspiring with the god Gronoch to smuggle bones from the pits. Ghulk has been sentenced to life in prison for grave desecration and the murders of Humble Visseract, Thulogian Silas, and Sergan Mire."

"Holy shit," Asta whispered, his eyes wide. "I really did miss a lot."

"We're still not sure how Silenced people are being used to make weapons," Grell went on. "The bridge is still looking a bit dim, so I'm afraid it's ongoing. We have someone who is actively working on a theory."

"Who?"

"Professor Emil Kunst."

"Hello!" Kunst said, his orb lighting up. "Greetings, Your Highness!

"What the fuck is that thing?" Asta blinked, stretching out and batting playfully at Kunst's orb.

"Ahem! Do you mind?" Kunst floated out of the way with an indignant huff.

"Nope." Asta wiggled his butt, preparing to pounce like a cat.

"Leave him be," Grell warned. "He's our new Royal Occult Advisor."

"We have one of those?"

"We do now." Grell returned to lounge in his throne, summoning a tumbler of whiskey and rubbing his temple as he sipped. "Professor Kunst, if you'd be so kind as to explain to my son your little theory about his visions and the bones."

Ted didn't think an orb could show joy, but there it was.

"Absolutely, Your Highness," Kunst said eagerly. "It would be my pleasure! Ah! Well, as we all know, the bones of the Asra are powerful catalysts for astral projection—"

"What's your name again?" Asta blinked. "Because it totally sounds like cun—"

"Kunst! My name is Kunst!" Kunst snapped. He cleared his throat, continuing as calmly as he could, "The sheer volume of Asran bones that Gronoch stole suggests he was trying to force a god—"

"Wait, wait!" Asta interrupted again. "How many bones were taken? Whose bones did they take?"

Grell's expression softened, sadness in his eyes as he replied, "Most of the ancient crypts were pilfered, and the royal chambers—"

"Mommy," Asta said, suddenly scared and tearful. "Did they…?"

"Asta, please listen to me," Grell began.

Asta was already gone through a portal, no doubt headed down to the pits to see for himself.

"Fuck," Grell muttered, downing his drink and holding it up as he continued to chug.

"Right, so maybe I'll try to tell him later?" Kunst asked quietly.

"Uh, much later." Ted noticed that Grell hadn't stopped drinking. "Okay? Please? I think we need to have some family time."

Kunst didn't move.

"Some *private* family time."

"Ah, yes. Well, as you wish," Kunst said, his orb hovering low as if he was sulking before he slipped away.

Ted came over to right Grell's glass and spare his liver some significant damage—if that type of thing was possible for an Asra. "Hey, hey, easy, big guy. Why don't you go down there and talk to him?"

"And tell him what?" Grell asked flatly. "That despite searching the castle and every last inch of Xenon, we were never able to find all the bones, including but not limited to his mother's? No, I think I'll be skipping that conversation."

"Well, hey," Ted tried again, "shouldn't we find out why he came back? He was supposed to be watching over Jay! Why is he here?"

"He left your dear roommate in the care of a god and one of the most powerful witches that's ever lived." Grell snorted. "I think he will be just dandy."

"Well, I wanna know," Ted huffed. He grabbed Grell's arm and tugged. "Come on. Get up."

"I dun wanna," Grell protested, sticking out his lower lip.

"I'll give you head," Ted promised with a coy grin.

"Both cocks?" Grell continued to pout.

"Yes, for fuck's sake, let's go."

Grell was cheerier as they headed down into the pits, resuming his cat body and slinking beside Ted as they walked back to the royal crypts.

Ted was thinking of this like a removal for work to maintain his confidence—except there was no body to pick up and the angry next of kin was a young cat monster who might try to eat him.

As they came to the end of the crypts, he heard Asta's sobs before he saw him, but already knew by the sound that he'd transformed.

Asta's feline form was as lean as his human body, sleek and shining black. He had gold ornaments like his father, though not nearly as many. He was curled up in front of Vael's slot, still empty except for the music box.

Grell hesitated to get any closer, nudging Ted ahead of him.

"Hey!" Ted protested, trying to keep his voice down. "You're coming with me!"

"I brought you here!" Grell hissed back quietly. "I didn't agree to talking!"

"Talk or no you-know-what!"

"That's just evil."

"You're a dick!"

"Tease!"

"You know I can hear you idiots," Asta drawled.

Clearing his throat, Ted tiptoed toward Asta. "Right, look. I guess we got off to a bad start. Like, a lot. But I'm... I'm really sorry about Vael. Like, so fucking sorry."

Asta scoffed, turning to stare Ted down. He was poised as if to pounce, and there was nothing playful about it.

Ted was very certain his bites would be much more painful now.

"And you know," Ted continued nervously, "that probably sounds like bullshit. I had to tell people that I was sorry for their loss all the time with my old job, and it didn't feel real. I wasn't honestly sorry the dead person had, well, died.

"Because I didn't know them. I wasn't genuinely sad they were gone because I wasn't gonna miss 'em. It always felt so fuckin' fake. But I'm thinking now I'm still sorry. Yeah, I didn't know them, just like I didn't know Vael, but I'm so goddamn sorry that you guys lost him."

Ted poured his heart into every word, and the silence that followed was absolute torture. He held his breath, waiting for Asta's response.

Some of the tension eased from Asta's shoulders, and he finally settled back down. He turned his head away, sweeping a paw over his face with a sad little purr.

Ted remembered to breathe again, grateful for Grell nuzzling up to his side in a show of silent support.

"You shouldn't be down here," Asta mumbled at last to break the silence, his lashing tail proving that not all of his fight had left him. "You're not family."

"Through a very weird set of circumstances—not my fault, totally your father's—"

"Hey!" Grell griped.

"I sort of might be, you know, one day." Ted shrugged awkwardly. "I mean, if I accept his engagement thing officially."

"Did he get you to help move a body?" Asta raised his brows, a curious-looking expression on his feline face.

"Wait... how did you know that?"

"That's how he got my mother." Asta scoffed, and then he actually laughed. "Old man used the same trick twice!"

"That is not what happened!" Grell argued loudly. "Vael knew the consequences—"

"What the hell?" Ted demanded, unable to resist grinning at Grell's obvious misery.

"When my mother's favorite uncle died, he wanted to help take him down to the pits," Asta replied. "And that old bastard over there is all, 'Oh, but it's dirty and gross and you don't wanna do that,' just playin' it up."

"Mmm, did he now?" Ted batted his eyes.

"Yeah," Asta said, almost smiling now. "My mother's stubbornness was legendary, and the best way to make him do something was to tell him not to do it."

"So you courted your future husband by telling him moving bodies was gross, which made him want to move a body, and that's how you got engaged?" Ted grinned. "Kinda sweet."

"Perhaps I was a very nervous and shy little prince at the time and was having a bit of trouble asking the very hot man out on a date," Grell said, holding his nose up in the air.

"You? *Shy?*" Ted scoffed. "Bullshit."

"No, it's true," Grell replied firmly. "I was quite awful. Braces, pimples, just wretched. I had explained to Vael that helping with the entombment would mean an engagement, obviously, and he said, 'Oh, but yes, I would just love to be married to you,' and that's about how it went."

"He's a liar," Asta drawled.

"I know," Ted said with a smooth smile. "I didn't know about the engagement body thing until I was in court fighting for my fuckin' freedom."

"And I already told you that I didn't think anyone would bring it up!" Grell fussed. "I apologized and have given you many orgasms to make up for—"

"Okay, okay, yes, and I get that, still a little salty because it was a fuckin' dick move."

"You two are fuckin' perfect for each other," Asta said, shaking his head and turning back to look at the empty slot. He grew quiet again, and Ted thought he heard a soft sniffle. "Have fun getting married."

"Thanks," Ted said, hating how easily he still blushed thinking about it. "I mean, I still haven't said yes. We're, you know, seeing how things go. But...." He smiled. "I'm really happy."

"Good for you, Kicker of Cats."

"So am I, if anyone is wondering," Grell piped up.

"No," Asta snorted.

"I do," Ted said sweetly, reaching up to scratch behind Grell's ears.

"Hmmph. Thank you."

"So. Whose stupid idea was this?" Asta mumbled, his grumpy tone betrayed by the reverence with which he touched the music box.

"Mine," Ted replied, unsure of what to say except to keep being honest. "I thought it could be a promise, uh, that we're gonna keep trying to find them. Grell picked out the music box."

"It was a birthday gift," Asta said with a little smile, glancing back to Grell. "It was my idea, and Daddy had it made for him. Mom always kept his jewelry in here, my baby teeth...." He turned back to the box. "This sucks."

"Agreed," Grell said.

"So." Asta stood up, padding back toward them with a flash of his teeth. "Shots?"

Grell bowed, bumping their heads together. "That's my boy."

Ted stepped back, letting father and son have a tender moment. He could hear Asta whispering, but only caught part of it.

"...it's like losing him again...."

"I know," Grell soothed, purring sadly. "I know...."

Asta pulled away quickly, shaking it off as if they weren't just being sweet. "Let's go get fucked-up!"

"Let's." Grell swished up against Ted's side and ported them out to the pool. There was a line of colorful umbrella drinks and a large bottle of liquor waiting for them, and Ted laughed when he looked down and saw Grell had given him unicorn swimming trunks.

Grell's matched, naturally.

Asta turned back into a human and put on shorts after Grell yelled at him for being naked, and they shared a toast. The alcohol never stopped flowing, and Asta spent every second spilling every juicy and embarrassing story about Grell that he could.

Grell grumbled and fussed, but he honestly just seemed happy to see Asta smiling again.

Ted tried to maintain a respectful distance—wouldn't it be weird to be all over Grell when his son was right there? But Grell wasn't having any of that and dragged Ted right into his lap so fast that the eels scattered.

As the hours ticked by, Grell summoned food for them to help ease the booze's grasp, and Ted was ever so happy to see a tray of big cheeseburgers just for him.

Grell left abruptly for some royal emergency, promising to return soon, and left the two of them alone to finish their meals.

"You're not that bad," Asta said, slurring a little as he ate some bright pink cheese. He reached out and nudged Ted's shoulder. "For a douche who kicks cats."

Ted wasn't even going to argue, raising his glass to say, "Thanks, dude. I appreciate that."

"You really like my dad, huh?"

"It's a bit more than 'like,' you know," Ted replied with a bashful grin. He ran his fingers through his hair and sighed. "It's… complicated. He's fuckin' complicated."

"You make him happy," Asta said, the drink having loosened his tongue, and laughed loudly. "Fuck, I haven't seen him this happy in fuckin' centuries. Maybe like, eh, when he discovered cable? No, wait, not even close."

"Thanks, man." Ted grinned. "I guess I owe you for sending me through that portal. I mean, I could have done without the murder charges, but—"

"You're gonna marry him, aren't you?" Asta demanded, suddenly quite serious.

"I still… uh…." Ted became flustered. "I haven't given an official answer to the court yet."

"The fuck are you waiting for?" Asta complained.

"That… that is a good question," Ted said, smothering his doubts into the last bite of his burger.

Asta was relentless, pressing, "Well? It's not like you have forever, you know. You've got what, ten years, maybe?"

"What the fuck?" Ted mumbled through his food, trying to hurry up and swallow to reply. "Hey, humans do live for a decent little while, you know!"

"Whatever," Asta scoffed. He looked up as Grell reappeared. Eyes narrowed stubbornly, he jabbed Ted's shoulder. "Maybe you should use what time you have left being happy, huh?"

"Right." Ted knew better than most how fragile life was.

He had seen for years how quickly and unexpectedly it could be taken away, even from people in their prime. He couldn't say how long he had left, but then again who really did? Wasn't that enough of a reason to seize the moment and do what was going to make him happy?

"Nice to see you two getting along," Grell declared, slipping back into the pool and grabbing a fresh drink topped with fruit slices.

"Is everything okay?" Ted asked. "What was the big royal emergency?"

"Look," Grell replied, pointing out to the night sky.

The bridge, once flickering and dim, was now flooding with new light. The illumination was moving slowly, but as the moments ticked by it was fully lit up and glittering with a rush of scattered spheres dancing across it.

"What's… what's happened?" Ted gulped, both bewitched by the bridge's restored beauty and terrified of the possible cause.

"All of those missing Silenced people on Aeon, wherever they were, have finally passed on," Grell explained somberly. "The bridge is back up and running at top speed, it seems."

"But that means a whole shit-ton of people just died," Ted said quietly, reaching for Grell's hand as his heart sank.

"I don't know what Gronoch was doing with them, but I have a feeling that death may be a welcome change."

"Shit," Asta whispered, his big eyes staring down the bridge with a loud gulp. "Jay. I should probably get back to Jay. Make sure he's okay."

"Go on," Grell urged, "but be safe. No doubt Gronoch is behind this."

"No problem. I'll track down Starkiller and Azzy, see what's up. I'm gonna ask them about the bones too." Asta blinked out of the pool, naked once more with his sunglasses reappearing on his face. "I'll be back as soon as I can." He pointed at Ted. "And you! What's your answer gonna be?"

"Well… it's… I'm—" Ted floundered to reply.

"Yeah, that's what I thought," Asta said with a toothy grin. "Congrats, you crazy kids! See ya later!" He disappeared into a bright portal with a quick pop.

"Why does he always travel naked?" Ted wondered out loud.

"Loves the whoosh down on his bits," Grell said with a laugh, tugging Ted back over into his lap. "It can be quite refreshing."

"I'll take your word for it." Ted laughed, kissing Grell warmly. "Mmm. Missed you."

"I wasn't gone so long, love," Grell said, smiling.

"Well, there's something I wanna talk to you about," Ted said, holding his head high and trying to be serious.

"Oh?" Grell looked intrigued. "Is it something perverse?"

"No!" Ted scolded. "Our engagement."

"Oh?" Grell still seemed interested. "What about it?"

"I was talking to Asta, and he kinda gave me some perspective about my squishy mortal life," Ted replied. "Got me thinking about what I want for the future."

"Does this mean you're accepting?" Grell asked patiently, his hands lightly stroking Ted's hips.

"It means I'm willing to accept being permanently engaged for the near future while we figure our shit out," Ted said carefully, "because somewhere along the way, in spite of all the murders and blood and shit, your insane charms actually got me kinda hooked."

"I am quite charming. That's very true," Grell said proudly, kissing Ted's lips. "Mmm, so it's a yes?"

Ted's cheeks promptly caught on fire, and he took a deep breath. He'd spent so long being alone, and he was absolutely crazy about Grell. Fuck it. He was going to go for it.

"It's a yes," Ted confirmed.

Grell cackled triumphantly and swept Ted into a passionate kiss. "Oh, my love, my beautiful love. You've just made me the happiest man in all of Xenon."

"Oh yeah?" Ted teased, his heart so full that he thought it was going to burst inside of his chest. He leaned in close, nipping at Grell's ear as he whispered, "Take me to bed, and I guarantee I can make you even happier."

"Just when I think you can't get any more perfect, there you go, proving me wrong." Grell held Ted close, preparing to blink them away. "Ready, my love?"

"Fuck, yes." Ted smiled. He was ready for anything: for the promise of awesome sex that was about to be fulfilled, for a life waking up every day next to this handsome king, and for making the most out of each and every moment.

Asta was right, that little shit.

Life was too short not to be happy.

K.L. "Kat" Hiers is an embalmer, restorative artist, and queer writer. Licensed in both funeral directing and funeral service, she's been working in the death industry for nearly a decade. Her first love was always telling stories, and she has been writing for over twenty years, penning her very first book at just eight years old. Publishers generally do not accept manuscripts in Hello Kitty notebooks, however, but she never gave up.

Following the success of her first novel, *Cold Hard Cash*, she now enjoys writing professionally, focusing on spinning tales of sultry passion, exotic worlds, and emotional journeys. She loves attending horror movie conventions and indulging in cosplay of her favorite characters. She lives in Zebulon, NC, with her husband and their children, some of whom have paws and a few who only pretend to because they think it's cute.

Website: http://www.klhiers.com

A SUCKER FOR LOVE MYSTERY

ACSQUIDENTALLY IN LOVE

K.L. HIERS

"A breezy and sensual LGBTQ paranormal romance."
—*Library Journal*

A Sucker For Love Mystery

Nothing brings two men—or one man and an ancient god—together like revenge.

Private investigator Sloane sacrificed his career in law enforcement in pursuit of his parents' murderer. Like them, he is a follower of long-forgotten gods, practicing their magic and offering them his prayers… not that he's ever gotten a response.

Until now.

Azaethoth the Lesser might be the patron of thieves and tricksters, but he takes care of his followers. He's come to earth to avenge the killing of one of his favorites, and maybe charm the pants off the cute detective Fate has placed in his path. If he has his way, they'll do much more than bring a killer to justice. In fact, he's sure he's found the man he'll spend his immortal life with.

Sloane's resolve is crumbling under Azaethoth's surprising sweetness, and the tentacles he sometimes glimpses escaping the god's mortal form set his imagination alight. But their investigation gets stranger and deadlier with every turn. To survive, they'll need a little faith… and a lot of mystical firepower.

www.dreamspinnerpress.com